Lawless

Lawless

K'wan

www.urbanbooks.net

Urban Books, LLC
300 Farmingdale Road, NY-Route 109
Farmingdale, NY 11735

ISBN 13: 978-1-60162-124-5
ISBN 10: 1-60162-124-8

First Trade Paperback Printing February 2019
Printed in the United States of America

10 9 8 7 6 5 4 3 2 1

Distributed by Kensington Publishing Corp.
Submit Orders to:
Customer Service
400 Hahn Road
Westminster, MD 21157-4627
Phone: 1-800-733-3000
Fax: 1-800-659-2436

Lawless

by

K'wan

PROLOGUE

"Fire Bug make the trap go boom!" the youngest of the Savage boys sang while dancing in the passenger seat of the Yukon he was in. He watched with childlike amusement as the truck sitting on the corner a block away went up in flames. On his lap was the remote detonator for the explosives he had planted under the hood of the truck the day before. Fire Bug had been itching to hit the switch, but they had had to wait for the proper time.

"That's a mighty fine piece of work you done there, Bug," Big Money Savage said from behind the wheel. They called him Big Money, but he never seemed to have much of it. He was Bug's first cousin, but he wasn't a killer like the rest of them. Still, he was a Savage, and they wouldn't leave him out in the cold. He was the odd jobs' man of the family.

"Fucking right it was. I'm a damn perfectionist," Bug told him.

"Well, this one didn't go so perfect, seeing how you killed the wrong person," Big Money told him and pointed a few feet to the left of the burning truck. The target, a man named King James, was still very much alive. Two of his henchmen were trying to restrain him as he attempted to run to the burning truck. There wasn't much they could do for the boy inside, yet he still felt compelled to try.

"That lucky muthafucka!" Bug raged. He pulled his gun out from between the seats. "Big Money, pull up on this nigga so I can blow his brains out. The Savages ain't never fucked up a hit, and we ain't gonna start now."

"Save it for another day, Bug. After an explosion like that, the police and everybody else are gonna be crawling over the block in a few ticks," Big Money told him.

"I can take him, and we'll be gone before anyone knows what happened," Bug insisted.

"Bug, if you wanna go to prison, you can do that on your own time. Ain't no way I'm gonna be the one to tell your mama that you got knocked over some dumb shit." Big Money started the engine. They slowly pulled out into traffic.

The Yukon carrying the two arsonists rolled slowly past what was left of the burning truck. King James was on his knees a few feet away, sobbing uncontrollably, while his men stood around him. Seeing the self-proclaimed king of Harlem in such an emotional state gave Bug a cheap thrill. He may not have killed King, but he had sure as hell broken him. Bug continued to watch as two men helped King to his feet. Bug didn't know who it was who had died in the explosion, but from King's reaction, they must have been close. That at least made Fire Bug feel a little better about messing up the hit. As they passed the grieving soldiers, Bug and King James made eye contact. Not being able to resist the temptation of kicking a dog when he was down, Bug blew King a kiss before the Yukon peeled through the light and disappeared. Bug didn't know it at the time, but the mocking gesture would set off a chain of events that would change his family forever.

PART I

Opening Statements

CHAPTER 1

Charles Johnson was what you would call a less than average Joe. He was an unassuming young man of twenty who lived in his mother's basement. Three days per week, he rode his bike back and forth to his job at Home Depot. Outside of the people he talked to at work and the professors who taught some of the night classes he was taking at Atlanta Technical College, Charles had no social life to speak of. He was what you would call an unimportant man. So unimportant that if he up and dropped dead, it was doubtful that anyone but his mother would miss him. And that was only because he wouldn't be around to kick in his monthly payment for the rent she charged him. Charles was an invisible man that no one ever saw.

That all had changed six weeks ago. In the blink of an eye, he'd gone from obscurity to being the meat in a newspaper byline about a man charged with armed robbery and attempted murder. According to the police, Charles was one of several men who had got it in their head to rob a liquor store in Bankhead. The owner, an older white man, had ended up taking a nonlethal gut shot and had been able to point the police in the right direction and identify several suspects. Charles hadn't originally been one of them, but it hadn't taken long for his *codefendants* to point their finger at him unanimously. Charles was the only black man in the group. It hadn't helped matters when the store owner accused Charles in court of being the one who had shot him. Charles was being singled out and railroaded, and it appeared that only a miracle would be able to save him. Luckily for Charles, the law office he'd stumbled into happened to employ a miracle worker.

Keith Davis was an up-and-coming defense attorney who worked for the firm of Hunt, Lehman, and Gold. It was one of the top law firms not only in the city of Atlanta but also in the state of Georgia. The firm was built on the résumés of the partners, but their stellar reputation came from the stable of young lawyers they kept in rotation. It was a collective of some of the sharpest legal minds in the state, but Keith was by far the sharpest knife in the drawer.

Being the color of milk chocolate, standing six feet two inches tall, with rich black hair that rolled over the top of his head in waves and with engaging brown eyes, Keith was someone who would look more comfortable in a catalog than he did in a courtroom. Writing him off as a pretty boy with a degree was why prosecutors often found themselves caught off guard when he walked into a courtroom and almost effortlessly punched holes in their cases against his clients. Keith had an intimate understanding of the law, which made him an authority on manipulating it to win a case.

Keith sat listening to the prosecutor babble, but he was only half paying attention. He kept casting anxious glares at the courtroom doors to see if his paralegal, Susan, had arrived yet, but there was still no sign of her. If she didn't show soon, Keith would have to improvise. It wouldn't be the first time he had to work on the fly, but he preferred to go into battle with his guns fully loaded.

The prosecutor, Allen Glen, was a legend in the halls of courtrooms across the state of Georgia. They called him the Black Death, because he had a reputation for burying minorities in the deepest and darkest holes, never to be seen again. On the stand sat Glen's star witness and the lead detective on the case, Roy Graves. He was both a smug bastard with a splotchy record and a card-carrying member of the good old boy network . . . a true son of the South. Graves and Glen had been playing Batman and Robin throughout the whole fiasco, going above and beyond to punch holes in Keith's case, and for the most part, they had been successful.

When Charles was fifteen, he had been arrested for assault when he took part in a fight that had broken out at a high school basketball game. Charles had only been defending himself against members of the opposing team when they attacked him, but at the urging of his legal aid attorney, he'd pleaded guilty to the charges in exchange for probation and a felony conviction. Charles had been a minor at the time, and legally, Glen couldn't use these old charges in the case, but during cross-examination, he had conveniently let it slip out that Charles had an arrest record. Planting that seed made it easy for Glen to demonize Charles in the eyes of the jury and feed the notion that he was some common thug who was capable of committing the new crime he was being accused of.

Keith glanced over at his client, Charles, who was so terrified that he could barely keep his knees from knocking together. He was nervous, and rightfully so. The deck was stacked so high against him that it was almost a sure thing that prison awaited him in the future unless something short of a miracle happened. Luckily for Charles, miracles were what Keith specialized in.

When Glen finally got tired of hearing himself talk, he rested his case and opened the floor for Keith Davis. "Game over, hotshot," Glen said slyly while passing Keith on the way back to his side of the courtroom.

Keith took a second to pat Charles's hand reassuringly before standing up from the table. He spared a last glance over his shoulder, but still no Susan. He was on his own. Taking a deep breath, Keith stepped from behind the table and prepared to address the court. His manicured fingernails glistened in the pale light of the courtroom as he buttoned the blazer to his tailored dark gray suit. The pink shirt beneath was freshly pressed, and his charcoal tie was knotted perfectly. Though Keith appeared to be the perfect picture of calm, his mind was racing at a million miles per minute. He could feel the eyes of his boss, Theodore Hunt, boring into him from a few seats back. He didn't have to see him to know that he was watching. Theodore always seemed to be watching him. No doubt he was probably wondering if the seemingly hopeless case would finally be the one to smudge Keith's pristine track record.

Theodore had been the most animate about Keith not taking the case to begin with. "You're setting yourself up for failure, kid," Theodore had told him that morning in his office. He'd been more concerned about how Keith losing the case would reflect on the firm than about the young man whose life hung in the balance. This had only made Keith more determined to take the case, just to prove his overbearing boss wrong. Now, drawing closer to the moment of truth, he began to think his ego had painted him into a corner he wouldn't be able to get out of.

With the last card he had to play seeming to be missing from the deck, Keith now took a deep breath and prepared to mount as best a defense as he could. He had gone all in and now had to finish playing the hand. Just as he was about to open his mouth to start his cross-examination, the courtroom doors swung open and in stumbled his ace.

Susan Delany came stumbling into the courtroom, carrying a stack of folders, which threatened to spill from her grasp. She was a frumpy woman, twentysomething, with curly blond hair and clear blue eyes behind wire-framed glasses. Susan Delany was one of the paralegals who worked for the firm and was Keith's go-to person. Her uncanny knack for fact-finding and her attention to detail had pulled Keith's ass out of the fire on more than one occasion.

Susan hustled down the aisle, offering mumbled apologies to those whose feet she stepped on and those she accidentally slapped with her trench coat, which flapped behind her like a superhero's cape. Her theatrics, though not intentional, caused quite a commotion, to the displeasure of the judge.

"What in blazes is going on?" the judge snapped.

"A moment please, Your Honor?" Keith asked, trying to hide his excitement.

"Mr. Davis, you had better have a damn good reason for disrupting my courtroom!" the judge spat.

"If God has seen fit to smile on me today, I will," Keith said, moving to meet his paralegal. "Did you get it, Susan?" he asked her when he reached her side.

"Yes. It took some doing, but a friend of a friend was able to help me out, if I promised to go on a date with him," Susan said, balancing her folders with one hand and digging in her satchel with the other. From it, she produced a green folder, which she handed to Keith.

Keith took a few seconds to flip through the folder to make sure it had what he needed inside. When he laid eyes on the documents, his lips parted into a wide grin, showing off two rows of perfect white teeth. "Susan, I owe you one for this." He kissed her on the forehead.

"You owe me more than *one*," she whispered. "You should see the guy I had to agree to date in order to get you this stuff. He's got a unibrow, for Christ's sake!"

"Mr. Davis, do you plan to cross-examine this witness, or would you like to waste more of this court's time?" the judge barked at Keith.

"My apologies, Your Honor. I do intend to cross-examine Detective Graves, but I plan to make it short and sweet," Keith said with an easy smile, which made Prosecutor Glen nervous. "Detective Graves," he began, "I'm going to begin with asking you a very simple question. Can you say without a shadow of a doubt that the right man was arrested for this crime?"

"That's what my report says," Detective Graves replied in a smug tone.

"Right, your report. The same report that has my client being positively identified by the store owner as well as one of his codefendants, correct?"

"Yup," Graves answered.

"Is there any scientific evidence to support this? Camera footage, ballistic evidence maybe?"

"No, the cameras in the store relay only live feed, and as far as ballistic evidence, by the time we tracked Mr. Johnson down, several days had passed, so any trace evidence we could've used was long gone."

Keith raised his eyebrow. "So, your testimony is based on hearsay?"

"My testimony is based on an old man sitting in the hospital with a gut shot, a man who fingered that colored fella as the shooter." He jabbed an accusatory finger in Charles's direction. "Hell, even his friend said he done it."

A confused expression crossed Keith's face. "So, what you're saying is that this whole case against my client is based on the word of a traumatized old man and an informant who you've promised only God knows what to place the blame on Mr. Johnson?" Keith shook his head pitifully. "Shame on you and the Atlanta Police Department for wasting this court's time, Detective Graves."

Detective Graves's eyes narrowed to slits. For a brief second, he couldn't hide the contempt he felt for the well-dressed African American attorney. "Look, *boy*, I don't know what you're fishing for, but—"

"I haven't been a *boy* in quite a few years," Keith said, cutting him off. "And I'm not fishing for anything. I'm digging a hole and this"—he raised the folder Susan had given him for all to see—"is my shovel." Keith approached the bench, then handed both the judge and Detective Graves copies of one of the documents in the folder.

"Mr. Davis, what is this?" the judge asked, looking at the document strangely.

"I was hoping to let Detective Graves have the honor of explaining, but since he seems to be at a loss for words, I'll help him out." Keith turned his attention to the detective, who had suddenly turned as red as a tomato. Detective Graves opened his mouth to say something, but no sound came out. There was blood in the water, so Keith turned to the jurors and went for the kill. "Detective Graves, what you have in front of you is a photocopy of a desk appearance ticket for a drunk and disorderly that was issued on the same night of the robbery, only in the city of Savannah. Could you please read the name of the person this ticket was issued to out loud for the court?"

Before Detective Graves could answer, Prosecutor Glen was on his feet. "Objection, Your Honor! It's a little late to introduce new evidence, especially if we weren't made aware of it during discovery."

"If I'd had it in my possession at the time, I'd have observed protocol, but this information was just made available to me a few seconds ago by my legal clerk." Keith motioned toward Susan, whom he allowed the honor of presenting Prosecutor Glen with his copy of the document. "I assure you, Your Honor, I would not have disrupted these proceedings at the eleventh hour if the new information had been anything less than a game changer in this case."

The judge stared Keith down for a few seconds. He didn't particularly care for the young defense attorney, but he respected his tenacity. "It had damn well better be, Mr. Davis." He motioned for him to continue.

"The name, please, Detective Graves," Keith said, pressing his witness.

Detective Graves mumbled something that was inaudible.

"Could you repeat that so that the entire courtroom can hear you?" Keith cupped his hand to his ear.

"Charles Johnson!" Detective Graves repeated in a nasty tone.

The whole courtroom, including Charles, gasped, in shock.

"Bingo!" Keith snapped his fingers. "At the time of the robbery, my client was sitting in a holding cell nearly three hours away from the scene of the crime. Unless Mr. Johnson has figured out how to defy the laws of physics, it's impossible for him to have been in two places at once. So, I'll ask you again for the record, Detective. Are you sure the right man was arrested for this crime?"

There was a pregnant pause in the room, followed almost immediately by an outbreak of whispers. Keith studied the faces of the jury to gauge the impact of his words. He didn't need to sway them, only create the shadow of a doubt. Prosecutor Glen looked like he was ready to blow a gasket. As Keith strutted back to Charles's side, he stopped for a moment at the prosecutor's table and leaned in to whisper to him, "I hear that crow really isn't that bad if you drizzle it with a little hot sauce."

A few minutes later, Keith came out of the courtroom, leading Charles and his mother, Martha. For Keith's higher profile cases, there was always some sort of media waiting outside the courtroom, but Charles's case had been a passion project that nobody had believed in but Keith. There was no fanfare, only the satisfaction of knowing that he had given Charles Johnson a second shot at life.

Keith was standing in the hallway, speaking with Charles and Martha, when his boss, Theodore Hunt, came strutting out of the courtroom. His square jaw was covered in a rich, well-groomed dark beard. Theodore was now in his fifties, but at six feet two inches tall and a shade under 220 pounds, he was still an imposing figure. His broad shoulders strained against the fabric of his tailored black suit. Only a few knew that he got his suits cut especially close about the chest and shoulders to make himself look bigger. When he trolled the halls of their law offices, he gave off an almost ominous feeling.

Trailing him was his pet ferret, Julian Sands, one of the junior partners. He was Theodore's fly on the wall and keeper of secrets. Julian was an excellent lawyer but a horrible person, and he wore this fact proudly. Most of the lawyers at the firm feared Theodore Hunt, but they unanimously hated Julian Sands.

When Theodore's dark eyes landed on Keith, the younger attorney straightened himself and waited for his boss's inevitable critique of his performance in court. Theodore demanded the highest of standards from all the attorneys under him, but he seemed to be especially hard on Keith. No matter what Keith did, Theodore always found something he could've done better. Theodore stopped in front of Keith, and much to Keith's surprise, he simply gave him a curt nod of approval and kept walking. That was the closest Theodore had ever come to complimenting Keith's work. Keith wished he had a camera to record the rare moment, because when he recounted the story, no one would ever believe him.

"I can't thank you enough for what you've done for my son. God bless you, Killer," said a teary-eyed Martha, drawing Keith's attention away from Theodore's departing back.

"It's *Keith*," he said, correcting her. Killer was a name that he'd buried long ago, and he planned to keep it that way. "And I'd do no less to stand for anybody from the same soil as me. We kin, baby," Keith told her, letting slip the faintest traces of the Southern drawl he'd worked so hard to suppress. It was an involuntary reflex that sometimes manifested itself when his path crossed with those of people he knew from back home, which was very rare.

Keith was the last person Martha Jones had expected to run into, let alone take up her cause, when her son had gotten into trouble. Her search for representation had brought her into the offices of Hunt, Lehman, and Gold, where she'd pleaded for someone to hear her out about the mess her troubled son had gotten himself into. It had been divine intervention that Keith had happened to be on his way out to lunch as Martha was being stonewalled by the receptionist.

Over a cup of coffee in one of the conference rooms, Martha had laid her troubles at Keith's feet. Things were tight for her financially, so there was no way she could pay the retainer, but what she lacked in money, she made up for in the belief that her son was innocent. Keith hadn't seen Martha in years, but they had a history that went back to when he was just a nappy-headed kid in the South, trying to carry a name that was too heavy for his shoulders. He hadn't even had to think twice about agreeing to take on Martha's case pro bono. His decision to try to rectify this dire situation, for free, no less, hadn't earned him any favor with the partners, but Keith didn't care. He felt Martha's pain over her son because he, too, was from a demographic in which it was up to women to ensure the survival of their sons.

"We aren't completely out of the woods just yet, Martha," Keith said as they stood in the hallway outside the courtroom now. "We've got another court date next month, and hopefully, by then this mess will be completely cleaned up, and your boy properly exonerated. Think of this as a temporary reprieve, and until it's official, I'm going to need Charles to keep his nose clean."

"You won't have to worry about that. I'm confining his ass to the house twenty-four–seven. He might not be in prison, but it's sure as hell gonna feel like it," Martha said.

"Come on, Mama. I'm twenty. How are you gonna put a grown man on punishment?" Charles asked with an attitude.

Martha's lips drew back into a sneer, showing the gold cap on one of her incisors. "Don't you go giving me no lip! You weren't grown when your ass was in that cell, crying like a baby and begging me to help your monkey ass get out of this mess. Had it not been for Keith's kindness, you surely would still be rotting in that cell, because I ain't have no damn money to spring you. If I were you, I'd try to be a little more appreciative, Charles. Do you understand?"

"Yes, ma'am," Charles said in a soft tone. His mother had always had the power to make him retreat into his childhood ways by simply changing the pitch of her voice.

"Martha, I need to talk to you for a second, and then I need a minute with Charles before my lunch meeting," Keith said. Then he led Martha out of earshot of Charles. "Listen, Martha, I'm glad I was able to help you, but I'm afraid I'm going to need something from you in return."

Martha gave Keith a suspicious look. "Killer, I told you before you took the case that I was uptight for money, and you said it wouldn't be a problem," she reminded him.

"*Keith*," he said, correcting her again. "And it's nothing like that, Martha. It's just . . ." He searched for the right words. "I've gone through a considerable amount of effort to put some distance between who I was and who I'm striving to be. I have a new life here in Georgia."

Martha chuckled. "I kinda guessed that when we met at your office that second time." Martha recalled the morning she had gone to meet Keith at the firm to go over some last-minute details of Charles's case. His office door had a sign that said K. DAVIS, which had her slightly confused. She had wanted to ask him about it but hadn't wanted to pry and run the risk of him changing his mind. "We all running from one thing or another, Kill . . . I mean, Keith."

"I'm not running from anything, Martha. I'm running toward something, and I don't need anything getting in the way of that, feel me?"

"If you're worried about me knocking some bones loose from those skeletons in your closet back home, you needn't be. Keith, you gave me my son back, and you asking for your privacy to be respected in return is a small price."

"Thank you for understanding, Martha."

"Something has been puzzling since you agreed to take Charles's case."

Keith raised his eyebrow. "And what would that be?"

"Well, I wasn't being nosy or anything, but I was sitting just in front of your boss, Mr. Hunt, while we were inside the courtroom, and I overheard him talking to the other man he was with," Martha told him.

"And what was he saying?" Keith asked, preparing himself for whatever dirt Theodore or Julian might've thrown on his name.

"I ain't gonna go into the whole conversation, but from what I hear, you 'spend more time trying to save babies in the ghetto than you do working the big cases.' His words, not mine," she said. "Seems I'm not the only mother you've given back her son to."

"Don't worry about that stuff, Martha," Keith told her.

"Oh, I'm not worried, especially since my ghetto baby is one of the ones you were able to help. I was just a little surprised by it. The Keith I remember from back home was more worried about chasing money and women than helping people. Now here you are, a big-time lawyer who could be making only God knows how much money on these cases, but you leave it on the table to help strangers. Why?"

Keith thought long and hard about it before answering. "I'm paying my blessings forward," he said simply.

Martha nodded. "Fair enough. Either way, I'm thankful for your mercies, Keith *Davis*." She winked. "I'll be outside. Send Charles out when you're done with him. I've got to get to my second job." Martha gave Keith one last hug and headed for the exit.

Keith waited until Martha had gone before he walked over to where Charles was standing. Before the young man could open his mouth, Keith had him by the arm and was dragging him to a quiet corner near the vending machines. Charles tried to protest, but Keith's hand clamped his windpipe, making it nearly impossible for him to speak.

"Shut up," Keith snarled. His smooth demeanor had vanished, replaced by a hard face and sharp words. "If you open that lying-ass mouth one more time without me telling you to, I'm going to smack the taste out of it. You understand me?"

Charles opened his mouth to say something but then thought better of it and just nodded in response.

"Let's establish two things off the muscle." Keith released his grip on Charles's throat. "One, I hate liars, and two, I know you were at that robbery and not in Savannah that night," Keith revealed to Charles, who was so shocked that his jaw dropped. "Close your mouth, boy. You're letting the flies in." He tapped Charles's chin with his finger.

"Listen, Mr. Davis, I can explain—"

"Please don't," Keith said, cutting him off. "You've already proven to me that anything that comes out of your mouth is suspect. Let me paint a picture for you, shithead, and feel free to stop me when I'm wrong. Those idiots from your job, who you thought were your friends, concocted this robbery scheme, and even though you knew it was a dumb idea, you went along with them. Probably didn't want to look like a punk to your boys. Things take a wrong turn, and when the old man resists, one of you panics and shoots him. Now, I'm not sure who fired the gun, but I know it wasn't you. From the bit of time I have spent around you while working this case, I can tell you ain't no shooter. You being the weakest link in your crew, it only made sense to pin it on you. You were the most likely to let the DA spook you into going along with whatever he said. The next thing you know, these guys you were so desperate to be accepted by are feeding your stupid ass to the dogs to save their own skins. Sound about right?"

Charles lowered his head in shame. "How do you know I ain't the one who shot the old man?"

Keith used his finger to lift Charles's head so they were looking at each other. "Because you ain't got no stains. I been around killers, Charles, and to the trained eye, them stains burn bright as halogen lamps. You ain't no saint, but you ain't slipped to the point of no return just yet."

"You probably think I'm a punk or something now, huh?" Charles asked, unable to hide the shame in his voice.

"Nah, little brother. Dumb as all hell, but not no punk. You're just a kid who made a stupid mistake. Ain't no shame in making mistakes, but there is shame in not learning from them. You're going to be okay, Charles. I'm sure of it."

Charles nodded. "Say, man, if you knew all this, why'd you still help me?"

Keith shrugged. "I don't know. Part of it is because me and ya mama go so far back, but I guess it's also because I'm tired of seeing young men of color get buried in the system because of stupid mistakes. Believe it or not, I was once young, dumb, and confused. If someone hadn't taken a chance by trying to save me, maybe I'd be the one sitting in your chair, and there would be no Keith Davis to do for me what I just did for you."

"I'm going to fly straight, Mr. Davis," Charles promised.

"Of this I'm sure, because I'm going to be hovering over you to make sure you do. You may not have been guilty of the shooting, but you're still guilty of being an accessory, and for that, you owe society a debt. I'm going to make sure you pay this debt in full. Come Monday morning, I want you at my office first thing. Report to Susan, my legal assistant. I'm not sure what she's going to have you do, but I'm sure it'll be unpleasant. I'm going to pay you two hundred dollars per week, minus forty percent. That forty will go into an account, which we'll use to anonymously start making restitution payments to the store owner."

Charles did the math in his head and frowned. "Man, those are slave wages!"

"And it's still more than what you would've made while working one of the prison jobs they'd have offered you. Look, li'l buddy, this is nonnegotiable. If you get it in your mind not to show up for work, I'm gonna come find you and beat the brakes off you, before I turn you over to these white folks you wronged and let them treat you to some Southern justice. Feel me?"

"Yes, Mr. Davis," Charles replied.

"And, Charles, if you happen to think that ass whipping I promised you is an idle threat, when you get home, ask your mother about Killer from the Lower Ninth. Now get going. I have a lunch meeting to catch."

Charles turned to leave but stopped short. "Mr. Davis, can I ask you one last thing?"

"Sure, kid."

"How did you make it look like I was really in Savannah during the robbery?"

Keith chuckled. "Thank the universe for that one, with a little help from your older brother Mike. He managed to get himself arrested that night too. Busted some guy's jaw in a bar fight near Savannah State and spent the night in the drunk tank. Him being a city employee, his name popping up in the system would've cost him his job, so instead, he gave them your name when he was booked. It was a greaseball move, but it ended up saving your ass, so I'd call it even."

Charles was stunned by the revelation. His older brother Mike was a straight arrow. He had a good job, women loved him, and he had always been popular around town. His mother had always praised Mike for being perfect, but it seemed he wasn't so perfect, after all. "I guess you learn something new every day."

"Very true, Mr. Johnson. Now get going, and I'll see you Monday morning."

Keith came out of the courthouse in time to catch a last glimpse of Charles and his mother. She was giving him some last-minute words before opening the car door for him. For good measure, she slapped him in the back of the head as he was getting in the car. She must've felt Keith's eyes on her, because she turned around and gave him a smile before jumping behind the wheel and pulling off. He wasn't sure, but it seemed that the sun had started to shine a little brighter after her smile.

It did Keith's heart good to be able to help a family in need, especially one that came from what they came from. Charles reminded Keith of himself in a lot of ways. He had been far more street poisoned by the time he was Charles's age, but he'd still been just as desperate for acceptance by his peers. It saddened him the way that the judicial system was locking away kids like Charles. These kids acted tough for their friends, but they were hardly built to survive harsh prison conditions, and the psychological trauma of being incarcerated changed them, often for the worse. They went into prison as scared young kids and came out monsters.

A lot of the youth were being written off before they were even given a proper chance, and Keith had made it his mission to help change that. Keith understood that some of the kids were too far gone for him to do much good, but if you caught them young enough, there was still time to rewrite the narrative of their lives. He was a firm believer in second chances, because many years ago he'd been given one, and it had changed everything.

Keith was born and raised on the streets of New Orleans, and he lived a good chunk of his formative years in the Lower Ninth Ward. To say that he wasn't a handful at that age would be a lie, but he wasn't quite as far out there as the kids he hung around with. When he was a teen, his list of offenses was limited to petty crimes, which he committed in an effort to fit in with his friends more than anything else. His heart was more into books than breaking the law back then. The heavy stuff wouldn't come until later in his life.

What very few knew in those days—including those teachers for whom he played dumb—was that Keith was a brilliant young man. But where he was from, brilliance wasn't celebrated. It was targeted. Keith had seen, and sometimes had participated in, the bullying of smart kids in his neighborhood, and he wanted no part of the receiving end of that kind of punishment. It especially wouldn't go over well with his family, who were considered hood royalty throughout the wards. Being crushed under the weight of family members' reputations sometimes led Keith to do things he really didn't want to do just to prove that he belonged.

Keith's academic brilliance might've been lost on his family and friends, but some of his teachers took note. One in particular, Mrs. Winston, stayed on Keith's back about continuing his education after high school. He'd never put much thought into going to college until she planted the seed in his head. Mrs. Winston was relentless in badgering Keith about not wasting his gifts, and she even went as far as picking him up the morning he was to take his SATs, just to make sure he didn't back out. He ended up with the highest scores of all the students in three parishes, and this only increased Mrs. Winston's pressure on Keith to go to college. To him, college wasn't a realistic goal. He was from the mud, and kids from the mud didn't get to go to college. They merely survived. Though Keith wasn't interested in college, he wasn't thrilled about the alternative, which was going into the family business. He didn't have the heart to do what his brothers and uncles did, but he reluctantly accepted the fact that it was what was expected of him. That was before the night that would change everything.

Keith had let his friends talk him into going to a party in a neighborhood that Keith's older brother had warned him to stay out of because of mounting tensions between two rival gangs in the area. War was imminent, and everybody on the streets knew to steer clear. This didn't stop Keith from following his friends into the hot zone in search of a good time. Sure enough, halfway into the party, an altercation broke out, and during it a young man was shot and Keith was left holding the smoking gun. The gunshot victim's crew wanted Keith dead, and it didn't matter who his family was. The only thing that foiled the execution was Mrs. Winston calling in a favor on Keith's behalf.

It came as a surprise to Keith when he found out Mrs. Winston was the one who had got the contract on his life canceled, but it was more of a shock to find out how she'd pulled it off. As it turned out, Keith wasn't the only one living in his family's shadow. He would find out later that Mrs. Winston was the granddaughter of a man known around the city as Father Time. Time was an old-school gangster whose résumé stretched as far back as the 1960s. He'd been retired for decades, but his name still carried more weight than even that of the mayor in the city of New Orleans. With one phone call, Father Time had given Keith his life back, but the favor would come at a price.

In exchange for Father Time's pass, Keith found himself the property of Mrs. Winston. She continued to stay on him during school hours, and she forced him to stay after school three days per week to work as her teacher's assistant. Eventually, Keith stopped looking at the extra time spent with Mrs. Winston as a punishment and recognized it for the blessing that it was. Keith would gradually put distance between himself and the streets and would focus more on finishing school. Removing himself from the madness allowed him to reevaluate his life with fresh eyes, and he finally started to believe that life had more to offer him than being a gangster

from the Lower Ninth. Not only had Mrs. Winston saved
Keith's life, but she had also changed it.

After graduating from high school, Keith left New
Orleans, and the sins of his family, behind him, in search
of a fresh start. It was a bold move on his part, as he had
never been out of New Orleans or away from his family,
but putting distance between himself and his past was
the only way to truly make a clean break. His travels carried him first to Texas, where Mrs. Winston helped him
get into Texas A&M. Halfway through his sophomore
year, his past caught up with him, and he was forced
to leave school. He next found himself enrolled in the
army, where he would spend the next few years, before
settling in New York City. Once again Mrs. Winston came
through for him, pulling a few strings to help him get
into NYU, where he was able to finish his undergraduate
education and then get his law degree. Shortly before
graduation, Keith received a devastating piece of news:
Mrs. Winston had been killed.

The murder was committed by two high school students that Mrs. Winston had been trying to help the
same way as she had done with Keith. Mrs. Winston
would have students over to her home for study groups.
After one of the sessions, the boys killed her and bur-
glarized her home. She died for a couple of hundred dollars and her 1999 Saturn. The police managed to capture one of the boys who was involved, but the second
one wasn't so lucky. The rats who lived in the abandoned
house on Conti Street, where the boy was found, didn't
leave much of him to identify. He was severely beaten
before having his throat slit and his hands chopped off.
To this day, the police hadn't found his hands or his
killer. There was quiet talk on the streets about who was
behind the deed, but the authorities could never prove
it, nor did they really care to. Mrs. Winston was a saint,

and one of her killers got just what he deserved . . . street justice.

Two people went into the ground when they laid Mrs. Winston to rest: his guardian angel and the monster that he had once been, the one she had spent years trying to help him exorcise. That day was the last time he had set foot on Louisiana soil. As far as he was concerned, there was nothing left there for him but a ghost and the memories of what he had once been.

CHAPTER 2

Bacchanalia was a restaurant located in downtown
Atlanta. It was an exclusive spot where power players
often gathered to talk business over high-priced meals
and aged wine. Keith was supposed to meet his fiancée,
Bernie, there at noon, and it was now twenty minutes
past the hour.

Bernadette, known as Bernie to her loved ones, wasn't
hard to spot. She was the most beautiful girl in the room,
at least to Keith. She was sitting at her favorite table near
the window. It gave her a clear view of the street. She
and Keith would sometimes sit there and people watch.
Trying to guess the life stories of the different people that
walked by was their game. Bernie was far better at it than
Keith. She had a wild imagination, and Keith often joked
that she should give up her job in marketing to become a
writer. On this day, she was dressed in a peach-colored
skirt suit with a low-cut white blouse that showed just
a hint of cleavage. The sun shone brightly through the
window, framing her caramel-colored face and giving
her an angelic look. Every time Keith saw her, his heart
skipped a beat, and this day was no different.

She wasn't wearing much jewelry, nothing but the two
crystal-clear diamonds in her ears and the canary stone
on the fourth finger of her left hand. The ring had been
a gift from Keith on the night when he got on one knee
and asked her to be his for forever and a day. From the
first time Keith had seen Bernie, at a social gathering

hosted by the firm he worked for, he knew she had to be his. Keith had slept with scores of women since moving to Atlanta, but none of them moved him both physically and emotionally the way Bernie did. She stood five-eight and had deep brown eyes and a curvaceous body. In addition to being physically attractive, Bernie had a beautiful mind. She had a quick wit and a personality that allowed her to thrive in most social circles. Keith had never known true love until the moment he met Bernie.

"Late as usual, Mr. Davis," Bernie said, looking up from the glass of wine she had been sipping. From the slight flush on her caramel-colored cheeks, Keith knew it wasn't her first.

"Sorry, baby. I got tied up in court a little longer than I expected to." Keith planted an apologetic kiss on her rose-colored lips.

"I'll let you make it up to me later." She reached up and used her thumb to wipe away a smug of her lipstick from Keith's lip. "I hope you don't mind, but I ordered for you already."

"That's fine, because I'm starving." Keith sat in the chair opposite Bernie and slipped his suit jacket off, then hung it on the back of the chair. "I hope you ordered me some real food, and not that rabbit bait you love so much."

"Keith, just because it's not that heart attack food that you're constantly shoving into your body doesn't make it nasty. I'm a firm believer in a clean diet equaling a clean life. If you ate a little cleaner, then maybe you'd be able to win a game against me without wheezing like an old man." She was referring to their Sunday pickup basketball games at the park.

"So says the all-American starting point guard of the Ole Miss Rebels," Keith retorted, reminding her of her college athletic career.

Bernie had been an outstanding athlete in college, improving her team's record in each of the four years she played for Ole Miss. She could've had a career in sports, but she'd opted to enter the field of advertising. Just as she had been a star on the basketball court, Bernie was fast becoming a star in the corporate world, having been named one of the youngest elected vice presidents at the firm she worked for.

"I'll bet there are NBA players who'd be hard pressed to win a game against you without working up a good sweat," Keith added.

"Cut it out, Keith. I haven't played organized sports in years. Besides, skill is only part of the game. You've got to have the stamina to outlast your opponent," Bernie told him.

"I go like a champion when it counts." Keith ran his finger across the top of her hand seductively.

Bernie snatched her hand away playfully. "Don't start something you can't finish, Keith. Though after your day in court, you do deserve a little something."

Keith leaned back in his chair. "News travels fast in the ATL."

"You know I've got the inside track. Even Daddy was impressed."

In addition to being Keith's fiancée, Bernie was also Theodore Hunt's daughter. This sometimes made things awkward for Keith at the office. Though he had never come out and said it, Theodore had never really warmed to the idea of Bernie dating Keith. Keith was a promising young attorney and had never treated Bernie with anything but respect, but he didn't quite fit the mold that Theodore had envisioned for the princess of the Hunt clan. From the time they were little girls, he had been adamant about his daughters marrying men from families just as prestigious as theirs. Keith, a street rat from the bottom of the map, didn't meet the criteria.

Keith snorted. "I could tell. He actually gave me a nod, but then he barely spared me a second look when he walked out of the courtroom."

"Daddy has never been good at expressing his emotions. Take it from someone who knows," Bernie said.

"Well, he expresses them pretty well when he's chewing us out in the office. I swear, it seems like he hates everybody except that two-legged pet rat of his, Sands," Keith spat.

"Cut it out, Keith. Julian isn't that bad. Why is it that you seem to hate him so much?"

"Because he's a snake," Keith said plainly. "He's always slithering around, spying on people and reporting back to your father. He seems to be especially fond of trying to dig up dirt on me. Julian has never been able to get over the fact that I stole you from him."

"Keith, you did not steal me from Julian. He and I went on one date. We were never in a relationship," Bernie said, correcting him.

"That's still one date too many." Keith was unflappable in court, but he could be crazy and inexplicably jealous when it came to Bernie.

The waitress finally arrived with their food. She was a cute young woman, with light skin and twinkling brown eyes. "A salmon plate for the lady, and fried chicken for the gentleman," she announced as she placed the meals in front of them. Bernie noticed her eyes lingering on Keith a little longer than she was comfortable with.

"So, how is your day going so far?" he asked, drawing Bernie's attention from the waitress.

"Great actually. We were finally able to get a commitment from NYAK." Bernie beamed. Her firm had been trying to secure a deal with the pharmaceutical company for months. NYAK was a relatively new company, but it was making waves and money faster than anyone had expected. When Bernie wanted something, she was like a bulldog on a bone, and she wanted that NYAK deal before one of the other firms snatched it up.

"Good! Over the past few weeks, that negotiation has been getting more of your time than me," Keith said, thinking of the long nights she had spent on her laptop, working on the NYAK deal, instead of lounging in his bed.

"Baby, when you see my commission for the work I put in on this deal, I think you'll agree those few nights you suffered through blue balls were worth it," Bernie teased.

"So now that you balling and stuff, what we getting? New Benz? Bentley maybe?" Keith joked.

"Actually, I was looking at a property over in Boulder-crest." She pulled a printout from her purse and handed it to Keith. On it was a picture of a house. It was huge but falling apart. "They're selling it for next to nothing."

"I'll bet. You do know what goes on in Zone Six, right?" Keith asked. The Eastside of Atlanta boasted one of the city's higher crime rates.

"I was born and raised here. Of course I know what goes down on the Eastside, which is all the more reason I want to make the investment. That place is a mess, but only because the people currently living over there don't have the money to bring it up. At the rate Atlanta is being gentrified, I doubt it'll be like that for long. This property might not look like much now, but in about five years, it'll be worth triple what they're asking."

"Sounds like you've given this some thought already."

"You know I don't do anything without a plan, Keith." She gave him a wink. "Speaking of plans, what are yours for tomorrow night? Your presence has been requested."

"By who?" Keith asked suspiciously.

"My father. He wants us all to get together at Sasha's house for dinner. She wants to introduce us to her new suitor." Sasha was one of Bernie's older sisters.

"Another one? Man, y'all been trying to get that girl married off since the Bush administration!" He laughed.

"Stop trying to act like my sister is loose. I know she's had quite a few guy friends since you've known her, but she seems serious about this one. She's making a big production of it and wants everyone to see it."

"Do I have a choice?" he asked unenthusiastically.

Bernie gave him a look.

"I'd love to, but I kind of have plans with the fellas. Carl has tickets to the Hawks game."

"You can play with your friends any night, Keith. This is important."

"So is the game. It's the play-offs! Do you know the last time the Hawks made the play-offs?"

"Go to your stupid game, then, I guess." Bernie folded her arms and glared at Keith from across the table. Keith was smart enough to read between the lines.

"Don't act like that, sweetie. For as hyped as I am about going to the game, I also wanna be there for my friend." He paused for a moment. "You know Carl always gets in a funk around this time of year," Keith reminded her. His friend Carl had lost his mother two years prior and still hadn't quite come to grips with it.

"Jesus, I'm sorry, Keith. I completely forgot. Go to the game with your friend. I know that's important to you."

"What you want is important to me too," Keith countered. "Tell you what, how about a compromise? I'll hit the game with Carl and them, but I'll leave during halftime so I can still catch dinner with your people."

Bernie's eyes lit up. "You'd do that for me?"

"That and then some. Never underestimate a man in love." Keith gave her a wink.

"You know, this situation with Carl has got me thinking. Mother's Day is coming up in a few weeks, and I've got some vacation days to burn. Maybe we should take a trip down to New Orleans to visit with your mom."

"I don't think that'd be a good idea," Keith said flatly.

"And why not? You said yourself that it's been ages since she's seen you, and it'd be a nice surprise."

"My mother isn't big on surprises. Besides that, I've got that big case coming up around that time. I'll need to be here to prepare."

It was a bullshit excuse, and Bernie wasn't buying it. "Keith, why do I get the feeling you're stalling when it comes to introducing me to your mother?"

"You're bugging, Bernie. Why would you think that?" he said innocently.

"Because we've been together over two years and I have yet to meet anyone in your family besides your sister, Maxine. You even tried to avoid that meeting, waiting until the day before she was supposed to leave to even tell me she was here. We hardly got to spend any time getting to know each other. What is it? Are you embarrassed of me or something?"

"No, it's not like that, baby . . . it's just . . ."

"Just what, Keith? Give me one good reason why I haven't met your mother."

He searched for the proper words. "I don't know, Bernie. My family is just a bit . . . different."

A silence inserted itself between them. Bernie had questions etched across her face, while Keith sported answers across his . . . answers that he wasn't sure he was ready to give her yet. They'd had this discussion several times in the past, but Keith had always avoided total disclosure. He loved Bernie and wanted to share everything in his life with her, including his secrets, but how would she respond?

"Bernie, I'm sorry that you don't understand—" he began, but she cut him off.

"I'm even sorrier that you aren't trying to help me to understand," she said. "We're supposed to be a team, but there's always a line drawn in the sand when it comes to your family."

Just then the waitress came back. "Can I get you guys anything else?"

Keith opened his mouth to speak, but Bernie beat him to the punch. "Just the check, please."

"No coffee or dessert?" the waitress asked politely. Again, her eyes were on Keith.

"What part of 'just the check' didn't you understand?" Bernie snarled.

The waitress took the hint. She firmly placed the bill on the table and scurried off, but not before giving Bernie a dirty look.

Keith spoke up. "You were kind of nasty to that girl."

"I'm in a nasty mood," Bernie replied.

"And that's my fault, right?"

For an answer, Bernie rolled her eyes.

"I see where this is going," Keith snorted. Bernie was in one of her moods. Much like her father and her sisters, she could get real pissy when things didn't go her way. It was a Hunt family trait.

"I wish *I* did. I guess I'm just a fool in love, huh?"

"So, being in this relationship makes you a fool?" Keith asked.

"Nope. Flying blind does. But it's fine, Keith. Keep your secrets."

"I'm not keeping secrets," Keith assured her.

"You're not being truthful, either, but it's cool." She stood to leave.

"I don't like open-ended discussions."

"Neither do I, so give me a call when you're ready to close it." Bernie slapped two hundred-dollar bills on the table. "Lunch is on me today, Counselor."

Keith sat there watching Bernie storm out of the restaurant. He wanted to chase her down, but it would do him no good if he wasn't ready for total disclosure, which he wasn't. Bernie was pissed and likely would be for a long time. But what could he do to soothe her fears outside of opening a box that was best left closed?

Another one-sided argument.

Another open-ended conversation.

There was no way Keith would be able to go back to the office and focus on work after this. He was too wound up. The perfect remedy for what was ailing him was two hours in the gym, followed by a bottle of bourbon. *Fuck the rest of the day!* No sooner had that thought crossed his mind than his cell phone rang.

CHAPTER 3

Bernie's lunch meeting with Keith hadn't gone quite how she had expected it to. When she had originally suggested that they do lunch, it had been the first step of an attempt to convince him to have dinner with her family. Being around Bernie's family wasn't one of Keith's favorite things to do, so it always took advanced preparation when she needed him to make an appearance: after a good meal, maybe some bomb sex, he was usually more agreeable about undertaking the task. Keith and the Hunts had never quite seen eye to eye, and this was especially true when it came to Keith and her father. In the halls of the firm, they were professionally courteous to each other, but socially they couldn't be in the same room for very long without tensions mounting. You could see the fuse to the powder keg aflame, and the only thing that stopped the keg from blowing was their mutual love of Bernie.

It hadn't always been that way between them, though. Theodore and Keith had never been friends to speak of, but each recognized the other for what he was, and that had created a quiet respect. Keith acknowledged that Theodore was the elder statesman and a legend in legal circles, and Theodore recognized that Keith was the promising young upstart who carried a chip on his shoulder every time he stepped into a courtroom. Keith had been brought into the firm by one of the other senior partners, Martin Gold. From the start, Theodore thought Keith was a bit on the cocky side, but he knew the first time he saw Keith litigate that the young lawyer was going to be special. He worked hard, showed up early, and never cut corners on his cases. Theodore had been happy that Keith landed at their firm up until the moment he discovered Keith was dating Bernie. That was when everything went to shit.

It wasn't that Keith wasn't a good man. He was educated, financially stable, and focused. He brought everything to the table that a father could want from a man who was courting his daughter—except the one thing that Theodore valued above everything else . . . pedigree. It was important to Theodore that his daughters married well, meaning that they took a name that was as prestigious as his own. This would strengthen their legacy through the generations. Keith didn't have that. He was a product of the ghettos of New Orleans, and he had managed through hard work and the grace of God to claw his way to a promising life. It was an admirable story, but it didn't make him good enough to marry one of the Hunt daughters.

Theodore was sure that Keith dating Bernie would eventually lead to problems at the firm, so he had been doing his utmost to encourage Keith to quit. Theodore had gone out of his way to make sure all the worst cases were dumped on Keith's desk, and he purposely never credited him for his work on high-profile cases when speaking to the media. But his efforts to pull Bernie and Keith apart had only pushed them closer together. When they announced their engagement, Theodore had decided to resort to a tactic that he hoped would taint the perfect image his daughter had of Keith.

He'd reasoned that if Keith was going to be a fixture in his daughter's life, then he needed to know more about him than what they had in his human resources file. Theodore had gone behind Bernie's back and had launched an investigation into Keith's past. This was when things had gone from bad to worse. For all the resources Theodore had at his disposal, his best efforts hadn't been able to dig up any dirt on Keith. Outside of a few parking tickets and his military discharge papers, there was nothing on Bernie's future husband. He was clean . . . almost too clean. This had only made Theodore more suspicious. Either Keith Davis was a ghost or someone had gone through a great deal of trouble to scrub his past.

When Bernie had caught wind of her father's little backdoor operation, she was livid. Not only was it an invasion of her man's privacy, but it was also just a low thing to do. Thankfully, she'd put an end to it before Keith found out. It would've surely caused irreparable damage to their relationship. The stunt had changed the way Bernie looked at her father and had put a strain on their relationship. Eventually, they'd been able to start mending what was broken, but things would never be the same between them. Though Bernie loved her father, she no longer felt like she could put anything past him.

Bernie pushed the thoughts of her two warring loves from her mind and turned her attention to a more important matter—herself. She had the rest of the afternoon off and decided to put the downtime to some good use. What she needed at that moment was some retail therapy. She was in the mood to murder a store or two, but she would need an accomplice.

By the time Bernie made it to Lenox Square, an upscale mall in Buckhead, Lulu was already there, sitting inside the Cheesecake Factory, nursing a drink. Lulu was a thick girl, tipping the scales at just under 240 pounds, but she carried herself with the confidence of a woman half her size. She was big, beautiful, and proud, qualities that she wore on her sleeve. Lulu had never been afraid to let the world know who she was, and this was why Bernie loved her.

At present Lulu was currently occupying the attention of the light-skinned young man who had helped himself to the seat across from hers. He wore skinny jeans, which sagged off his ass, and a pair of expensive red sneakers that looked a size too big. He was definitely young, which didn't surprise Bernie one bit. Lulu liked her men like she liked her steaks, tender. Bernie watched in amusement as her friend bewitched the young man to the point where he couldn't seem to stop smiling. No doubt she was whispering things to him that were so vulgar that Bernie, as a good Christian, wouldn't dare say them to a man. When Lulu noticed her standing there, she slid a business card across the table and dismissed him. If the boy was smart, he'd dump the card into the nearest trash can and forget the chunky cougar from the mall, but Bernie knew he wouldn't. They never did. When Lulu was done with him, the boy would end up another blocked phone number and a nasty story for their next girls' night.

"You done playing in the sandbox?" Bernie took the seat the boy had vacated.

"He's thirty, if you must know," Lulu replied with a roll of her eyes.

"Bullshit."

"Twenty-six. I just rounded up." Lulu snickered. "So, to what do I owe the pleasure of being offered a surprise shopping excursion? And before you say anything, you know I don't get paid until Thursday, so I ain't got no money."

"Didn't I tell you I got you?" Bernie reminded her. "Not too much to it. I was in the area and decided to catch up with my girl. I haven't seen much of you since you got that promotion at your job. So, how does it feel being a senior editor for a major publisher?"

"Just like being an editor for a small publisher, only with more vacation days," Lulu joked.

"You always were the bookworm of the crew, so it is really no surprise that your career path would take you down a literary road. Who knows? Maybe one day you'll even start your own publishing house."

"The hell I will!" Lulu sucked her teeth. "This industry is a damn headache. I love to read, but I don't have time for the politics played between these publishers and authors."

"Is it that bad?" Bernie asked.

"Girl, this game is worse than when I used to strip back in college. Just the other day we rescinded an offer we made to this really talented woman because she got into a public argument on social media with another author. If I was getting five- or six-figure checks to make up stories, I'd be more worried about where I was taking my next vacation than what the next muthafucka is doing! But enough about me. What's going on with you? I'm surprised Keith isn't joined to your hip this afternoon."

"We met for lunch earlier, but he had to go back to court. I swear, sometimes that man can be a pain in my ass." Bernie sighed.

"Trouble in paradise?"

"A small thing to a giant. We got into a little argument."

"Over what?"

"What else? His mother again. Every time the subject of meeting his family comes up . . ."

"He gives you the runaround," Lulu said, finishing her sentence. "You and Keith have been playing this game since things got serious between you. Why do you insist on beating a dead horse?"

"Because I think it's total bullshit that the man I'm supposed to marry doesn't think I'm good enough to meet his family!" Bernie fumed.

"You ever stop to think that maybe it's the other way around?" Lulu countered. "Outside of the fact that he is originally from New Orleans, has been in the military, and graduated from NYU, how much do you really know about Keith's past?"

Bernie thought about it. "Keith has always been pretty open with me about his past. He didn't have the best upbringing, so I know there are some lingering resentments toward his mother and his siblings. That's the reason why he settled in Atlanta after graduation. He wanted a fresh start."

"In my experience, people looking for fresh starts are usually trying to shake bad endings," Lulu told her.

Bernie had never thought about it that way. "You think he's already married? Or maybe got a baby mama tucked away somewhere?"

Lulu gave a throaty laugh. "No, I wouldn't take it that far. One thing I can say about Keith is, his love for you is genuine. Only a man in love would put up with the Hunts and y'all bullshit. He's probably worried you won't approve."

"But I'm marrying him, not his family."

"Girl, you know all that comes with the package. Keith is the one you'll be exchanging vows with, but his family is still going to have to pass Theodore Hunt's five-point inspection. He still gives Keith the side eye, so imagine how he'd treat his family if they're anything other than upstanding."

"But, damn, they can't be that bad," Bernie observed.

"That's true. But you've met some of my cousins from Mississippi, and I ain't gotta tell you how ratchet them Mississippi niggas are. And let's not forget how judgmental you Hunts can be. Keith's probably embarrassed because his family is a little ghetto."

CHAPTER 4

New York's Little Italy . . .

"I'm glad I caught you before you closed!" Carol said, with a sigh of relief, when she slipped inside the fish market.

"No worries, Carol. We know you come in every Friday for the same thing. We'd have stayed open all night for ya if need be," Jimmy said with a sly wink. He was a sweet older Italian man with thinning white hair and a nose that resembled a bell pepper. Some called him "Old Man." "Two pounds, right?" He began heaping large shrimp onto the metal scale.

"Yes, and thanks, Uncle Jimmy." Carol began rummaging through her purse for her money.

Jimmy placed a hand over hers to stop her. "Don't insult me, sweetie. We're family, and you know family takes care of family at the Fulton Fish Market." The fish market had been there since before Carol was born, and it was part of history for the people who had grown up in that neighborhood. "If you wanna do something for me, you bring the kids around more often to see their uncle," he told her while taking the shrimp off the scale and wrapping it in newspaper.

"You've got it. And thanks, Uncle Jimmy," Carol said gratefully. When Jimmy was done packing her shrimp, Carol collected her bag and headed for the exit. Just before she reached the door, it swung open, and she

was run over by three assailants who were storming the
market.

There were two men leading the charge, with a woman
bringing up the rear. The first man was tall and thin, and
he wore a ski mask over his face. The second man was
much shorter, standing barely five feet, and he had broad
shoulders. In his meaty palms, he held an old-school
tommy gun. He, too, wore a mask. The woman, who was
older, was the only one who hadn't bothered with a mask,
but a pair of dark sunglasses covered her eyes. She had
smooth chocolate skin and full lips, which were pulled
back in a sneer, showing off the two gold crowns on her
incisors. Atop her head of silver curls was an army-issued
beret that sat cocked to one side. From the way the men
stepped aside to allow her to get in front of them, you
could tell she was the leader of the bunch. She was small
in stature, but she was carrying a very big shotgun.

"Okay, muthafuckas." The older woman cocked the
slide on the shotgun. "You all know what this is and how
it goes. Show me your hands or show me your brains."

"Lady," Jimmy said as he came around the counter,
with his hands raised, "I think maybe you're looking
for the bank down the street. This is a fish market, and
I doubt you'll find enough cash here to be worth the
trouble that's going to come with it."

The woman cracked Jimmy in the jaw with the butt of
her shotgun, sending him spilling to the floor. "This ain't
no more a fish market than I'm a twenty-year-old video
vixen. You boys are running a Laundromat for dirty cash,
and I'm here to pick up some dry cleaning. Now, run it,
before I find myself at a loss for words and let this pump
speak for me."

A brave, yet foolish, worker wearing a white smock and
rubber boots saw this as his opportunity to play tough
guy. Before Jimmy could shout a warning to him, he had

already drawn the gun they kept behind the counter and was making his move. He never even had a chance to chamber a round before the short man cut loose with the tommy gun and damn near split him in half.

"Y'all think we fucking around?" the tommy gun–wielding robber yelled as he stormed forward. His eyes made a quick sweep over the small crowd of shoppers in the market before landing on Carol. He reached up and grabbed a fistful of her hair, then dragged her into the center of the room. From behind the holes of his ski mask, lifeless eyes stared down at Jimmy. "You got two choices, old-timer. Give us the paper and let us bounce." He pressed the hot barrel of the tommy gun against Carol's cheek and singed her soft white flesh. "Or I'm gonna rock this bitch to sleep."

Jimmy had been around for a long time . . . long enough to know the difference between a threat and a promise, and what the short man was giving up was hard facts. "Okay," Jimmy finally agreed. "The money is in the back. Just take it and go."

The tallest of the robbers took a step toward the back room, but the woman in the beret stopped him with a firm hand to his chest. "What, you looking to die early? You don't never rush foolishly through a door when you don't know what's on the other side," she scolded him.

"I'll go with him," the robber with the tommy gun volunteered. "You got this out here?"

"Yeah. I think they've gotten the idea of how we give it up. Ain't nobody gonna break stupid," the older woman said confidently. Fear was etched across the faces of everyone in the room, including Jimmy. "Go get that cash for Mama, but take the white bitch with you for insurance."

The two robbers made their way toward the back room, with Carol leading the way. They had been gone for only a few seconds before the sound of gunfire split the air. There were two short pops, followed by the familiar rattle of the tommy gun, and then eerie silence fell over the store. Everyone, but especially the older woman, held their breath to see who would emerge from the gunfight. She bit her lip in nervous anticipation, hoping she hadn't sent the boys to their deaths. A few minutes later the two masked men resurfaced. As he dragged a black trash bag behind him, the shorter one was supporting the weight of the taller one, who appeared to have suffered a gunshot wound to the gut.

"You were right about the ambush, Ma," the taller one joked, trying to hide the world of pain he was in from the hole in his stomach.

Ma didn't miss his slip of the lip, but she ignored it. "Don't worry, son. We're gonna get you patched up." She turned to the shorter robber. "Get him outside and the money into the van. I'll cover our exit."

Tommy Gun nodded and helped his partner outside. He didn't like the idea of leaving the older woman in there alone to watch their backs, but Pearl "Machine-Gun Ma" Savage wasn't the type of woman you could argue with and expect to win. Besides, she could handle a gun better than anyone he knew, including himself. If anyone decided to buck, there was no doubt in his mind that he or she would meet a swift end.

Ma backed cautiously toward the door, shotgun sweeping back and forth, keeping everyone on the floor. Jimmy lay there, staring daggers at her. She knew exactly what he was thinking and how things would play out, because the taller robber had been sloppy when he called her by name. She knew that no sooner would they leave than Jimmy would be on the phone with his bosses to report the robbery and share what he had heard. It wouldn't take a rocket scientist to put it all together, and she and her boys would find themselves on a Mafia hit list.

Better safe than sorry, she thought. She braced the shotgun against her shoulder and blew Jimmy's chest open.

When Machine-Gun Ma came outside, she expected to see the getaway van waiting, but instead, she saw a black on black Caprice car pull to a screeching halt a few yards away. Even if someone had heard the gunshots and had called them in, blue and whites would've likely been the first to respond to the crime scene, not an unmarked car. Ma cursed herself for not factoring in that an establishment such as the one they were robbing would have cops on the payroll who would respond at a moment's notice if something went down. Somebody must've signaled to the cops while they were robbing the joint. It was too late to worry about it now; escape was the only thing that mattered from here on out.

"Die pigs!" Ma bellowed before cutting loose with the shotgun.

Seeing his mother engaged in a gunfight, Tommy Gun, who was actually named Big John Savage, went into kill mode. Abandoning his wounded partner and the bag of money, he brought his tommy gun into play and made Swiss cheese of the windshield of the unmarked car. He was able to get the cops off his mother's back long enough for her to join him behind the parked car he had been using for cover.

"Where'd these pigs come from, Mama?" Big John asked.

"From the goddamned bacon fairies! How the hell should I know?" Ma barked, letting off another round from her shotgun. The gun battle, waged in broad daylight, quickly brought more cops to the scene. They were pinned down. "We need an exit, ASAP!"

"I'm on it, Ma!" Big John said, retrieving the two-way radio from his pocket. "Fire Bug, are you there?" he shouted into the radio.

"What you need, big bro?" said a voice over the radio. From the crunching sound, you could tell he was eating something.

"I need you to stop stuffing your face and get us out of here." Big John ducked just as a bullet shattered the windshield of the car they were hiding behind. "Them *people* got us trapped, and they ain't taking no prisoners. Make these muthafuckas jump for 'em one time!"

"Say no more," Fire Bug said excitedly. That was the order he had been waiting for. A split second later there was a series of explosions that started at a trash can sitting outside the fish market. Next, two cars on opposite sides of the street went up in flames at the same time, sandwiching the police in a shower of glass and metal shards.

"Fire Bug make the trap go boom!" Fire Bug sang over the radio, like it was the hook to a rap song.

"I hate that damn song," Big John said over the ringing in his ears.

Before the dust could fully settle, a black van with tinted windows pulled up. Behind the wheel sat a young light-skinned man with dusty brown hair and a freckled nose. "Beautiful," Fire Bug said breathlessly, looking at the smoldering mess of bodies and rubble, as if he was in a trance.

"That's Mama's baby," Ma said as she climbed into the back of the van. "Get that bag and let's go," she told Big John.

Big John tossed the bag into the back of the van, then prepared himself to go back for the wounded robber, but Ma stopped him.

"What are you doing? We can't just leave him here for the police," Big John said.

"Of course not," Ma said. Then she cocked her shotgun and hit the wounded robber with both barrels, shocking Big John.

"What'd you do that for, Mama? He was my friend!" Big John protested.

"But he wasn't one of us. He ain't no *Savage*," Ma said by way of an explanation. "Now, you wanna keep arguing about family loyalties or get your ass in the van so we can skedaddle and split this bread three ways instead of four?"

Big John didn't reply. He got in the back of the van and disappeared with his mother and brother.

"You didn't have to do that, Ma," Big John said once they were away from the crime scene.

"Sure I did. That boy was about as sharp as a wet bag of hair and could've gotten us all murdered because of his big-ass mouth. I killed him to save us," Ma said, settling into the passenger seat next to Fire Bug.

Big John shook his head. "He had a wife and kid."

"And we'll make sure they're nicely compensated for their loss," Ma shot back. "If you're trying to make me feel guilty about this, Big John, it ain't gonna work. That boy was a liability and should've never been with us on a job this important, anyhow. You were the one who recruited him, so if you wanna blame somebody, then blame your damn self."

"I wouldn't have brought him in if Big Money had shown up," Big John snapped, giving Fire Bug a dirty look. Big Money was Fire Bug's partner in crime and their cousin.

"Don't put this on me!" Fire Bug complained from behind the wheel. "I ain't seen Mama's favorite nephew since we handled that piece of business in Harlem. I've been trying to call him, but he ain't picking up. Knowing Big Money, he's probably laid up with some bitch!"

The older woman's hand moved so fast that Fire Bug didn't realize he'd been slapped until the van swerved.

"I ain't one of your hood-rat friends, Bug! Watch your damn mouth when speaking in front of me!" Ma barked. She then turned to Big John. "And as far as your little boyfriend is concerned, ain't no sense in crying over spilled milk. You say he got a family, right? Then we'll break them off a nice severance and be done with it. Now, the both of you shut the hell up, and let's push back to the house and count this money. Once we get this out of the way, I want you boys to hit the streets and find your cousin. He'd better have one hell of an excuse for leaving us hanging on this job."

CHAPTER 5

When Big Money Savage awoke that morning, he knew one thing without question: it was going to be a great day.

When he stretched to loosen the muscles in his broad shoulders and back, one of his meaty palms connected with something in the bed beside him . . . or rather someone. She was a brown-skinned girl of about twenty, and her name escaped him. Not that her name was important to him, though. For two hundred dollars she had spent the night sucking, fucking, and doing whatever else he had asked of her. The girl had allowed Big Money to do things to her that she had never done with another man, including her steady boyfriend, who was no doubt somewhere wondering where she was. The foolish young woman never suspected that it was the half gram of Molly that he'd slipped into her champagne that had pushed her to go the extra mile.

"Wake up." Big Money slapped her across her bare ass. The girl jumped from her sleep and looked around as if she was trying to remember where she was. "Time for you to go, shawty."

"Jesus, my head hurts." She rubbed her temples. She felt like she had just been in a prizefight.

"Probably because yo' drunk ass swigged down nearly two bottles of Moët all by your lonesome," Big Money told her while hauling himself out of bed. He was a slob of a man who was allergic to exercise.

"You got any food?" she asked.

"Sho' do, but we ain't got time for all that. I got places to be, and so do you, like out of my pad." He tossed her the slinky dress she'd been wearing the night before.

With an attitude, she slipped into her dress and put her shoes on. "Well, can you at least call me a cab or an Uber?"

"Trust that whatever I call you, you ain't gonna like it." Big Money plucked his bankroll from his nightstand and peeled off a twenty, which he balled up and tossed at her.

"You're one low-ass nigga, Big Money," she hissed.

"Tell me something I don't know." He laughed. "Now you can leave through the door, or I can toss your funky ass out the window. Your call."

The girl stood there trembling with rage. Her friend had tried to warn her about the piece of shit who called himself Big Money, but she wouldn't listen. She'd been too blinded by the jewelry and the seemingly countless bottles he was popping to see anything but a good time. She had thought he would be her come up, but she had ended up with nothing but a sore pussy and a severe case of embarrassment. She wanted to cry but wouldn't give him the satisfaction. With her head held high, she made for the door. Before she left, she had some passing words. "Karma is a bitch!"

"And so are you. Now beat it, whore," he yelled, dismissing her.

After getting rid of the girl, Big Money checked his phone. He saw that he had five missed calls from his cousin Fire Bug. "Shit," he cursed. He'd completely forgotten than his aunt needed him on a job. She was going to be pissed that he never showed, but when he explained to her what he had going on, she would understand. Money was always a surefire way to smooth things over with Ma Savage, and he had plans to lay his hands on quite a bit of it.

He showered and took his time dressing. He slipped into a pair of crisp black slacks, an electric-blue blazer, and black wing tips. He stood in front of his full-length mirror and admired himself. He looked like a boss, which was what he was on the fast track to becoming.

It was hard to believe that only a few weeks ago, he had been but a soldier in a small crew of bandits. That was until he and his had unleashed hell up in Harlem. That was the job that had pushed them to the next level. The execution hadn't gone quite as planned, though. Instead of their target, an innocent kid had died, but the fact that they had leveled an entire street corner in the process had put them on the radar of some major players. It seemed like people had been lining up to work with him after that, which was the reason he was up and dressed in his Sunday best today. He had a meeting with a man who needed some work done and who was willing to let Big Money write his own ticket on it. Big Money had considered calling in Bug to help out, but then he'd decided he didn't want to split whatever he made on the contract. He'd let his cousin eat with him on the next one.

The sun shone down brightly on Big Money when he emerged from his building. *Another good sign*, he thought to himself. He stepped out to the curb and held his hand out for a taxi and managed to get one to stop on his first attempt. That was a hell of a feat for a black man in New York City. Big Money barely spared the driver a glance when he jumped into the back of the taxi and rattled off the address to where he was going. He was preoccupied with his phone. A text message had just come through. Someone wanted to commission him for another job. Yes, New York City was definitely proving to be fruitful for him. "Karma," he said in a low voice and chuckled as he recalled the girl's warning. Didn't she know that he was a Savage? His last name put him above the law, even that of karma.

If Big Money was not so busy basking in his own glow, he'd have noticed the milky-white eye of the taxi driver glaring at him through the rearview mirror.

King James stood at the mouth of his empire, the General Grant Housing Projects in Harlem, staring aimlessly out at the street. He was deep in thought as he waited for his delivery to arrive. At his sides were one of his lieutenants, a kid named Dee, and his second-in-command, Lakim. It was a tense moment, and no one was quite sure what to say. It was Lakim who broke the silence.

"You sure about this, King?" Lakim asked, hoping King would change his mind. He could see the moral struggle going on in his friend's eyes.

Before King could reply, the car he had been waiting for pulled to a stop at the curb. Leaving Lakim's question unanswered, King went out to meet it.

Climbing out of the car were the twins Cain and Abel. They were two young dudes from the neighborhood whom King sometimes called on to handle especially nasty jobs. They were fraternal twins, and their personalities were just as different as their appearances. Abel was the fair-skinned, outgoing lady's man, and Cain was the dark-skinned introvert. Both brothers were gifted at violence, but it was Cain whom men feared. He had a soul as ugly as the scar that marred the left side of his face, the result of a childhood accident that also left him partially blind in one eye. His mother called the scar the Mark of the Beast. It made him hard to look at, but it also added to his menacing persona. Like his biblical namesake, Cain was born to commit murder.

"So what up?" King asked, cutting to the chase.

Cain smirked, causing the scar tissue just above his lip to wrinkle. "Little piggy went to the market and never came home." He handed King the keys to the car.

King popped the trunk, revealing the cargo he had sent the twins to fetch. Inside it was a pudgy man. He had been stripped down to his boxers and hog-tied at his wrists and ankles. A strip of duct tape covered his mouth, muffling whatever it was he was trying to say. King James expected a man in his position to show signs of fear, but there were none. His cold eyes stared up accusingly at King James.

King ripped the tape from the hostage's mouth. "So you're Big Money Savage?"

"If you know my name, then you know my relations," Big Money replied. "You know what will happen if I'm returned to my people in anything less than one piece."

"Why should I show you the courtesy when you didn't do the same for my little homie?" King James asked him. He was speaking of a fallen comrade whom everyone called simply Shorty. He had lost his life in a death trap that had been set for King James. A car bomb had splattered him all over 124th Street, and word had it that it was Big Money who had set it up and his cousin Fire Bug who had planted the bomb. "He was just a kid, barely old enough to have gotten his dick wet, and y'all sent him back to his mama in pieces. Why should your limbs show up still attached to your body?"

"On my life that wasn't for the youngster, but I think we both know that. My hands are dirty, but yours ain't clean, either, King. You brought a child into a war and made him a casualty," Big Money said. It was more an observation than an accusation.

In response, King James slapped him viciously across the face, sending blood flying inside the trunk. "How dare you speak to me like you're a stand-up nigga, you fucking baby killer!" He slapped him again.

"Are you going to beat him to death or stick to the script?" Cain asked sarcastically. A look from King James silenced him.

"Tell you what, Big Money. Tell us where we can find Fire Bug, and I'll make sure the twins give you a quick death," King offered.

Big Money let out a nervous laugh. "I think we both know that ain't gonna happen. So, do what you gotta do."

"Spoken like a man with the heart for this shit." King gave Big Money an approving nod. "Cain." He turned to the scarred twin. "Since Big Money's got so much heart, make sure it's the first thing you cut out of this fat tub of shit." He turned and walked away.

"Wait. Wait. I can—" Big Money began, but his words were cut off when Cain slammed the trunk shut.

Lakim caught up with King James. "King, I know you tight, but let's think about this. Big Money definitely needs to feel that pain, but you sure about killing him? Don't get me wrong. I'm not denying the fact that Big Money is a fucking greaseball and gotta get his justice, but he's still a Savage."

"And?" King questioned.

"I'm just saying . . . after all the bullshit we just went through with the Clarks, I don't think it benefits us to make new enemies, especially them. Big Money's family name carries a lot of weight."

King studied his friend. He and Lakim had been running together since they were kids, but they'd always had differing opinions when it came to principles. "Yes, Big Money has a name, but Shorty had a name too. I'm going to make sure Big Money's people remember it."

CHAPTER 6

By the time Keith arrived on Atlanta's southwest side, his mood had gone from bad to foul. After getting into it with Bernie, he had planned to work out, then go home and drink himself stupid. However, he had gotten a phone call from a young man named Dante. Dante Archer, formerly known as D-Stone, was one of Keith's legal clerks. After Susan, Dante had been with Keith the longest. Keith had first made the young man's acquaintance while defending him on an attempted murder charge. Back then Dante had still been a notorious hothead and a shot caller for one of the local Blood sets. He'd been on a date at the skating rink with his girlfriend when he'd gotten into an altercation with several members of a rival gang. They'd tried to earn some clout by jumping Dante, but all they had ended up getting was their asses kicked. One of them had even ended up in the hospital from Dante bashing his skull in with a roller skate. Keith had been able to work his magic and get the charges reduced to simple assault, and Dante had ended up with probation instead of jail time.

While working on Dante's case, Keith had gotten to know the young man behind the laundry list of charges he'd racked up over the course of his young life, and he'd taken a liking to him. Despite Dante's reputation as a thug, he was really just a kid trying to make the best out of the bad hand life had dealt him. Dante was rough around the edges, but Keith felt like he genuinely wanted to make a positive change, so Keith provided him with an opportunity by giving him a job.

Dante was yet another wayward soul that Keith was attempting to save by keeping him out of harm's way, but considering the fact that the call he just got had come from a police station, it seemed Keith was doing a piss-poor job. Once again Keith was called on to put on his Superman cape and pull Dante's ass out of the fire. It was the last thing that he wanted to deal with, considering everything else that was going on, but he felt obligated. Dante was a pain in the ass, but he was still one of Keith's wards and therefore was under his protection.

When Keith entered the police station, he was greeted by a red-faced desk sergeant wearing a uniform that looked a size too small. Given the fact that he was looking at Keith like he was shit on a stick and the fact that he had the Confederate flag tattooed on the interior of his forearm, Keith knew the officer wasn't going to make things easy.

"Help you, boy?" the officer asked with a thick drawl.

Keith ignored the urge to snatch the officer from behind the desk and kept things professional. "Keith Davis. I got word that you're holding a client of mine, Dante Archer."

"Sorry. Doesn't ring a bell," the officer replied coolly.

"I imagine not, since I doubt your brain is big enough to have memorized the names of all the detainees you've got back there. Why don't you be a good public servant and check the system for me? Thanks, pal," Keith remarked.

The officer gave Keith a dirty look before letting his fat fingers dance across the keyboard of his computer. He half looked at the names. "Sorry. Don't see no Danny."

"I said *Dante* . . . Dante Archer," Keith said, correcting him.

"Sorry, son. Maybe you've got the wrong precinct."

"Or maybe you're just too lazy to do your damn job!" Keith said heatedly.

The officer leaned forward, and his cold blue eyes bore into Keith. "You think that fancy suit will keep me from coming around this desk and kicking your ass?"

"No, but the fact that I have a law degree and a brown belt in jujitsu may give you some food for thought before you try it. Now, we gonna keep playing dumb, or am I going to have to get a judge to explain to your country ass what obstruction of justice means?"

"You black son of a bitch!" The officer stood up and headed around the desk, but a voice from behind them brought everything to a halt.

"What the hell is going on here?" A tall man who had salt-and-pepper hair and who was wearing a white uniform shirt stood in the doorway, looking at Keith and the sergeant like they'd both lost their minds.

The desk sergeant stood at attention. "Sorry, Lieutenant. Just trying to clear up a little misunderstanding, is all."

"Is that right?" The lieutenant looked at Keith.

Keith let the question linger for a beat. "Sure, just a misunderstanding. Seeing how you're the resident voice of reason, maybe you can help. I'm here to see my client, Dante Archer, but he seems to have gone missing," he said sarcastically.

The lieutenant looked to the desk sergeant for an explanation.

"As I was just trying to explain to Mr. . . ."

"Davis," Keith said, filling in the blank. He handed the lieutenant one of his business cards.

The lieutenant immediately recognized the name of the firm on the card. Most of the local law enforcement knew about, or at least had heard of, Hunt, Lehman, and Gold. Anybody associated with that firm was a problem the lieutenant didn't want in his precinct. "We holding this man's client?" he asked, looking to get Keith out as soon as possible.

"I didn't see his name in the system," the sergeant huffed.

"Then maybe you need to check in the back," the sergeant replied sharply.

A sharp reply formed on the sergeant's lips, but he held it back. "Sure," he grumbled and headed off toward the holding cells.

Twenty minutes later the sergeant came back out with Dante. He stood a head taller than the sergeant and had broad shoulders and long dreadlocks that touched the small of his back. His thick arms were covered in tattoos that told the story of a life spent around violence. The minute Keith saw his battered face, black eye, and split lip, he understood why the cops didn't want him to be seen.

"What happened to you?" Keith asked as he inspected Dante's bruises. It was a question Keith already knew the answer to before he asked. The police had found time to throw him a beating before trying to lose him in the system.

The sergeant answered for him. "Seems he resisted arrest. We found your boy here hanging around a housing complex that we've got marked as a known drug area. When the unit rolled up to ask them for ID, everybody turned rabbit."

"What's the charge?" Keith asked.

"We haven't officially 'charged' him yet," the sergeant said as he made air quotes with his fingers. "He got a little feisty when they were bringing him in, so we put him in a cage to cool off. Your boy has a real problem with authority."

"No, I just got a problem with pigs who like to whip on niggas for sport," Dante spat.

"Not another word, Dante," Keith warned. The more Dante spoke, the worse they could hurt him. He turned to the sergeant. "Twenty minutes ago, you claimed you'd never heard of Dante Archer, but now you know his story?" Keith cracked a cunning smile while waggling his finger accusingly at both the cops. "I know I don't have to tell either one of you what this looks like, right?"

"Mr. Davis, I can imagine what you're thinking, but—" the lieutenant began, but Keith cut him off.

"No, you can't, because if you could, you'd have those cuffs off Mr. Archer and your PBA rep on the phone."

The lieutenant motioned for the sergeant to remove the shackles. He reluctantly did so and shoved Dante toward Keith.

"You good?" Keith asked.

Dante nodded.

"Considering how small the charges against Mr. Archer are, I think we would be comfortable releasing him to your custody, with a future court date. He keeps his nose clean for six months, and this will all go away. Be like a bad dream," the lieutenant promised.

Keith knew he was being played and called the lieutenant on it. "Right, sweep another black man getting his ass kicked by the police under the rug, huh? Well, not on my watch. Somebody is gonna wear this."

"Mr. Davis, let's not go getting too big for our britches. The only reason I'm being so amicable about this is as a courtesy to the firm you represent. I suggest you exercise some restraint before you go poking a hornets' nest," the lieutenant warned.

"And I suggest you boys get your story straight," Keith shot back. "The next time you see me, it'll likely be through the hail of fire and brimstone I'm going to rain down on this department. You boys enjoy the rest of your day." He grabbed Dante and steered him toward the exit.

Keith was fuming when he stormed out of the precinct. That lieutenant had some balls thinking that he would just sweep what they had done to Dante under the rug. Keith wasn't dumb enough to think Dante was an angel, and he knew that Dante had possibly invited this trouble, but that still didn't make it right. Law enforcement was getting out of hand with its treatment of minorities, not just in Atlanta but all over the country.

"Man, Mr. Davis, you let those pussies have it!" Dante said proudly once they were inside Keith's Mercedes and away from the precinct. He went on and on with his spiel about being a victim, but Keith said nothing. A smart man would've picked up on the tense silence coming from the attorney and let it be, but Dante was too full of youth and adrenaline to notice and kept going. "Bitch-ass police always on some bullshit. I'm telling you, if they didn't have them badges and guns, I'd . . ."

"You'd do what? Get your ass kicked again?" Keith said sarcastically.

"If I'd had my strap on me, things would've played out different," Dante said in a tone that gave Keith a chill. He had gotten so used to looking at Dante as his troublesome little brother that he sometimes forgot the kid had a reputation as a killer.

"What's the one thing that I always stress to you guys who work for me at the firm?" Keith asked.

"Mr. Davis . . ."

"What do I tell you, Dante?"

"Don't give them a reason," Dante said, repeating the quote that he heard from the lawyer at the end of every workday.

"Yet you take off running from them like that can't get you killed in this day and age. I guess you don't watch the news anymore, huh?"

Dante didn't answer.

"What were you doing hanging in the trap, anyhow?" Keith paused for effect. "I gave you the morning off because you said you had to go with your mother to a doctor's appointment," Keith reminded him.

"I did, Mr. Davis. After I handled business with my ole bird, I stopped to check in on some friends. The police were sweating us because we were outside drinking beers."

"Which is illegal, not to mention you were doing it in a high-traffic drug area," Keith pointed out.

"It's also the neighborhood I grew up in," Dante reminded him. "I know what it looks like, but on the set, I wasn't doing anything illegal. I was just kicking it with the homies."

"The same homies who couldn't even help your mother raise your bond the last time you got locked up for *kicking it*?" Keith asked. "If you hang around nine dudes with no aspirations, you're bound to become number ten."

"And what's that mean?"

"It means you are who you keep company with. Dante, you're twenty-three years old, a grown-ass man. If you wanna piss your life away, I won't stand in your way. Just don't waste my fucking time in the process. There's at least a dozen other kids who'd kill for the opportunity I've given you. Get your shit together, or find another guardian angel."

For the next few miles, they rode in silence. Keith would catch Dante shooting glances in his direction, but he didn't say anything. Dante was pissed, and rightfully so. Keith probably didn't have to go so hard on him, but he desperately needed Dante to understand what was at stake. In a perfect world, a kid could enjoy a cool drink on a hot day in the company of his friends without getting his ass kicked, but the world they lived in was far from perfect. Police mistreatment of men like Dante was at an all-time high, and because of it, the country was trapped in a bubble of tension that threatened to burst at any moment. When the cops looked at Dante, they didn't see a frightened kid; they saw a threat. This time Dante had lost only a bit of skin and some blood from running from the police, but the next time he could lose his life.

"Thanks, Mr. Davis . . . for coming to get me and all," Dante said, breaking the silence.

"Oh, don't thank me just yet. I'm going to work your ass like a slave all next week for this," Keith promised.

Dante laughed. "I don't doubt it. But thanks, anyhow. Say, can I ask you something, Mr. Davis?"

"Sure. What's up?"

"How do you do it?"

"Do what?" Keith wasn't sure what he was getting at.

Dante paused for a moment to find the correct words to articulate what he was trying to ask. "Keep giving a fuck," he said flatly. "I know you may not know it, but I pay close attention to you. You work twice as hard and twice as many hours as any of them funky-ass lawyers at the firm, and they still don't treat you any better than a nigger working in the mail room. If it was me, I'd probably be tweaked the fuck out and hurt somebody, but you do this shit day in and day out and never complain. Doesn't it get frustrating?"

"All the time."

"Then why keep at it? Why continue to try to prove that you belong among muthafuckas who will probably never accept you?" Dante asked.

Keith thought about it. It was an excellent question, one that he had asked himself on more than a few occasions. "I guess because I'm trying to prove it more to myself than to them."

Dante nodded but said nothing. For a long while, he was silent as he stared out the window, as if reflecting on Keith's answer.

"You good?" Keith asked when they pulled up in front of Dante's apartment complex.

"Yeah, I'm straight," Dante said, but Keith didn't believe him.

"So, what are you gonna tell your mom about the bruises?" Keith asked.

Dante shrugged. "I'll tell her I got into a scuffle."

"She's gonna be angry at you for fighting."

"I think she'd be more pissed if she found out I got arrested."

"She's going to find out eventually. I was serious about you suing them."

"I know you were, Mr. Davis, and we'll cross that bridge when we come to it. For today, let my ole bird have her peace." Dante paused for a beat. "You're a good man, Mr. Davis. At least better than most I've ever met. You're always first in line to offer folks a helping hand, even if maybe they don't deserve it."

"I guess it comes with the job. Years of defending others and all, ya know?" Keith said, downplaying it.

"Maybe, but I think it has less to do with your occupation and more to do with what's in your heart. You're a man of high character, and character is something that you can't learn. You have to be born with it."

Keith smiled, as he recognized his own words. "I guess you do pay attention when I talk."

Dante shrugged. "Sometimes. One of these days it'll be your turn for someone to do you a solid for once, and when that time comes, I hope it's me that the honor falls to. See you Monday morning, Mr. Davis." He saluted him, climbed out of the Mercedes, and ambled off toward his apartment complex.

Keith sat there watching Dante for a time. The young man's shoulders sagged a bit under the weight of what he had just endured, but he tried not to show it. Keith admired Dante's strength. With all he had gone through, with the biggest battle yet to be fought, his main concern was not wanting to disappoint his mother. It was a sentiment that Keith, above everyone else, could identify with.

CHAPTER 7

After the robbery, Ma and her sons had retreated to the place that served as their headquarters on the East Coast. It was an unassuming three-story house located in Westchester, New York. Normally, Ma and her crew kept temporary residences in whichever cities they were plundering, but when business had started picking up in the tristate area, she had decided that purchasing something small and out of the way was more financially sound. The neighborhood was home to mostly working-class families, who kept to themselves. For all they knew, she was a retired widow from down the street who spent her days watching game shows and occasionally baking goods for neighborhood functions. None of them had any idea what kind of illicit business was being conducted right under their noses.

By the time Ma and her boys got done dividing the spoils from their heist, night had fallen. She was tired, and her bones ached. All she wanted to do was take a hot shower and lie down for a few days. She quickly undressed in her bathroom, ran the water in the shower, and stepped in. As she showered, she took stock of her cuts and bruises.

They had barely made it out with their lives. After forty years of playing high-stakes games, she was beginning to wonder if she was getting too old to keep playing the game. Then she thought about all the cash they had just counted up, and pushed the thought from her mind. She was born by the gun and would die by it.

Her thoughts drifted to her eldest boy, Big John Savage. He had been in a sour mood the whole ride back. Fire Bug had tried to chat him up a time or two to break the tension, but Big John had been unreceptive. All he'd done was stare out the window, averting his gaze only to shoot murderous looks at his mother. When they arrived at the house, he had stayed only long enough to shower and then had rushed off to God only knew where. He'd left in such a huff that he hadn't even bothered to take his cut from the heist. For Big John Savage to leave money on the table meant that he was really in his feelings. All Ma could do was shake her head as she stood in the shower. Her eldest boy was one of the most dangerous men she knew, but he could also be an emotional son of a bitch.

Big John had been against coming north from the start. He hated New York, preferring the familiarity of New Orleans, where he ran the Savages' other criminal enterprises. A few days ago, she had called him in to help out on the Mob heist. It was going to be an important job, and she needed her most reliable son to watch her back. Of course, Big John had pitched a bitch, but all Ma's children knew better than to argue with her. He had wisely got on the next flight to play his role like a good son. As a result, he had lost a close friend. She wished it hadn't gone that way, but it was Big John's own fault for bringing the boy. You couldn't trust outsiders, and that was exactly what he was. Ma didn't care how well Big John knew him or how trustworthy he claimed he was. The boy wasn't a Savage, and therefore, he was expendable.

Ma longed for the days when she didn't have to rely on hired help and reluctant children to pull heists. When the family was whole, things went according to plan, but the family hadn't been whole for quite some time, and she was partially to blame. She ran her family with an iron fist, but sometimes heavy hands bruised hearts.

Ma was just toweling herself dry when she heard the doorbell ringing. It seemed that she could never have even the smallest moments to herself without someone intruding. She tried to ignore the doorbell, hoping Bug would get the door, but the ringing continued. "Hold on!" she shouted, slipping into her robe. She shuffled through the house in her furry slippers, wondering where her youngest child was and why he hadn't answered the door. Ma had just crossed into the foyer when the ringing graduated to a banging. "I said I'm coming, damn it!" she cursed and swung the door open angrily.

On the other side was a man wearing a brown UPS uniform and hat. The hat was pulled down low, covering most of his face, but it did little to hide the nasty scar near his eye.

"What the fuck do you want?" Ma Savage asked suspiciously.

"Package for the Savages, ma'am." He nodded toward the parcel on the doorstep. It was about the size of a hatbox and was wrapped in plain brown paper. "I just need your signature right here." He handed her the clipboard.

Ma Savage snatched the clipboard, scribbled her name on it, and slammed it back into the deliveryman's chest. "Here. Now get the hell off of my property before I put a hole in you, ugly!"

The deliveryman tipped his hat. "You have a good one, ma'am." He smiled and left.

Ma Savage picked up the box and noticed that it was a lot lighter than she had expected it to be. She carried it into the living room, where Fire Bug was sitting on the floor, wearing a pair of headphones, with his eyes glued to the big-screen TV. He was so engrossed in the video game he was playing that the roof could've fallen on his head and he probably wouldn't have noticed. She gave him a sharp slap to the back of his head to break his trace.

"Didn't you hear the doorbell?"

"No, ma'am. Can't hear much with these new Bose headphones," Bug said, rubbing the spot where she'd hit him.

"See, that's the slacker shit I be talking about. A good soldier is on point at all times. For all you knew, that could've been the enemy at our gates. They could've killed me and been gone before anybody noticed," Ma scolded him.

"If it had been the enemy, I seriously doubt they'd have rung the bell first. And they might've made it in." He reached into the pocket of his hoodie and pulled out one of his homemade explosive devices. "But they wasn't gonna make it out."

The older woman took a cautious step away from her son. "Didn't I tell your little ass not to play with your toys in the house?"

"Relax, Ma. This one ain't live, but the six I got buried in the front yard and the backyard are. Anybody try to come round here without an invitation gonna go boom!" He slapped his hands together for emphasis, scaring the hell out of his mother.

"I know I shouldn't have smoked weed when I was pregnant with you," she mumbled. "Bug, you shut that game off and go disarm that minefield this instant. The last thing I need is for you to bring the law down on us for blowing one of these good white folks up by accident!"

"Yes, ma'am." He paused. "So, what's in the box?" he asked, changing the subject.

"I was about to ask you the same thing. You're the one who keeps getting things delivered to this address, when I keep asking you not to. I swear, if you ordered some more of that black-market internet shit and had it delivered to this house, I'm going tan your yellow hide!" She fished a blade from a pocket of her robe and sliced the box open. When Ma Savage peered inside the box, her face turned as white as a sheet. She clasped her hand over her mouth and staggered backward.

Curious, Bug approached the box. What could've possibly drawn that kind of reaction from steel-willed Machine-Gun Ma Savage? When he peered inside the box, Fire Bug almost threw up the sandwich he'd just eaten. Resting in a container of dry ice was the severed head of his missing cousin—Big Money Savage.

CHAPTER 8

It was well into the night before King James finished counting up the take from that morning. Even with the help of the two girls he had working in the trap house, the task still took hours. By the time they wrapped it up, they all had paper cuts on their thumbs, but seeing those stacks of cash made it worth it. Business was good and would only get better when they pushed through with their planned expansion. At the rate King was moving product, he not only would be rich but would also be able to upgrade the lives of those around him. Those who armed themselves every day in the name of his cause and those who had lost their lives for it. He was well on his way to living up to the name King, but his ascension hadn't been without its obstacles.

King James had been barely a teenager when he began his tour of the New York State correctional system. A stupid mistake he made in high school had left a young man dead and had snatched seven years of his life. When he was finally released, he hit the ground running. While he was away, he had soaked up as much game as he could from the old heads and hustlers who had come before him. He'd studied them like a college student studied for finals, determined not to make the same mistakes again. One inmate in particular who'd helped him was a con everyone called Old Head. Old Head was the one who had given King James the blueprint to build his empire.

When King was finally released from prison, he had five hundred dollars to his name, Old Head's plan, and memories of going to sleep hungry. That was all he needed to hit the ground running. In the beginning, it was just King and three of his close friends from childhood, Lakim, Shabazz, and Dump, but as his ambition grew, so did his team. Soon King James had locked down two city housing projects and was working on a third. They weren't quite big time yet, but the streets were talking. This was what put him on the radar of the reigning king of New York, Shai Clark.

See, Old Head had been able to teach him the game, but what he had been able to teach his protégé was etiquette. King James was moving through the streets like a bull in a china shop and was unintentionally stepping on toes in the process. When Old Head caught wind of it, he wrote King from prison and tried to school him on protocols, but it was already too late. The monster Old Head had created had already been unleashed, and King James wasn't ready to go back in the box.

It didn't take long for the inevitable to happen and the paths of King and Shai to cross. The very first time King met Shai Clark, he knew he didn't like him. Shai was young, standoffish, and had an ego that could fill a room. King James tried to present himself to Shai with respect, but Shai brushed him off like he was a peasant. At the time King didn't understand that because of Shai's status, he couldn't risk certain types of exposure. King was a known drug dealer and killer, while Shai was working to clean up his family's image. King took the slight personally, and as a result, he started doing things to spite the young boss, like encroaching on drug territories that he had been warned not to enter. King was out of control, and his antics forced Shai's hand.

The war between King James and Shai was hailed as one of the most violent since Crazy Joe Gallo lead the rebellion against Joe Profaci. Blood and bullets rained down on the streets as the two sides went at it seemingly night and day without rest. Shai had the soldiers and the connections, which put him at a clear advantage, but what King James and the few who followed him lacked in numbers, they more than made up for in heart. They were ready to die down to the last man, and they would have had it not been for a headache bigger than the two sides warring entering the picture. Its name was Animal.

Animal was to the streets what the bogeyman was to unruly children. He was death in the guise of a man and had been responsible for taking down men who had been considered untouchable until crossing paths with him. A stray bullet sent by one of Shai's shooters landed Animal's girlfriend, Gucci, in the hospital and Shai Clark in the killer's crosshairs. Even with the killer on King James's side, Shai's forces still proved to be a challenge for King's army. In the end, it was Animal who came up with a way to end the war when bullets failed . . . blackmail. He found himself in possession of information that, if it became known, would shatter Shai's façade as a legitimate businessman and expose him to the public as the dope-pushing monster that he was.

In the end, Shai reasoned that maintaining his public image was more important than wiping out the young upstarts. So thanks to Animal, an uneasy truce was reached between King James and the Clarks, but this didn't mean that there still didn't have to be compensation for all the trouble King James had caused. King James and his crew would be allowed to continue their operation under two conditions: they would now buy their drugs from the Clarks, and all loose ends as a result of the war had to be tied up. One of those loose ends was Big Money Savage.

In truth, King James could've let Big Money live. Big Money had tried unsuccessfully to assassinate him, which was a slight King wouldn't forget, but Big Money was a nobody. He didn't have any real power outside his family, and even in the Savage hierarchy, he was little more than a foot soldier. Had King willed it to be so, Big Money would've faded into obscurity, but because of what he had done to Shorty, even if by accident, he had to die.

King had taken the accidental murder harder than he let on. Though he hadn't hit the detonator on the bomb himself, he might as well have. Shorty had looked up to King and had always been hanging around. The boy had been way too young to be in grown folks' business, but King had thought that by keeping him close, he could keep Shorty safe. But it had backfired. King had been meant to die in that explosion, but it had taken Shorty out instead. King couldn't help but think that if he had only chased Shorty off the block and sent him home, where he belonged, then he might still be alive. Though King would never admit it to his crew, Big Money's execution was just as much an effort to ease his own guilt as it was a way to avenge Shorty's death.

When they were done counting the money, King secured the stacks with rubber bands and then shoved them into an old green duffel bag. It was the only thing he had kept from his days in a prison yard. It was a constant reminder of what was waiting for him if he slipped in the streets.

"I'm going to tuck this. I'll be back through here in a few hours," he announced as he slung the heavy bag over one of his muscular shoulders.

"You gonna walk through the projects by yourself with all that money?" Bunchie asked nervously. She was a curvaceous, light-skinned girl of about twenty. She cooked drugs for the crew and let King lay with her when he got a mind to.

King James smirked. "Any nigga fool enough to test me don't love his life," he told her and left.

He took the stairs down from the eighth floor. As a rule, he avoided taking the elevator whenever possible, especially if he was carrying money. It was too easy to get trapped in one. As he went down the stairs, he cursed when he accidentally stepped in a puddle of piss, which splashed the front of one of his Timberlands. One thing he could never understand was why the residents had such little regard for the place where they laid their heads. King had been born and raised in the projects, but his mother had always taught him to respect where they lived. He never threw trash on the floor or pissed in stairwells. He would even reprimand his soldiers when he caught them doing it. It irritated him to no end. King had a nice apartment on the Upper East Side, which only a few close members of his crew knew about, but he was hardly ever there. The hood may have had its flaws, but it was the only place he felt totally comfortable.

Instead of going out the front of the building, King James slid out the back. It was a nice night, and he knew the front of the building would be teaming with people enjoying the weather. Seeing him with the duffel bag would put people deeper into his business than he was comfortable with. He made it a point to stay low key. Of course, everyone in the hood knew King James was getting money in the hood, but none of them had any clue as to the scale.

When he stepped out the maintenance door in the back, he found a young man loitering nearby . . . as he knew he would. King made sure he kept a set of eyes at the back of every building he did business out of. That night the task had fallen to a kid named Genesis. Genesis wasn't from their hood. He'd moved there from North Philly about a year ago with his mother and sister. There was no father in the house, at least that King James knew of. This was part of what made Genesis stand out from the others. While most hustled for gear or status, Genesis was out breaking the law to put food on the table for his family. Lakim had been the one to recruit him, but King had taken a liking to the boy. Genesis was a cool young dude who, for the most part, stayed out of the way and did what was asked of him without asking too many questions. In a way, he reminded King of Ashanti. He didn't have the same homicidal tendencies, but King could see in his eyes that he would get busy if the circumstances were right. He planned to test his theory about the boy in the field the moment the opportunity presented itself.

"Sup, King?" Genesis nodded from beneath his gray hoodie, his youthful, tan face hidden within the folds. It was too hot for the garment, so whatever weapon he was packing had to be big enough to require extra cover.

"Peace." King gave him dap. "Everything a'ight out here?"

"Quiet," Genesis said with a shrug.

"Where's everybody else?"

"Dee slid off with some *jawn*, and Lakim went to the store to grab some roll ups," Genesis told him.

King stood there shooting the shit with Genesis for a few minutes. At some point in their conversation, King heard the distinct sound of Genesis's stomach growling. When the boy realized his boss had heard it, he lowered his eyes in shame.

"How long you been out here?" King asked.

"About four or five hours," Genesis replied.

King went into his pocket and fished out some cash. He peeled off forty dollars and extended it toward Genesis. "I'm gonna send one of the young boys back here to relieve you. I want you to go grab yourself something to eat."

"Don't embarrass me, man. I ain't with no handouts," Genesis said, refusing the money.

"This ain't a handout. Consider it an advance on your pay. You're no good to me if you're passed out back here from hunger."

Genesis reluctantly took the money. "Thanks."

"You really wanna thank me? Start listening to your body when it's trying to tell you something." King patted him on the shoulder. Before walking off, he had some parting words for the young hustler. "After tonight you're off the door."

"C'mon, King. You know I need this money. If I did something wrong, tell me what it is, and I'll fix it," Genesis pleaded.

"I'm not firing you. I'm *promoting* you," King told him. "See Dee in the morning, and he'll explain your new duties."

"Thanks, King. I won't let you down!" Genesis promised.

"If you know what's good for you, you won't," King replied. It was more of an affirmation than a threat.

As King James was walking out of the projects, his best friend, Lakim, was coming back in. He was jawing away with someone on the phone. Lakim was a straight goon and a man who rarely smiled, but whoever he was speaking to on the phone had him showing the entire gold bridge that covered his top row of teeth. He had just reached King when he ended the call.

"Money or pussy?" King asked. Those were the only two things he could think of that elicited that reaction from Lakim.

"Both. That package got delivered," Lakim told him. King knew without Lakim having to say that he was speaking about what was left of Big Money Savage. "I can only imagine the look on ole girl's face when she got it."

"I should have told Cain to take a picture."

"That crazy muthafucka probably would've. I hear he carried out your directions to a T. Messed that boy up something awful," Lakim said, recalling the story he'd gotten from Abel.

"That's why I asked him to do it instead of you. Cain is the only one who could properly convey the type of message that I was trying to send," King said. "Did you tell them what I said about getting low for a while?"

"Yeah, I hit them with some paper and dropped their asses off at the Amtrak."

"Good." King nodded. "I'm sure Cain was careful, but he's got a face that isn't easy to forget. Best he not be around for a few days."

"I feel you, King, but I don't think that was a good idea. There's gonna be blowback behind this, and now we're short two of our best soldiers," Lakim said.

"You still talking that revenge shit?" King gave Lakim a disapproving look. "If those country muthafuckas know like I know, they better chalk this up as an eye-for-an-eye situation and stay in the woods."

"I hear you, but I know how these people move. Had we just knocked off a soldier, I could see it, but we've spilled their blood. The old woman ain't gonna let this go. Her honor won't allow it."

"Fuck it! Let 'em come," King said. "Muthafuckas hear the name Savage and bitch up like they don't bleed too. I'm a fucking gladiator, and so is every man on this team, or so I thought." He gave Lakim a questioning look.

"All I'm saying is it's best we be prepared for anything," Lakim said.

"And I always am." King rolled his broad shoulders. "Ain't a muthafucka who grew off that family tree ready to box with God."

CHAPTER 9

Keith made the trip from Dante's apartment complex to his place in Brookhaven in record time, just under forty minutes. It was an abandoned warehouse on the outskirts of town that he had purchased and renovated when his star first began to shine in Georgia. As he turned into the cracked driveway on the side of the house, his tire hit a dip, reminding him that he needed to call someone out to fill it. He'd been dumping every loose dollar he had into the renovation of the space in an attempt to turn it into what he envisioned as the ultimate bachelor pad. It had been an impulsive and unnecessary purchase, but at the time he had still been stuck on trying to prove that he belonged among Atlanta's elite. In the end, he'd end up with a bad investment and too much pride to say "I fucked up."

The motion lights cast Keith's shadow on the side of the brick building while he fumbled with his keys at the front door. No sooner had he crossed the threshold than he was greeted by his two miniature pinschers: Bonnie and Clyde. Bonnie barked her head off to protest the fact that he'd left them alone for so many hours. She was maybe ten pounds, soaking wet, but she carried herself like a certified killer and would go head up against a man or a beast of any size. Clyde, as usual, was silent as the grave, but his eyes followed Keith intently as he wearily kicked his shoes off at the door. Keith had discovered the dogs while on a fishing trip. The burlap sack their previous owner had tried to drown them in had got caught in Keith's fishing line. Of the five newborn pups in the sack, only Bonnie and Clyde had survived the assassination attempt.

Keith spared both dogs pats on the head before shuffling into his living room. Of all the rooms in the house, he always felt most comfortable in this one. It was the one room of the house that had been robbed of all color. Everything, from the walls to the furniture, was white. It was his clean slate and the place he went when he needed to zone out. He plucked a bottle of Johnnie Walker Red from the bar in the corner and flopped on the couch, totally spent. Between having an argument with Bernie and having to rescue Dante from the law, he had nothing left in the tank for the day. All he wanted to do was drink and watch ESPN until he fell into a dreamless sleep. However, this wasn't to be.

Instead of rolling waves of drunken unconsciousness, Keith experienced nightmares and fits of tossing and turning, which caused him to keep waking up throughout the night. He finally got out of bed at six o'clock the next morning, drenched in sweat and shaking like a leaf. Most of the nightmares were random and hardly worth remembering, but the last one, which had hitched a ride back into the conscious world, got his attention.

It was more a memory than a nightmare. He was a boy of maybe ten or eleven at the time of the incident. His dad and his older brother Dickey were gearing up to go on a fishing trip. Normally, Keith was allowed to go, but for some reason, this time his dad forbade him. Keith, never being one to take no for an answer, stowed away on the trip. He buried himself under some blankets and fishing gear on the floor of the backseat of the truck. It wasn't the best hiding spot, and when his father found him, he would surely rain hell down on him for disobeying, but by the time that happened, they'd be too far from home for him to send Keith back.

They'd been riding about an hour when Keith started to feel like something wasn't right. It never took them that long to get to the lake, which was only a few miles from the house. From beneath the blankets and gear, he could hear the truck's front doors open and close and braced for the beating that he surely had coming. To his surprise, they never stopped at the backseat but went right to the trunk. Keith peeked out from beneath the blankets and discovered that they were nowhere near the lake but were parked at the edge of the swamp.

Through the back window, he spied his father and Dickey struggling to pull something from the trunk. It was an old carpet, and judging by the fact that it took both of them to carry the thing. it had to be heavy. The father and son half dragged, half carried the carpet into the brush. Keith's instincts told him to remain hidden, but curiosity pulled him from the truck. He peered through the weeds and watched as his dad and Dickey pulled the carpet through the mud and toward the murky water. From his position, he could hear Dickey say something about gators, which drew a throaty laugh from their father. The humorous moment was broken up when something unexpected happened. The carpet moved! More like thrashed, really.

Keith watched in confusion as his father wrestled in the mud with the thrashing carpet, while Dickey beat it with a stick. Finally, the carpet stopped its thrashing, and they were able to dump it into the swamp. The moment it touched the water was when Keith noticed the blood. It fanned out like a crimson cloud on the water as the carpet began to sink. Then came the gators.

Keith didn't need to see any more. He crept as quickly as he could back to the truck and buried himself again beneath the blankets and gear. During the ride home, his knees knocked together so bad that it was a wonder no one heard them. No matter how hard he tried, he couldn't get what he had just seen out of his head. Keith was young, but he wasn't dumb. He suspected that his father and Dickey had driven out to the swamp to get rid of more than just an old carpet. Keith's parents had never made it a secret to their kids that their family was *different*, but it wasn't until that morning at the swamp that he began to understand just what that meant.

Keith shook off the memory of that morning when Bonnie and Clyde started to stir on the bed. Since he was already up, it made no sense to waste the daylight. Keith jumped into his sweat suit, grabbed the dog leashes, and headed out for his morning walk. While scrolling through his phone as he walked, he noticed he had missed two calls from his sister, Maxine, while he was sleeping. Of all his siblings, she was the only one he kept in semi-regular contact with. Keith and Maxine were the closest in age and had spent a lot of time together. After his dad got killed, his older brothers had taken to the street, and his mother had never seemed to have time for him, so it had been left to Maxine to look after him. She was the one who had taught him how to ride a bike and even how to put on a condom properly. Keith loved Maxine and would do anything for her.

He was just about to check his voicemail when his phone rang. When Bernie's picture popped up on the screen, a smile spread across his face. He knew she could stay mad at him.

"Good morning, beautiful," he answered in a silky tone.

"Hi, Keith. I'm just checking to make sure you haven't forgotten about dinner at Sasha's tonight," she said, her response dry.

"Yeah, I got you, babe," he replied.

"Thanks. I appreciate you doing this for me."

"You know there's nothing I wouldn't do for you, baby. Listen, about earlier—" he began, but she cut him off.

"Listen, I hate to rush off, but I'm about to get in traffic and don't want to talk while driving. I'll see you tonight." Bernie ended the call before Keith could reply.

It was safe to say that she was still pissed.

His journey took him a mile down the road to the local 7-Eleven, where he grabbed a coffee, a bottle of water, and a newspaper. As he was waiting in line to pay for his goods, two females walked in. One was tall and light skinned, with legs that looked like they went on for days and shorts so tiny they didn't leave much to the imagination. The other was brown, with an ass so big that he wondered how she kept her balance. The tall one made eye contact with Keith, then whispered something to her friend, which made them both snicker before they disappeared down the snack aisle.

He was outside, feeding the bottled water to his two pinschers, when the girls came out of the 7-Eleven and headed in his direction. As soon as Bonnie spotted them, she started in, barking and snarling. She lunged forward to nip one of the approaching girls, but thankfully, Keith had a firm grip on the leash.

"Cut it out!" Keith gave the leash a firm tug. "Sorry about that," he said to the two girls.

"It's all good. She's just marking her territory. Can't say that I blame her." The tall one eyed Keith. "So, is she the lady of the house?"

"Yes, but if you're asking me if I'm single, afraid not. I have a girlfriend," Keith said, cutting right to the chase.

"But you ain't married. I'm thinking maybe we can be friends too?" the tall girl replied, pressing.

For just the briefest of moments, Keith thought about it. The girl was definitely sexy as hell, and he could only imagine the raunchy things they could do behind closed doors, but then he thought of Bernie. "Nah, I don't think that would be healthy for either of us."

"A loyal one, huh?" the tall girl smirked. "I respect it. I hope your girlfriend realizes how lucky she is."

"Me too," Keith mumbled.

"Well, if you ever change your mind about us being friends, come see me. I dance at the Blue Flame. Ask for Kat," she told him before sauntering back toward her car with her friend.

Keith stood there for a time, watching the girls leave. Were he the Keith of old, he would have taken Kat down, and probably would have brought her friend along for the ride. They'd have made for a hell of a war story to tell Carl and Nate. Bonnie barking brought him out of his daydream. She gave him a look, as if she knew what he was thinking.

"You're right, girl. No more living in the past."

On his walk back home, Keith thumbed through the newspaper to see if there was anything interesting going on in the world. It was mostly filled with articles about how poorly the country was being run, though it also contained the few pieces about the upcoming mayoral election. Nothing Keith hadn't seen before. He was about to toss the paper when something caught his eye. It was a small article about a shooting in NYC.

Keith read the details of the shooting. Apparently, a heist had taken place at the Fulton Fish Market in Manhattan and had left several people dead, including the owner, Jimmy "Old Man" Gissepie. Keith knew the Fulton Fish Market well from back when he was still living in New York. He had accompanied his friend Willie Boy there a few times when Willie needed to *handle business*. The Fulton Fish Market was a Mob front owned and operated by gangsters. It was like holy ground in the underworld, and Jimmy had been respected like a priest. Whoever had hit the place was either very stupid or very brave. Either way, there would likely be hell to pay for killing the old mobster. The shooting was just one more reason Keith was glad he had moved out of New York. He missed the excitement of the Rotten Apple but not the violence. This wasn't to say that Atlanta was without crime, but it was nowhere near the level of New York. That city had a way of bringing out the worst in people, which was why Keith had to leave.

Keith found parking on the street and walked the few blocks to Philips Arena. He refused to pay the outlandish rates at the arena's lot. It wasn't that he couldn't afford it; he just wasn't willing to fork over that much cash to park. He was frugal like that when it came to his finances. Keith found Carl and Nate waiting for him with their tickets near the will-call counter. Next to Bernie, these two men were the closest thing he had to loved ones in Atlanta. Carl, he had met through Nate when he moved to Atlanta. He was an accountant who worked at an office downtown, not too far from where Keith's firm was. Carl was a soft-spoken man who always smiled and shied away from confrontation. He was like the little brother of the crew, and Keith was very protective of him. Nate, on the other hand, was a man in no need of protecting.

Keith's friendship with Nate went back to his days in the army. They had been a part of the same Ranger unit, with Keith being the new guy and Nate the hardened soldier on his second tour. They had grown quite close, Keith, Nate, and Willie Boy, who was from Harlem and was also in their Ranger unit. They were kindred spirits and complimented each other's unique skill sets. Keith would scout the targets, Nate would blow them to hell, and Willie Boy would exterminate anybody who was unfortunate enough to be left standing. The three of them had done some very dark things in the service of their country, and the scars had lingered after their tours ended. When the fighting stopped, they had gone their separate ways: Keith left the military to finish his law degree, Nate reenrolled for his third tour of duty, and Willie Boy took to the streets, having learned how to turn a profit from what the army had taught him.

Nate was actually the one responsible for Keith moving to Atlanta. After his third tour, Nate had settled in Atlanta and had joined the police department. He and Keith had reconnected through Facebook. At the time Keith was still living in New York, where he worked at a small firm and hustled on the side with Willie Boy. Willie Boy had managed to get them into a situation that left Keith with only two options: relocate or do something that he couldn't take back. It didn't take much convincing from Nate for Keith to put in his two weeks' notice at the small firm he was working at and jump on the next thing smoking to Georgia.

"You owe me twenty bucks!" Carl was telling Nate when Keith walked up to them.

"What did you fools bet on this time?" Keith asked, watching Nate grudgingly part with the cash. The two of them were fiercely competitive and would bet on anything from sports to whatever fragrance a woman was wearing. Keith had never understood it, but they seemed to get their kicks from it.

"I bet Nate twenty bucks that you'd show up in a suit tonight, and sure enough . . ." Carl gave Keith's sleek black suit the once-over. "Who dresses like they're going to a funeral to see a basketball game?" He doubled over laughing.

Keith had to admit that he was a bit overdressed. He had planned to leave the suit in his car—for the dinner party later on—and change into after the game, but then he had decided a clothing change would cut into his time with his boys. Now that Carl had pointed it out, he did feel very overdressed. "Fuck you, man. I gotta jet to a dinner party after I leave you idiots. Bernie's sister invited us over."

"Leave him alone, Carl. You know when Massa Hunt cracks that whip, ole Keith gotta come running," Nate half teased. He loved Bernie like a sister, but he had never cared for her father. Nate had once locked a guy up for killing a kid in a dispute over drugs. Theodore Hunt had gotten him acquitted. The man had been back on the streets for less than a week before he killed someone else. This time his victim was a working single mother of two. Nate blamed Theodore for making those kids orphans, and to this day, he hadn't been able to let it go.

"So ya'll gonna stand here giving me shit all afternoon, or are we gonna go watch this game?" Keith asked.

"Yeah, but first, I got something that I think will loosen your tight ass up, Keith," Carl said. He fished around in his pocket and pulled out a ziplock bag containing broken pieces of cookie.

"Carl, you're such a cheapskate. You're sneaking your snacks in instead of buying them?" Nate teased.

"Oh, these aren't just any snacks. They're made with special sauce." Carl wiggled his eyebrows.

"Are those . . . ?" Keith began.

"Sure are," Carl answered before popping one of the pieces of cookie into his mouth and extending the bag to Nate.

"You must be out of your mind. You know I can't piss dirty." Nate shoved the bag away.

"Keith?" Carl offered.

"Nah, man. I don't want to show up high to Bernie's sister's house," Keith said, declining.

"Man, they're low dose. By the time we sit through the game, it'll probably be out of your system. If anything, it'll work up your appetite so you'll be able to stomach that bland-ass food Bernie's peoples are gonna make you eat." Carl laughed.

"Fuck you." Keith snatched the bag. He retrieved a piece of cookie and examined it. He smoked weed from time to time, but it wasn't really his thing. He reasoned an edible wouldn't hit him as hard as a joint. "Low dose, huh?" He looked at Carl.

"Barely a buzz," Carl assured him.

"Fuck it. Why not?" Keith tossed the piece of cookie in his mouth and prepared to enjoy the game with his boys.

Before going to their seats, Nate suggested they grab some hot dogs. Keith wasn't a big fan of processed meat, but the cookie was on his back, and he could feel the munchies settling in. He had at least two hours before he was to meet Bernie, and there was no way he'd be able to hold out that long before eating something.

The arena was crowded that night, so all the lines at the concession stands were long. They decided to split up, with Carl jumping on the beer line, and Nate and Keith securing the dogs. There were so many people crowding the halls that Nate and Keith had to elbow their way to the hot dog vendor. He noticed that Keith hadn't said so much as a word in the past few minutes, so he decided to pry.

"You good?" Nate asked.

"Yeah, I'm straight. Just had a little disagreement with Bernie earlier. You know that girl is always digging deeper than she needs to," Keith told him.

"As she should. You plan on marrying that girl, Keith. That means sharing physical space and head space. How long do you think you can keep that closet door closed before a bone comes falling out?"

"You act like it's that simple."

"It isn't that hard, either," Nate shot back before moving to the window to order their hot dogs.

Keith stood there, lost in his own thoughts. Since the arena was packed for that night's game, the local dope boys had come out in full force, dressed in gaudy jewelry and Atlanta Hawks paraphernalia. One particular group caught Keith's eye because they were passing through the hall and making more noise than they had to in an attempt to be seen. Their whole presence screamed trouble, and Keith hoped he and his friends weren't seated anywhere near them. Other than having youthful offender clients, Keith was disconnected from the younger generation. They had no moral code like the youth of his era had, and their lawlessness made them dangerous, so Keith kept his distance from the twenty-five-and-under crowd.

As the dope boys were passing Keith, Carl was making his way from the beer counter, trying his best to balance everyone's drinks. He tripped over his own feet somehow and accidentally splashed beer on the jersey of one of the young men who were passing by. Keith didn't have to be close enough to hear what was said to know what would happen next. Their body language told it all as the thugs circled around a frightened Carl. Without thinking twice, Keith moved to intervene.

"I told you I'd be more than happy to pay to get it cleaned if I damaged it," Carl was saying when Keith walked up.

"Fuck all that. It's ruined. You need to be buying me a new one!" the young man screamed in Carl's face.

"Look, li'l bro, why don't you calm down a bit?" Keith interjected.

The young man's cold eyes turned to Keith. "Nigga, you know me to be suggesting I calm down?"

"No, I don't know you, and I don't want to know you. I'm just trying to make sure everything is okay with my friend," Keith said in a calm tone.

"Ain't shit okay!" the thug barked. "Your boy fucked up my jersey, and he needs to cough up the bread for a new one." He tugged at the bottom of the shirt so that Keith could see the small wet spot on the fabric.

Keith pulled out a fifty-dollar bill and extended it to the thug. "That should be more than enough to cover the cost of getting your jersey cleaned, but as far as buying you a whole new one . . . that ain't gonna happen. I say you take this money and everybody goes their own way."

The thug slapped Keith's hand away. "And I say, 'Fuck you and your money. I want a new jersey.'"

Now that the thug had raised his voice, people started to pay attention to the altercation. They watched in anticipation of what would happen, some of them even whipping out cell phones to get footage of the impending fight. From the corner of his eye, Keith could see Nate moving stealthily toward them. The situation was about to go from bad to fucked up. Keith had tried to take the high road, but the thug was backing him into a corner.

"Homie," Keith said, slipping into his street drawl, "I'm gonna need you to turn that tough shit down before—"

"Before what?" The kid in the jersey lifted his shirt to show Keith the butt of his gun. How he had gotten it through the metal detectors was beyond Keith.

By then Nate positioned himself behind the young man's entourage. Keith knew what the old soldier was thinking without it having to be said. They were one ill-fated word from a shit show. Luckily, before the situation could escalate, two armed security guards came over.

"Everything okay here?" the first guard asked. His hand rested on his pistol.

"Ain't nothing." The kid in the jersey took a step back. "Just catching up with some old friends."

"Is this true?" the guard asked Keith. Since he was the one dressed in a suit, the guard reasoned Keith wasn't the aggressor.

"Yeah, just some old friends talking." Keith went along with the lie, but his eyes never left the kid in the jersey.

"If you've got tickets, then I suggest you get to your seats. If not, we have to escort you out," the second guard said, chiming in.

"It's all good. We going," Jersey said, motioning to his crew that it was time to bounce. "I'll see you again soon, tough guy," he snarled at Keith.

"You better hope not," Keith shot back.

Keith, Nate, and Carl stood there for a time, while the two guards trailed the thugs to make sure they didn't get lost along the way to their seats. Long after they had gone, the threat of violence seemed to still linger in the air.

"Jesus, that could've gone so bad." Carl let out a sigh of relief. "Keith, what were you thinking about, mouthing off to those guys like that?"

"I was thinking I was helping my pal out," Keith said. His voice was still trembling a bit from the adrenaline coursing through his veins.

"Thanks, man. For a minute, I thought someone was gonna get hurt," Carl said.

"They were," Nate said, catching the glint in Keith's eyes. He had seen that look many times when they were deployed into the field, and knew better than most what could've gone down. "You good, Keith?"

"Yeah, I'm straight. Let's just get inside and catch what's left of the game," Keith said, then walked ahead of them toward their entrance.

The Hawks game was a good one, one of the best games he'd seen the team play. They battled ferociously against the Chicago Bulls in game seven of the Eastern Conference semis. By halftime, the score was knotted up at fifty points, and the second half promised to be an all-out fight. Unfortunately, Keith wouldn't be there to see it. It was time for him to head out to Buckhead.

As Keith walked back to his car, he thumbed away on his cell phone, texting Bernie to let her know that he was on the way. She texted back a dry okay, at which he just shook his head. He was about to sit through what was sure to be a shit show of plastic smiles and bland food, and she was the one with an attitude? He had just arrived at the spot where he left his Mercedes when he felt the hairs on the back of his neck prick. His military training kicked in, and he spun in a defensive stance, ready to engage the threat. At first, all seemed quiet, but then he spotted them, three shadows doing a piss-poor job of concealing themselves. He knew who they were and why they had come long before they stepped into the light of the single streetlamp on the block.

"Where you off to, tough guy?" the kid wearing the jersey called out.

"Look, bro, I don't want any trouble," Keith told him.

"First off, I ain't your fucking bro. And second, where's all that tough shit you were talking back at the arena? You ain't so tough without them rent-a-cops to hide behind, huh?" Jersey taunted.

Keith could feel the blood begin to boil in his veins. They wanted trouble, and normally, he wouldn't mind giving it to them, but he had somewhere to be. "Okay, so what's it going to take for us to put this bullshit between us to bed?" he said, trying to bow out and hoping they'd let him.

Jersey looked at the shiny silver Mercedes. "I think your ride will do."

Keith looked from his car back to Jersey. "You're shitting me, right?"

A gun appeared in Jersey's hand. "Does it look like I'm shitting you? Run those keys!"

Keith had tried so very hard to avoid trouble while he was living in Atlanta, and until now he had been successful. He could tell that the only way out of this situation was to speak to the young men in a language that they understood. "Is this what you want?" He held up the small black box and hit the button to release the silver key. It glistened in the moonlight like a small dagger. "You got it."

CHAPTER 10

Nearly thirty minutes later Keith was burning up the road to Bernie's sister's house. He would arrive later than he had originally said he would, and this was probably already being chatted about among the Hunts. He'd have to think up a good excuse, because the truth certainly wouldn't do.

He adjusted the rearview mirror to examine the spot on his temple where one of the boys had sucker punched him. The blow had barely landed hard enough to make him stagger, but it had succeeded in making him angry, and that was when things had got nasty. Keith had set out to give the boys a good spanking just to teach them a lesson, but things had gotten out of hand. The first order of business was to separate Jersey from his knife, which was easy enough. He was a thug, not a highly skilled Ranger, so even though Jersey had a gun, he was still in over his head. It was hardly a fair fight. When Keith's car key bit into the muscles of Jersey's forearm, it caused him to lose his grip on the weapon. It was a minor wound that would heal in a week or so, but the two ribs Keith cracked when he slugged him in his side would probably take a bit longer to mend.

It was while he was busy with Jersey that one of the other boys punched him in his head. Keith respected the fact that this boy was trying to help his friend, but that didn't stop him from breaking the boy's jaw. When the third boy saw what had become of his friends, he took off running. His cowardice would probably earn him a nice ass whipping when his crew caught up with him, but Keith was more concerned about his three-hundred-dollar jacket, which had gotten ripped during the fight, than he was about what would happen to the coward. It was their own faults. They had come in search of prey and instead had found a predator.

It had been a long time since Keith had felt the soft tearing of a man's flesh beneath his knuckles. He had thought it would make him feel better, but it hadn't. In fact, he felt terrible. On that back street, he'd left two broken men, while he had walked away with a few aches and bruises, but he'd still lost the fight. Maybe not physically, but spiritually he'd gotten his ass kicked. For years Keith had fought so hard to suppress the old anger and find peace within himself, and in the blink of an eye, it had all been undone. Over what? Words? Pride? Or maybe it was as his mother's old words coming back to haunt him: "A man can change who he is, but what he is will always be."

When he pulled into the circular driveway of Sasha's plantation-style home, he found Bernie standing outside, waiting for him. She was wearing one of his favorite dresses, a short black number that dipped in the front, showing off her full breasts. Her short hair was loosely feathered, and a single red rose was nestled on one side. Standing there, arms folded and oozing sex appeal, she reminded him of Dorothy Dandridge when she played Carmen Jones. He gave himself the once-over to make sure there were no lingering signs of his scuffle and then got out of the Mercedes to greet his lady love.

"Damn, girl. You look good enough to eat." Keith went to plant a kiss on her lips, but she turned and gave him her cheek. "Oh, we still on that?"

"Please, let's not do this here," she said in a tired voice. "Where's your jacket? I thought I told you this was a formal dinner."

"I spilled mustard on it at the game," he lied. "I could always rock it as is, though." He faked like he was going back to the car to retrieve the jacket, hoping that she'd stop him.

"Just forget it. You're already late, and everybody is waiting so we can sit down and eat. Let's just go inside so I don't have to hear any more of my father's shit," Bernie said with a major attitude.

"We sho' don't wanna keep ole Massa Hunt waiting!" Keith said in his best slave drawl. He was trying to make a joke, but it was lost on Bernie.

"Don't do that, Keith. This isn't about my father complaining about you being late. It's about you respecting my family enough to be on time when you're invited to something important. If I'm ever fortunate enough to meet your family, I'll be sure to show them the same courtesy." Bernie stepped back. "And for the love of peace, please try to be nice. I can smell the alcohol on your breath, and you know you're a mean drunk."

Keith blew his breath into his hands to see if it was true. "I had only a half of a beer. I'm not even buzzed," he said, omitting the fact that he'd also partaken of a pot cookie. "And why wouldn't I be nice? Me and Sasha have always gotten along."

"I'm not talking about Sasha," Bernie told Keith while ushering him inside the house.

As soon as Keith walked inside the house, he understood why Bernie had been on him about being nice. One look at the cast of characters seated around the dinner table and he knew that it was going to be a long night.

As usual, Theodore sat perched at the head of the table, in all his omnipotence. His face was a blank slate, but Keith could see the judgment in his eyes as they washed over the assembled guests. His date for the evening was his current flavor of the month: a high yellow piece with bleached blond hair. Keith wasn't sure, but he thought he had seen her in a magazine ad somewhere. She'd spend the majority of the night scrolling through her phone, while occasionally raising her head to offer a fake chuckle at whatever Theodore said, funny or not. She was as plastic as her tits and was just Theodore's type. Since Theodore and his wife, Bernie's mother, had divorced several years ago, he spent most of his nights trying to recapture his youth in the wombs of women half his age. It was the first, and likely the last, time any of them would ever see the model.

When Theodore spotted Keith, he gave him a curt nod. Skulking in Theodore's shadow, as usual, was the reason Bernie had warned Keith to behave himself . . . Julian Sands. When Julian and Keith made eye contact, a mutual hatred passed between them.

"I thought this was a family function," Keith whispered to Bernie through clenched teeth.

"It is. Julian has been with my father for years. You know he's like family to us."

"He ain't no kin of mine, and if he keeps looking over here like he's getting big ideas, me and him are gonna go out in the yard and have a conversation," Keith said seriously.

"Keith, please!" Bernie tightened her grip on Keith's hand.

"You got it, babe," he conceded.

Sitting on the other side of Theodore was Bernie's oldest sister, Estelle. She was the lightest of the three sisters. In fact, in the right light, Estelle could pass for a white woman, and sometimes she acted like her fair skin gave her a sense of entitlement. Of all Theodore's daughters, she was the one who had been created most in his image. In fact, she'd even branched out and started her own legal practice down in Augusta, Georgia. She was a hard woman who was difficult to like, which was probably why she was the only one at the party without a date.

When Estelle saw Keith walk in, she looked at him like he was shit on a shoe, and he returned her glare. From the daggers they were shooting at each other, one would never guess that at one time they had actually been pretty cool. This was before Keith had discovered the truth about why Estelle couldn't seem to keep a man. After divorcing her first husband, Arnold, who was a well-to-do Jewish accountant, Estelle had played the field, going through man after man, discarding them all like broken toys. According to her, none of them could live up to her high standards, which was why she hadn't bothered to settle down yet. It was a good enough excuse to keep her father from pressuring her into getting married again, but it was only partially true. The men Estelle dated did fall short of her standards, but that was only because she had acquired a taste for something a bit different.

Keith had discovered Estelle's secret one night when he happened to be in Magic City, a strip club in Atlanta. He was there to double-check some information that one of the dancers had given him for a case that he was working on. He was on his way out after the follow-up conversation with the dancer when he spotted his future sister-in-law huddling in one of the darkened VIP sections. Seeing Estelle's uptight ass in a strip club was surprising in and of itself, but watching her in a lip-lock with one of the dancers left him speechless. When she finally came up for air, she spied Keith watching her and made a speedy exit. Keith had no plans to expose Estelle, but she was so afraid that he would, she started throwing dirt on his name to her sister in an attempt to break them up. In spite of Estelle's petty tactics, Keith had never revealed her secret, but the fact that he could kept Estelle on edge whenever he was around.

Next, Keith focused on Bernie's other sister, Sasha,
which was easy, since during dinner, Sasha made sure
that the attention never stayed off her for long. She
looked like an older version of Bernie, but her skin was
slightly darker, and gravity had begun to tug at her tits
and ass. The golden ball gown she wore and the matching
elbow-length gloves were a bit much, but Sasha wouldn't
be Sasha if she didn't overdo it. Keith sat there listening
to her go on and on, dishing all the latest tea being poured
around the Atlanta social scene. The girl seemed to know
everything and probably could've had a successful career
in journalism had she only been willing to put forth the
effort. That was the difference between the Bernie and
Sasha: Bernie was more than willing to go out and make
her own way, while Sasha was content to live off her
family's name and wealth.

To Sasha's credit, she had gone all out for her dinner
party, as she did with most things. Whenever she threw
a dinner party, she went with a theme. This time it was
an ode to the South, and she had poured it on thick.
Probably too thick. The entire waitstaff was composed
of black folks, with the men dressed in shirts, tails, and
white gloves, while the women wore traditional black-
and-white maids' uniforms. They bustled around the
room, carrying platters of fried pork skin, which they
offered to the guests, along with cool glasses of mint
julep. One of the male servers made eye contact with
Keith, and he could've sworn the man was trying to signal
to him to run. Keith felt like he was in the middle of a
scene from the film *Django Unchained*.

Despite the eerie setting, Sasha did well when it came
to the food. The meal consisted of three courses, including dessert. To prepare it, Sasha had flown in one of
Memphis's top barbecue masters and his team. She'd
even set up a fire pit in the back to make sure all the meat

was perfectly smoked. The piece of cookie Keith had ingested at the game had him ravenous, and it showed in the way he tore through the ribs on his plate. Bernie even nudged him under the table and asked him quietly if he was high. Of course, he lied and said he wasn't, but that cookie was kicking his ass. "Low dosage, my ass," he mumbled.

Dinner with the Hunts was about as much fun as watching paint dry, and Sasha's flavor of the month didn't help make the evening any easier. His name was Broderick, but he insisted that everyone call him *Brick*. He was a well-built, light-skinned dude with slick hair and a cartoonish square chin. He reminded Keith of a black version of Dudley Do-Right. Whenever Brick opened his mouth to speak, he droned on mostly about himself, and it was irritating the hell out of Keith. He was almost as big a narcissist as Sasha, which was saying a lot.

Midway through the meal, Keith's cell vibrated in his back pants pocket. He slipped it out and looked at the caller ID. A phone number with a 337 area code flashed on the screen; it was likely someone calling from Lafayette or possibly Lake Charles. Thinking it may be his sister again, he was about answer when Brick stopped him.

"So, I hear you're a part of the family business too, Keith," Brick remarked.

"Not quite. I'm a defense attorney who just happens to work at Mr. Hunt's firm," Keith said, correcting him, while slipping the phone back in his pocket.

"Same difference." Brick shrugged. He hadn't meant his comment to be offensive, but Keith interpreted it that way. Brick was working his nerves.

"They call him the miracle worker," Estelle added, giving Keith a look. She was trying to get under his skin.

"Among other things," Julian mumbled.

"Did you say something, Sands?" Keith asked sharply.

"I was just commenting on your case from earlier. That was quite the feat you pulled earlier, getting that boy off when the DA surely had him dead to right. One who didn't know any better might think you found some way to rig the case." Julian's tone was almost accusatory.

Keith shrugged. "Sometimes justice actually prevails."

"Brick is also in law enforcement," Sasha announced.

"Really?" Keith faked surprise. "City or state?"

"Federal," Brick replied, then whipped out his badge and showed it to Keith.

"Must be exciting," Bernie chimed in.

"It has its moments, but Georgia has actually been pretty laid back, not like the last field office I worked out of."

"And where was that?" Keith asked. He really didn't care, but he was trying to make small talk.

"Louisiana . . . Baton Rouge, to be specific. Julian tells me you're originally from those parts," Brick informed him.

"Did he now?" Keith cut Julian a look.

"Yes. He was chatting about you quite a bit while we were waiting for you to arrive for dinner."

"I'll bet," Keith mumbled.

"Brick, do you know that Keith was in the service too?" Sasha offered.

"Is that right?" Brick asked, with an interested expression on his face. "Which branch?"

"The army. I was part of a Ranger unit," Keith said proudly.

"Now, that's some heavy stuff. I was a marine myself, but I was friendly with some Rangers. Real solid guys, and about as lethal as they came." Brick paused. "Did you see much action, Keith?" he asked.

"A bit," Keith said modestly. In truth, he had found himself in the middle of some really nasty situations, and there were times when he'd thought he'd never make it out alive. His time in the service was yet another part of his life that he didn't like to talk about.

"A straight arrow like you, I can't imagine you behind a gun," Brick teased him.

"I could say the same about you being behind a badge. Bet you work some nice desk job, huh?" Keith shot back.

"No, most of my work is done in the field. I've been the lead on a few organized-crime cases," Brick told him.

"I didn't realize they have mobsters in Louisiana," Estelle said sarcastically.

"Organized-crime syndicates aren't exclusively limited to Italians in suits running around New York and Chicago. There's an outfit for just about every color of the rainbow," Brick informed her.

"Baby, tell them about the man you were telling me about the other night. The serial killer," Sasha said excitedly.

"Oh yes. Eldridge Savage. Goes by the moniker Mad Dog."

Keith almost choked on his water.

"And he has totally lived up to the name," Brick continued. "Mad Dog comes from a long line of criminals who've been raising hell in the South since before I was born. Bank robberies, murders, drugs . . . You name it and the Savages have dabbled in it. That whole clan is dangerous, but in my professional opinion, Mad Dog is the worst of the lot. That boy's name rings through the legal system like church bells on a Sunday. His antics keep local law enforcement on their toes at all times."

"If this Mad Dog is a local problem, what did he do to get on the radar of the FBI?" Theodore asked. His curiosity was now as piqued as everyone else's.

"Well, I'm really not supposed to be talking about it, because it's an ongoing investigation," Brick said, as if he wasn't really dying to tell the story.

"Brick, don't keep all us assholes in suspense," Sasha said, urging him on, as he grabbed another drink from a passing waiter.

"Okay, I guess I can tell you guys the stuff that's public information," Brick said, finally giving in. "Well, there were these drug dealers who managed to get on the bad side of Mad Dog. I think it had something to do with them pushing junk to high school kids. Mad Dog approaches these guys and tells them to shut it down, but they didn't listen." He shook his head as he recalled some of the crime-scene photos he'd been shown. "To say Mad Dog rained hell down on them is an understatement. He wiped out just about every member of their crew. He even snuffed out a few of their family members, to make sure he got his point across. The only reason he made it onto the radar of the Feds was that one of the dealers he killed had been working as a confidential informant for the government. It was really just dumb luck."

"Did you guys ever catch him?" Keith asked, not sure he really wanted to know.

"Catching Mad Dog Savage is like trying to catch water in your hands," Brick said, cupping his hands for emphasis. "Every time we get close, he vanishes and pops up somewhere else. Mad Dog isn't the type to stay in one place for too long . . . a real nomad. Mad Dog is slicker than a pig in shit, but damn near every greased pig finds itself as bacon eventually."

"Sounds like a barbarian," said the model, finally speaking, and surprising everyone at the table. For a minute Keith had thought the girl was a mute.

"Quite to the contrary. During the investigation, I did some digging into Mad Dog's past. The boy has an IQ of one hundred thirty-seven. Even got a free ride to LSU," Brick said. "I could never figure out how someone with so much potential could throw it all away to become trash."

"You have any insight on that, Keith?" Theodore said, switching his attention to his future son-in-law.

Keith felt the color drain from his face. "How do you mean?"

"You grew up around those parts. I'm sure you have bumped into this outlaw clan or, at the very least, have heard of them."

Paranoia induced by the cookie kicked in, and Keith had the feeling that every eye in the room turned to him, including those of the *Django*-looking waitstaff. "Can't say that I have," he replied coolly. He was focused on his plate, but he could feel Theodore's eyes on him.

"Well, I sure hope this Mad Dog character never finds his way to Georgia. I shudder to think what kind of hell someone like that could bring to our quiet Atlanta." Sasha fanned herself dramatically.

"Don't you worry your pretty head about it, my love," Brick replied, patting Sasha's hand reassuringly. "People like Mad Dog and his family don't like change. They prefer familiar hunting grounds, so to speak. If you ask me, I doubt any of those bumpkins have ever been outside Louisiana or have the desire to go elsewhere."

"Even if they did, I'm sure Brick would lock the lot of them up straightaway," Estelle said sarcastically.

"Only for Keith to find a way to free them," Julian said, loud enough for Keith to hear.

Keith was two seconds away from reaching across the table and popping Julian in his mouth when Bernie cut in.

"As much as I'd love to stay and continue dishing about criminals, I've got an early meeting. We should be going." Bernie stood.

"On a Saturday?" Theodore asked suspiciously.

"You know I'm never really off the clock, Daddy," Bernie said.

"Don't be like that, Bernie. Keith just got here. At least stay for one last round of drinks," Sasha pleaded.

"I wish I could, sis, but I don't want to be dragging in my meeting. Let's do lunch tomorrow, though, okay?" Bernie planted two air kisses on either side of Sasha's face, then Estelle's, before moving to her father. "I love you, Daddy."

"Love you too, baby girl." Theodore hugged her. "Good seeing you again, Keith," he said in a less than sincere tone.

"Likewise," Keith answered, matching his tone. He said his goodbyes to everyone else before escorting Bernie to the door. Before he left, he looked back over his shoulder and found Theodore giving him a knowing smirk.

CHAPTER 11

"Thanks for the assist back there," Keith said as he and Bernie rode in his car, headed back to his place. He was behind the wheel, while Bernie rode shotgun.

"You know I've always got my man's back. Besides, I'd had about enough of Brick and his ego," Bernie said while slipping off her heels and putting on her flats. Her feet were killing her.

"*Brick*." Keith laughed at the name. "Sounds like a character in a Sweet Valley High novel."

"More like a washed-up porn star." Bernie snickered. "I want to apologize about that business with my father too."

"What business?" Keith asked, as if he was oblivious about what she was referring to.

"That whole 'Have you got any Mad Dog stories?'" she said, imitating her father's voice. "What was that all about?"

"It's cool," Keith said, downplaying it.

"It really isn't. I know you don't come from the most squeaky-clean background, but it bothers me when Daddy tries to insinuate that you still associate with that type of element," Bernie huffed.

"Maybe I do," Keith half teased. "But on the real, I try not to pay ole Teddy any mind. He's only doing what rich folks do, judge everybody who ain't rich. Folks with money will never truly understand the plight of people without. They ain't from what I'm from."

"Well, my father is!" Bernie announced. "Before my father made his bones in Atlanta, he was a poor kid from the sticks who was trying to make a better way for himself. You and he are actually more alike than I think either of you realize or will give each other credit for."

"I don't know what his problem is, but one day me and your daddy are going to have to come to some kind of understanding," Keith said seriously. He didn't like the games Theodore played, but because of Bernie, Keith had never called him on his bullshit, but his patience was wearing thin.

"Watch it, now. That's still my father. He can be a dick, but he's family. Unlike some people I know, I was raised knowing the importance of family," Bernie told him. From the tone of her voice, he could tell she was still in her feelings about their disagreement from earlier.

Keith drove the next few miles in silence. At one point he cast a glance over at Bernie. Her face was hard, but her eyes were soft, and it was clear that she was deep in thought. She wouldn't come out and say it, but he'd hurt her with his unwillingness to introduce her to his family. One thing Keith couldn't stand was to see Bernie hurt. It was like Nate had once said. *How long do you think you can keep that closet door closed before a bone comes falling out?*

By the time they made it back to Keith's place, the mood had lightened. Keith opened the front door, then held it open for her to go in first. As she passed him, he gave her a gentle pinch on her rear to check her temperature.

"Quit it." Bernie swatted his hand away.

"How long you gonna keep up this fake attitude?" he asked, sucking his teeth.

"Ain't nothing fake about it. Don't think just because we shared a laugh or two at the expense of my sister's boo that I forgot about your bullshit from earlier." Bernie waggled her finger at him like a mother scolding her child. Keith grabbed her about the wrist and kissed the palm of her hand. "Don't . . ."

"Don't what?" He kissed her fingers. Bernie let out a low moan. "Tell me that doesn't feel good." He slid one of her fingers in his mouth and sucked on it.

"See, now you're playing dirty," Bernie panted.

"That isn't dirty. This is . . ." Keith got on his knees and slid Bernie's dress up over her hips. He was pleased to see that she wasn't wearing any panties. He kissed her bikini line before easing his way south and lapping gently at her clit. Bernie's breathing was now heavy. He knew all the right spots. "Isn't this better than fighting?"

"Uh-huh," was all she could manage to get out by way of a reply. Her resolve was slipping. She shivered as he moved back up her body, setting fire to her skin everywhere his lips touched. Acting more from instinct than thought, she pulled his belt free and began working on the buttons of his slacks. She finally freed his cock and held it in her hand as it throbbed. She wanted him inside her more than she wanted to be angry with him. She was just easing him in when Keith abruptly stopped and pulled away.

"What the hell?" she mumbled.

"Shhh." He raised his finger for silence and cocked his head to listen. Something was off.

"What's wrong?" Bernie asked.

"You hear anything?" he asked.

"No."

"Exactly. Where are the dogs?" Bonnie and Clyde hadn't come to greet him when they came in. It was something they had been doing since they were pups, but there was no sign of them now. Keith moved to the picture of Johnny Cochran that hung on his wall, near the control panel for the alarm. Behind the picture was a wall safe where Keith kept his Glock 40.

"Keith, what's going on?" Bernie asked nervously as he retrieved the Glock. She had been to Keith's place dozens of times and never knew he kept a gun.

"Go wait in the car," Keith ordered, moving past her, with the gun at the ready. He first checked the living room and then the bedrooms, but he couldn't find the dogs. Stealthily, he moved toward the kitchen, where he could hear the distinct rattling of one of their collars. As he neared the kitchen, he picked up on a familiar smell . . . fresh-brewed coffee. Keith moved into the darkened kitchen and flicked on the light. He found his missing dogs, and they weren't alone.

The man sitting comfortably at his breakfast nook appeared to be somewhere in his forties. He had a headful of long black hair streaked with gray. Against his paper bag–brown skin, his hair made him look like a Native American. Resting on the table was a tattered black cowboy hat, with what looked like reptile fangs circling the band of it. Clyde sat at his feet, silent, while Bonnie rested on his lap. She wagged her stubby tail affectionately as he scratched behind her ear. It was as if he and the dogs were old friends.

"What the fuck are you doing in my house?" Keith barked, startling Bonnie and causing her to jump off the stranger's lap.

"Not quite the greeting I was expecting," the man replied.

"Answer my damn question!" Keith slammed his fist on the counter, rattling the cup of coffee the long-haired man had helped himself to.

The man ignored Keith's anger and kept his tone even. "If I'd had a choice in the matter, I wouldn't have just popped up. Your family has been trying to reach you for days. When nobody could reach you, your mama insisted I come investigate personally," he explained.

"My mother sent you? Is she okay?" Keith asked nervously. A feeling of guilt settled in the pit of his stomach from the fact that he hadn't seen her in so long.

"Your mama is fine, but this doesn't make this visit any easier. I'm here on urgent family business."

"Then you can save it. They don't rock with me, and I don't rock with them," Keith said.

The man, whose name was Asher, shrugged. "Everybody has got their own version of a story."

"How the hell did you get past my security system?" Keith asked.

"You should know better than anyone that they ain't invented a security system that I can't bypass. And yours is shit, by the way. I'm surprised somebody hasn't broken in here sooner and made off with some of your fancy stuff." Asher picked up an expensive-looking crystal vase and examined it.

" Keith . . ." Bernie's voice startled him.

"I told you to wait in the car!" Keith snapped.

"I would have, but you never gave me the car key," Bernie shot back. "What's going on?" She looked from Keith to the man, waiting for an explanation.

"I'm sorry. Where are my manners?" The man stood to his full height, about six feet four, and extended his hand. "I'm—"

"This is my cousin Asher," Keith said, cutting him off. "Asher, this is my fiancée, Bernie."

"Ah, the fiancée? Pleasure to finally meet you. I've heard nothing but good things about you," Asher said warmly.

"I wish I could say the same. Keith doesn't talk about his family at all," Bernie said, looking at Keith.

Asher laughed. "I'm not surprised. I'm afraid the family has failed to live up to Keith's new standards."

"Asher, if you've come here just to point fingers, then you can get the fuck out. Now, cut the shit and tell me why you're here!" Keith demanded. He wanted to cut to the chase and get Asher out of his home as soon as possible.

"It's like I said. I'm here on family business. It's kind of a sensitive matter." Asher cut his eyes at Bernie.

"I'm his fiancée. Whatever you have to say to Keith, you can say in front of me." Bernie hated to be pushy, but this was as close as she had come to solving the mystery of Keith and his estranged family in all the time she'd known him.

Asher looked at Keith. He was wearing a worried expression, but he didn't contradict what his lady had said. "Very well then. Your cousin Big Money has passed."

This news stunned Keith. Their cousin Big Money had come to stay with his family not long before Keith left home for good. From what he remembered, Big Money had been a jovial young man who loved a good laugh but had a nose for trouble. The last he'd heard he was in New York, playing gangster. "I'm sorry to hear it. Things are crazy up here with work, so I don't know if I'll be able to get to New York for the funeral."

"The funeral isn't in New York. It's in New Orleans. Ma wants to lay Big Money to rest in his native soil, as is our tradition when kin passes," Asher reminded him.

"I'm sorry, Asher. I've got just too much going on to leave Atlanta right now. At the very least, I can help with the funeral arrangements. Just let me know what you need, and I'll write you a check," Keith told him.

Asher's calm demeanor changed, and his face became hard. "Cousin, I'm afraid you've mistaken this for a request. Your mama has called a gathering to honor our dead. When the head of this family calls a gathering, *every* son of a Savage must answer. That includes the ones who are pretending they have forgotten who's blood pumps through their veins. Once Big Money is laid to rest, you can go back to playing make-believe with your new friends in Atlanta, but until such time, you will respect our family . . . *your* name, and answer the call. It's time for you to come home, boy."

PART II

Discovery

CHAPTER 12

"Ladies and gentlemen, we've just touched down at Louis Armstrong New Orleans International Airport. The local time is forty-thirty in the afternoon, and the temperature is a balmy ninety-two degrees. At this time, you may use your cellular devices. On behalf of Delta Air Lines and our entire crew, we'd like to thank you for flying with us, and we look forward to you flying with us again in the future. Have a blessed day and welcome to New Orleans."

Hearing the in-flight announcement filled Keith with a sudden sense of dread. It was like he was descending into the very bowels of hell. In a sense he was, because he was surely about to come face-to-face with the devil.

The forty-eight hours following Asher's visit had been the longest of Keith's entire life. If he'd been smart, he'd have kicked Asher out of his house and mailed a sympathy card to his family instead of planning to attend Big Money's funeral. Instead he'd done what he was bound by honor and blood to do: he'd heeded the call. *Every son of a Savage*, Keith had thought countless times, repeating Asher's words to himself. He hadn't been a Savage in so long that the name no longer sounded right rolling off his tongue.

When Keith had finally decided that he was done with his family and their bullshit, that meant that he had devised a plan to cut them out of his life in every sense of the word. This had included dropping his last name. The

Savage name was synonymous with criminal activity, and so long as he carried it, he would never be able to escape his family's reputation. So, Keith had legally changed his last name to Davis. Davis had been his father's last name. Keith's dad wasn't a Savage by blood; it was Keith's mother who descended from the long line of Savages. His father had been a street dude and had had his fair share of run-ins with the law, but his mother was the real gangster. Machine-Gun Ma had balls of steel, and anyone hoping to share a bed with her had to be just as hard. Keith's dad had died trying to prove that he was.

The death of his father had hit Keith harder than it had his siblings. Of all the kids, he was probably the one who'd been closest to their father. He had been Keith's everything, and in losing his dad, he had also lost a part of himself. Though it wasn't his mother who had put his father in the ground, a part of him still blamed her that he was gone. His father had crumbled under the pressure of trying to live up to the expectations that came with being the husband of a Savage. That had been a turning point for Keith. His father's death had made him realize that he didn't want to die trying to live up to his family's expectations. As soon as he was old enough, he'd left his family and his name behind.

Asher unearthing Keith's skeletons had hurt, but this was nothing compared to what he'd felt when Bernie confronted him that night. For a long while after Asher had gone, Keith and Bernie had just sat on opposite sides of his living room in awkward silence. Two things had been apparent in her eyes: her hurt and her questions . . . so many questions. In court, Keith had a response for anything that a prosecutor could possibly think to throw at him, but he'd faltered when Bernie asked, "Who are you?"

He opened his mouth to answer but was hesitant. Not because he didn't want to answer, but because he wasn't so sure that he even knew anymore. For years he had tried to convince himself that Keith "Killer" Savage was dead and buried, but in his heart, he knew it wasn't true. His mother's son still lived somewhere inside him, and it would only be a matter of time before he came out. He'd always planned to tell Bernie the truth about his past, but it would be on his terms. Asher had robbed him of the choice, and now he was left to pick up the pieces of the heart he had just broken.

"Bernie, if you give me a minute, I'll try to explain—" he began, but she interrupted him.

"You've had three years to explain. What I need from you at this point is the truth!" Bernie demanded.

Keith's mind raced for a lie, something . . . anything to soften the blow she was asking him to deliver, but he couldn't find one. Once again, he thought about what Nate had told him. *How long do you think you can keep that closet door closed before a bone comes falling out?* And Nate was right. If he had any hope of salvaging his relationship, he had to use the only weapon he had left at his disposal, the truth. For the next hour, Keith talked while Bernie listened. He told her about his childhood in New Orleans, about the exploits of his family, and the events that had led up to him eventually fleeing New Orleans. He was as truthful as he dared be, omitting only the things for which there was no statute of limitations. Those were secrets he would carry with him to the grave.

When Keith was done with his story, he felt like a weight had been lifted off his chest. He had been carrying the secret around for so long that he hadn't realized how heavy it was until he unloaded it. For a long while after he stopped talking, Bernie just sat there and stared at him. No doubt she was trying to process everything. He wasn't sure how he would take it if the roles were reversed and Bernie were the one to have her mask ripped off.

"It was never a secret that you had a sketchy past," Bernie said, finally breaking the silence. "I'm not naive enough to think you've been completely honest with me about whatever you went through that drove you away from your family, but I didn't see *this* coming." She shook her head in disgust. "I can't believe you lied to me all this time."

"I've never lied to you, Bernie. I only omitted certain things about my past," Keith said.

Bernie stormed over to the bookshelf and grabbed a lead paperweight that was shaped like a pony. "Keith, I swear to God, if you try to hit me with some bullshit lawyer spiel, I'm going to crack your skull," she snapped, threatening him.

Keith got quiet.

Bernie began to pace the living-room floor, still holding the paperweight. "I thought you loved me."

"I do!" he declared.

"If you truly loved me, then why not tell me the truth?"

"Because I didn't want to hurt you."

"And you figured me finding out from someone other than you that you were a part of a family of serial killers would be less hurtful?" she asked sarcastically.

"They're not serial killers, for the most part. And the way you're reacting now is the exact reason I kept it from you. Meeting you was the most amazing thing that's ever happened to me. We're building a beautiful life together, and I didn't want to taint it with this curse that I'm carrying. You see how your family reacted when Brick mentioned my brother Mad Dog, so imagine how they would've looked at me if they knew who I really was."

"In all the time we've known each other, you've never given a damn about how my family or anyone else felt about you, and now that's the excuse you're going to stand on?" she questioned. "Don't you see? This isn't about your family or mine. It's about us. We were the ones who promised to always be true to each other. We were supposed to be building a life together, but how can I build a life with someone I don't even know?"

"Bernie, I'm still the man you fell in love with. The only thing different about me is my last name," Keith insisted.

"You act like that's a small thing. If you lied about that, it makes me wonder what else you've been lying to me about. Did you ever really love me?" Her voice was heavy with emotion.

"I can't believe you're asking me that." Keith was hurt.

"I can't believe you've been living a double life," she fired back. "Jesus, and what am I supposed to tell people about our engagement?"

"Why do you have to tell them anything? I still love you and still want to marry you," Keith told her.

"Marriage?" she said, as if the word tasted foul in her mouth. "Keith, right now I can't even stand to look at you, let alone think about marrying you. I need to get out of here." She began gathering her things.

"Bernie, let's just talk." Keith reached for her arm, but Bernie snatched it away, as if he were holding a snake. When he looked into her eyes, there were no signs of love, only hurt. "What can I do to make it right?"

"The only thing I want from you right now is space." And with that, she was gone.

As he stood at the window, watching Bernie as she jumped into an Uber, with tears in her eyes, Keith couldn't help but feel that it was the last time he would ever see her.

The old woman occupying the window seat next to Keith gave him a slight nudge, and he snapped out of his daydreaming. He hadn't even realized the plane had taxied to a stop. He grabbed his bag from the overhead compartment and hustled toward the plane's exit. On the way, he was stopped by one of the flight attendants. She was a thick brown-skinned beauty with eyes that sparkled every time she smiled. Keith had spent most of the flight admiring her every time she walked up or down the aisle. She'd known he was checking her out, and she'd made sure to put a little something extra in her walk whenever she passed him.

"How was your flight?" she asked.

"Good," he said politely.

"Could've been better," she replied, giving him a sultry stare. She looked around to make sure no one was paying attention before pressing a business card into his hand. "I'm off for the next two days. If you find yourself in need of someone to show you around the city, give me a call."

Keith smiled, as he knew what that phone call would lead to. "I've been here a few times, so I'm familiar with the city."

"It's not the city you need to get familiar with. Give it some thought. If you change your mind, I'll be staying at the Hilton."

Keith blushed like a schoolgirl and departed the plane.

As soon as Keith powered his phone on, he was bombarded with notifications. Most were work-related emails, which he would deal with when he got back to Atlanta the following week. He had told his secretary he had to go out of town on a family emergency, and he had instructed her to reschedule whatever cases she could and to pass the ones she couldn't to an associate named John Green. John wasn't the sharpest knife in the drawer, but he was competent enough to handle some of the less demanding cases in Keith's workload. Some of the partners weren't going to take too kindly to Keith leaving so abruptly, but he had earned the time off, so there was nothing they could do other than talk about him behind his back, which was nothing new.

There was a text from Nate, checking to see if Keith had landed safely. Besides Bernie, Nate was the only one who knew where Keith was going and why. Keith had had a long talk with his old army buddy and had told him about everything that had gone down. He'd expected Nate to say "I told you so," but he'd been surprisingly understanding about the situation. Nate had let Keith bend his ear about his problems for the better part of an hour. He'd even offered to fly down to Louisiana with Keith to give him moral support and to watch his back, just in case, but Keith had declined. He would've liked nothing more than to have his old army buddy at his side, but he had to face what was to come alone. He texted Nate back to let him know he was good, and promised to call once he got settled.

Keith continued scrolling through his text messages, hoping that one would be from Bernie, but he was disappointed. He hadn't seen or heard from her since the night of their argument. He had reached out, leaving voicemails and texts, but she'd never responded. He'd even tried calling her office, only to be told that Bernie had taken a leave of absence, and no one could say for sure when she would return. His little secret coming out must've done more of a number on her than he had first thought. Once his business was done with his family, he was going to turn his attention to fixing things with Bernie, if that was even possible.

One Hunt was avoiding him, but there was another who seemed eager to talk to him. He did a double take when he saw the text from Theodore Hunt. Theodore never reached out to Keith unless it was work related, and even then, it was by email, never by phone or text. Keith hadn't even realized the man knew his number. We need to talk ASAP, was all the message said. No doubt Bernie had told him about their breakup, and Daddy was eager to defend his daughter's honor. Well, if he wanted to get on Keith's case about how terrible a person he was, he would have to take a number and get in line.

Keith had just grabbed his luggage and was headed to catch a cab to his hotel when he spotted a slender white man with a tapered red fade that blended into a scruffy beard of the same color. He was wearing a black suit, and in his hand, he held a sign that read SAVAGE. He hadn't told anyone in his family, including Asher, what day he was coming in, so it was a bit of a shock to see that someone had been dispatched to fetch him. He really shouldn't be surprised, though. There wasn't much that went on in the Big Easy that the Savages didn't know about.

"Welcome home, Killer," the man in the suit greeted in a heavy Southern drawl, which didn't match his clean-cut appearance.

"The name is Keith," he said, correcting him. "And you are?"

"The name is Ulysses." He extended his hand, but Keith didn't shake it. "Right then. I was sent by the family to pick you up and bring you to the house."

"Appreciate it, but I'm afraid you've wasted a trip. I'm gonna grab a taxi to the hotel and freshen up. You can tell my mother I'll be by soon."

"I don't work for your mother." Ulysses took Keith's bags and started for the door, leaving Keith with no choice but to follow.

The first thing Keith noticed when he got outside was the heat. He'd been gone so long that he'd forgotten how oppressive the weather could be. Atlanta weather was always warm, but New Orleans heat was on another level. It was like being wrapped in a blanket of hot mist.

"How'd you know I was here? Did my mother figure out a way to hack my credit card?" Keith called after Ulysses.

"I've been coming here three times per day every day since Asher let us know you were coming," Ulysses said over his shoulder. "And I told you, I don't work for your mother."

"Then who do you work for?" Keith asked.

"You'll see."

Ulysses led Keith outside, to where a white Maybach idled at the curb. Its windows were tinted so heavily that it was impossible to see who was inside. Ulysses loaded the bags into the trunk, while Keith watched the car suspiciously. One thing he had learned in his days of running the streets was not to approach cars without first identifying the occupants. A friend of his had lost his life that way. Keith hadn't been involved in the life in years, but he knew that his family had no shortage of enemies in New Orleans. Killing one of Machine-Gun Ma's kids would be quite a boon for some young shooter looking to earn his stripes. Keith tensed when Ulysses went to open one of the back doors, not quite sure what to expect. He found himself pleasantly surprised when he saw who was inside.

She oozed from the backseat with the fluidity of a shadow. Dark sunglasses covered her eyes. She was a tall woman, standing nearly six feet in her stiletto heels. She was a big woman. A tight white dress clung to her wide hips like a second skin, dipping low in the front, showing off her full bosom. Her neck, wrists, and ears were adorned with clear diamonds. When she smiled, the sun seemed to shine a little bit brighter. It had been a long time since Keith had seen that smile, and until then Keith hadn't realized how much he'd missed it.

"You gonna stand there looking like a star-stuck schoolboy, or you gonna come give your big sister some sugar?" Maxine greeted in her husky voice.

Keith nearly fell into her arms and wrapped his only sister in a tight bear hug. She smelled of jasmine and whiskey. "There's my favorite girl!"

"Ha, flattery will get you everywhere. I thought Bernie was your favorite girl? And what happened between y'all? You need to stop doing dumb shit, before you push that girl away," Maxine warned.

"Why do you naturally assume it's my fault?"

"Because I know you, Killer. Your solutions to all your problems are to put them off or run from them," Maxine said, sounding every bit the psychology major she had been during her college years.

"You analyzing me now, Doctor?"

"I used to change your shitty papers, so I know you better than anyone else. Besides that, I spoke to Bernie. She's not real pleased with you right now," Maxine said, pointing out the obvious.

This came as a surprise to Keith. He had no idea his sister and his fiancée had kept in contact after their brief meeting. "You keeping tabs on me?"

"No, just vetting the young lady my little brother planned on giving his last name to . . . well, a last name, at least. We don't talk all the time, but I check in with her every so often. I called when I found out you were coming home, because I wanted to plan some girl stuff for me and Bernie, so imagine my surprise when I got word that she was sitting the trip out and when I learned the reason why."

"So, you two girls been swapping secrets?"

"Relax, Killer. You ain't been honest with her about the family, so it wasn't my place to tell her, but I can't say that I'm not a little disappointed with you for the way you've chosen to go about it. Are you that ashamed of where you come from?"

"I'm not ashamed," Keith insisted.

"Then why keep up the lie? Let me tell you something, little brother. Relationships built on lies never last. Before you put that ring on her finger, you should've put some truth in her ear."

"I planned on it, but—"

"See, there you go, making excuses again," Maxine said, cutting him off. "I'm your big sister, but I'm also a woman, so I feel her pain. You weren't honest with that girl about what she was getting herself into, so she has every right to be mad at you. You should have laid your cards on the table and allowed her to make an informed decision. Had it been me and I realized you'd been spoon-feeding me lies all this time, I'd have cut your ass before I walked out on you. I don't know her like that, but near as I can tell, Bernie is a good girl, probably the best your sorry ass will ever have. If you leave things the way they are and let her slip away, you'll regret it for the rest of your days."

"So what do you suggest I do at this point?"

"Whatever it takes to make it right," Maxine replied.

Keith was in his feelings over the things Maxine had said to him, mostly because she had spoken the truth. He should've just been honest with Bernie, and either she would've accepted him, flaws and all, or she wouldn't have. He had just been so afraid of losing her that he had done what he built his career on and had bent the truth to suit himself. Now he had to figure out a way to undo the damage.

"Mind if I ask a question?" Ulysses broke the silence.

Keith didn't feel much like talking, but he didn't want to be rude. "Sure."

"How did such a clean-cut dude earn the name Killer?"

"Max gave it to me," Keith revealed.

"Sure did," Maxine said proudly. "I gave him the name the day I got this." She pulled up her dress and revealed the scar on her thigh.

Keith couldn't have been more than eleven or twelve at the time she got the wound that caused that scar. He and Maxine had been walking home from school, and she'd decided that they would take a shortcut through the back of an abandoned house. Keith had been against it, but Maxine had insisted, and of course, he did whatever his big sister said. What they hadn't counted on was a mangy German shepherd that had claimed the backyard of the house as its own. From the foam gathering at the corners of its mouth, they knew something was off about the dog. The two kids took off running, but Maxine twisted her ankle and fell. The dog was on her in an instant. Propelled more by instinct than anything else, Keith picked up a rock and threw it at the dog as hard as he could. The rock hit the dog square in the tip of its snout and broke a bone, which somehow pierced the dog's brain. Over the years stories had been told about Keith's deadeye marksmanship when killing the hound, but in truth, it had just been dumb luck.

"Well, we ain't cutting through yards no more. We flying these days, baby!" Maxine boasted, running her hand across the top of the Maybach.

"I see," Keith said, admiring the car. "I take it the game has been good to you these days."

"Let's just say that the demand for female companionship is at an all-time high." Maxine gave him a cunning smile.

"You can't park here." Their attention was drawn to a cop, who had just pulled alongside the Maybach. He was looking at the car enviously.

"We'll be pushing off in a minute, sugar. We just picking somebody up," Maxine told him.

"Then the next time I suggest you park in the designated area. I don't think the place you rented this car from will take too kindly to you getting it towed," the cop said.

Maxine removed her sunglasses and gave the cop a piercing stare. "Honey, you got me fucked up. I don't ride in or on nothing I don't own. So you can take that ticket and that slick talk and—"

"We were just leaving, Officer," Ulysses said, cutting her off. He knew how reckless Maxine's mouth could be, and he didn't want a situation. The cop let his glare linger on Maxine for a few beats longer before he moved along.

"There you go, exercising that white privilege again," Maxine teased Ulysses.

"You can make fun of my pigment all you want, so long as we're doing it away from this airport and all these damn police, Ms. Maxie," Ulysses said.

"Let's roll, baby. And when we rolling, I want you to make sure all these windows are dropped. I want the whole city to know my little brother is back home!" Maxine declared, loud enough for everyone at the airport to hear, before jumping in the back of the vehicle.

When Keith slid into the plush ride, he was surprised to see that there was someone else in the car. She was a petite light-skinned girl who wore a honey-blond wig. The short red dress she wore didn't leave much to the imagination. High on her thigh, Keith spotted a small magnolia tattoo. She was one of Maxine's girls. His sister made sure all the girls who worked for her wore her mark. Keith didn't like it. It reminded him of how slaves were branded, which was why Maxine did it. She made money by controlling women's bodies, but she had built her empire by controlling their minds. Maxine may not have been in the mental health field anymore, but her psychology degree definitely hadn't gone to waste.

"Keith, I hope you don't mind that my girl Tiny is riding along. Where I need to drop her off is on the way to the house, so I decided to kill two birds with one stone," Maxine explained.

"It's cool. Nice to meet you, Tiny." Keith shook her hand.

"Nice to meet you too," Tiny said. Her voice matched her name. "I've heard a lot about you. Max told me you were handsome, but damn!" She admired him openly.

"Bitch, turn yo' groupie down a taste. This ain't some john looking to run roughshod in that golden hole of yours. This here my flesh, ya heard me?" Maxine said, checking her.

"I didn't mean nothing by it, Max. Just paying a compliment, is all," Tiny said.

"We all right, baby. I just wanted to make sure you were aware of the score." Maxine ran a manicured hand over Tiny's thigh in an effort to reassure her. "Man, I sure am glad to have my old cut buddy back," she told Keith once they were out of the airport and in traffic. "You know, me and Dickey had a bet as to whether or not you'd ever set foot round these parts again. I didn't think so, but your brother held on to hope that one day you'd come back to us."

"Let's not get ahead of ourselves. I haven't come back for anything more than to pay my respects to Big Money. As soon as his service is over, I'm gone," Keith told her.

"The last time you guys had a home going, it went on for three days. I believe it was when Mrs. Handcock passed," Ulysses interjected. He was behind the wheel.

"Mrs. Handcock who owned the cleaners off North Claiborne?" Keith knew Mrs. Handcock well, as did most of the families in their neighborhood. She was a hard but well-liked woman who would offer her cleaning services to the families who didn't have the money or the means to clean their kids' school uniforms.

"Bless her heart." Maxine crossed herself. "Mama sent her out in fine style. Didn't skimp on a thing."

"Mama paid for her funeral?" Keith was surprised. "I thought she and Mrs. Handcock had been at odds over those rumors about her sleeping with Daddy back in the day?"

"True enough. Mama couldn't stand her, but she was still a part of the community. One thing ain't changed about us in all these years is our commitment to our own." Maxine looked at Keith.

"Say, do you remember you got so drunk that you tried to call that young girl out to a dance battle? You nearly broke your ankle, trying to keep up with her," Ulysses teased Maxine.

"I ain't the only one who ended up in a bad way. Pastor Johnson was about ready to lay hands on you for putting that pink pecker of yours inside his daughter. Only thing saved you from a date with the Horseman was Big John stepping in and squashing the fight," Maxine remarked. "Big John always did have a soft spot for you."

"You must have money running through your veins, because that's all my brother has a soft spot for," Keith said.

"Don't be speaking ill of Big John, and he ain't here to defend himself. I'd warn him of the same if the roles were reversed," Maxine said.

"How is everybody taking Big Money's passing?" Keith asked.

"You know death ain't nothing new to our clan. Seems every other day we're putting somebody in the ground. Some take it harder than others, but we're maintaining," Maxine replied.

"And Mad Dog? I know he and Big Money were close." Keith remembered how when Big Money first came to stay with them, it was Mad Dog who had taken him under his wing. It was Mad Dog who had given him the moniker Big Money.

Maxine shrugged. "We ain't been able to track him down to tell him. Nobody has seen Mad Dog in months. I know he ain't gonna take it too well when he does find out, but Mad Dog is a soldier. It's Fire Bug I'm most worried about. He and Big Money were thick as thieves. In fact, I hear tell that this came behind a job the two of them pulled up north."

"What do you mean, a job? Fire Bug's just a kid," Keith pointed out.

Maxine shook her head. "Fire Bug may be young, but he ain't been a kid in a long time, Killer. That boy has developed quite a reputation since the last time you laid eyes on him. Quite a bit has changed around these parts, but you'll see for yourself once we arrive."

CHAPTER 13

Keith was hunkered down in one of the plush leather seats, staring out the window like a kid who was seeing the city for the first time. New Orleans had changed quite a bit, especially after the hurricane. Buildings that Keith was used to seeing along the well-traveled route had either been washed away or rebuilt to the point where he didn't recognize them. They had been riding for only twenty minutes or so when Ulysses exited the highway near the business district and crossed into a section of town known as Black Pearl.

"I thought we were heading to the house?" Keith asked. He hadn't been gone so long that he didn't know they were headed in the wrong direction if they wanted to reach the Lower Ninth Ward.

"We are," Ulysses told him.

Keith looked at his sister.

"Been a while since Mama called our place on Benton Street home. She's got a place out in the Pearl now."

"Mama moved? You've got to be shitting me. The Lower Ninth has always been Savage territory," Keith said.

"Things done changed since you been gone, little brother. We still own the property on Benton, but it's too hot to lay our heads there these days. We've made some mighty powerful enemies over the years," Maxine told him.

"Powerful enough to run the Savages out of the Lower Ninth?" Keith asked.

"What can I say? The game done changed," she replied.

A few minutes later they were turning onto the dirt road that led to the new Savage stronghold. It was a white plantation-style house that stood deep in a wooded area. They'd made it halfway up the road when two men appeared from the foliage as if by magic. Keith wasn't familiar with their faces, but he was familiar with the high-caliber automatic weapons they brandished. Once the men realized it was Maxine's car, they allowed them to pass. Keith looked out the back window, but the men had vanished just as suddenly as they had appeared.

"We keep them around to manage the property when the family is away," Ulysses said, answering the question on Keith's face.

The front yard of the house was busy with people, mostly children running around playing. Maxine had barely made it out of the car before the children swarmed her, begging for kisses and the loose dollars they knew she had stashed for them.

"Simmer down, my loves. You know Auntie comes bearing gifts." Maxine beamed.

Keith stood awkwardly off to the side, watching Maxine interact with the children. It was amazing to him to see so many little faces that resembled his. With some of the kids, he could tell which cousin, aunt, or uncle they belonged to, but with others, he had to guess. Until he set eyes on the children, he had never realized how strong the Savage genes were.

Seeing them made him think of Bernie. They had often discussed having children after they got married. Those were happier times in their relationship, which now felt like a lifetime ago. He missed her so much that it hurt him physically. He was about to try to call her again when Maxine came over.

"Quit standing there like a guest. You're home, boy. C'mon and meet some of your kin." She grabbed him by the arm and pulled him into the cluster of children. "Kids, I want you to meet someone very important. This is my brother, your kin, Killer."

Hearing his name sent the children into another fit of squealing. From their reaction, you would've thought they had just met some sort of celebrity. Keith may have been removed from his family for some years, but his legacy was still very much alive.

A lanky youth of about fifteen or sixteen pushed his way through the crowd. He was fair of skin and had long black hair that he wore tied off in two ponytails. "Can't tell you how excited I am to meet the legendary Killer Keith!" He shook Keith's hand excitedly. "I'm your cousin Anthony . . . Asher's boy." Now that he had said it, Keith could see the resemblance.

"Nice to meet you too," Keith said warmly.

"You're a legend around these parts," Anthony told him.

"Nah, I'm nobody special," Keith replied modestly.

"The hell you ain't. All us kids done heard the stories about you. Say, is it true you once cut a man's head off in the Quarter for fucking with Auntie Maxine?"

"That's not quite accurate." Keith remembered the incident, but Anthony had exaggerated the details. Maxine had thrown a drink in a man's face, and in response, he'd slapped her. Keith and the man had started fighting, and during the fight the man had slipped and landed on a broken bottle, which gave him a gash on his neck.

"Man, you even talk cool!" Anthony said. "Maybe one day I can come up to Atlanta and hang out with you and some of your fancy friends. Can you introduce me to Gucci Mane? I know y'all tight."

"I . . . ah . . ."

"Hey y'all! Come in the back. Cousin Bug is about to show us a magic trick!" one of the little boys announced before running around the back of the house. All the kids took off after him.

Keith followed the kids around the side of the house to the backyard. It had been years since he had seen Fire Bug, and he was anxious to catch up with his little brother. He wasn't hard to spot, with his flaming mop of red hair, which looked like it hadn't been combed in some time. He was standing near the pool, with a crowd of kids around him. On a small table in front of him was a birthday cake, but instead of being decorated with candles, it was crowned with what looked like fireworks.

"Ms. Maxine," Ulysses began, "is he about to—"

"Damn that crazy boy! Kids, move back!" Maxine shouted, but her warning came too late.

Bug lit the homemade fireworks, and seconds later there was a thunderous explosion. It was so powerful that it knocked some of the kids to the ground. Birthday cake was everywhere. Ulysses, Keith, and Maxine rushed forward into the smoke to make sure none of the kids were hurt. Fire Bug was sitting on his ass, coughing. Smoke was rising from his hair, and one of his eyebrows was almost completely singed.

"You okay, kid?" Ulysses helped Bug to his feet.

The young man flashed a toothy grin and replied, "Now, that's how you make the trap go boom!" Then he doubled over laughing.

"Boy, you could've killed one of these kids!" Maxine slapped him in the back of the head.

"Man, them kids be all right. Wasn't nothing but some old gunpowder I found in the shed. It barely had any kick left," Fire Bug said.

"I see you still out here playing with matches." Keith stepped into view.

Fire Bug squinted his eyes. He still had a bit of cake in one of them. When he spied Keith, he lit up bigger than the fire he had just set. "Oh shit! Is that Killer?" He ran over and gave Keith a strong hug.

"Good to see you, Bug." Keith held him at arm's length so as not to get any cake on his suit. The last time Keith had seen Bug, he had been knee high; now they were almost the same height.

"Why didn't anybody tell me you were coming in today? I'd have rode with Max to pick you up at the airport," Bug said, disappointed.

"You know damn well your pyromaniac ass ain't allowed to ride in my car no more. Took them three days to reupholster the seat you burned up and damn near a week to get the smell of smoke out," Maxine reminded him.

"Don't blame me. Blame that cheap-ass leather." Fire Bug laughed. "Say, bro, I'm glad you're back with us. I know it won't be long now before we put them New York niggas to sleep!"

"Um . . . I don't know about putting anybody to sleep. I just came to see you guys and pay my respects to Big Money."

"Oh, I get it. We don't talk shop in front of civilians." Fire Bug gave him a stage wink.

"I know damn well that fool son of mine ain't in my yard, playing with explosives!" a familiar voice boomed from the house. A few seconds later Ma Savage appeared at the back door. She was wearing a housecoat, a hairnet, and fuzzy slippers. In her hand, she carried a small wooden baseball bat.

"You done fucked up now," Maxine whispered.

Fire Bug walked toward his mother with his eyes downcast and his tail between his legs. "Sorry, Mama."

"Not as sorry as you're gonna be if you don't get the hose and clean all this damn cake up!" Ma swung the bat at his head, purposely missing him. Fire Bug scurried off to do as he was told. "And as for the rest of you," she said, addressing the children, "carry your asses back around to the front of the house, and stop climbing on my lawn furniture like little monkeys!" The kids all scurried off. None of them wanted any parts of Machine-Gun Ma when she was in one of her moods. She was about to say something to Maxine when her eyes landed on Keith.

For a long moment, the mother and son just stared at each other in silence, neither really sure what would come next. She seemed older than Keith remembered, slightly grayer of hair, and she had lost some weight. Keith had mixed emotions about seeing his mother again after so long. He had been prepared for the old resentments to force their way back to the surface, but they didn't. He no longer saw the spitfire who was always on him for not being Savage enough. She was just a woman getting on in years.

Ma finally broke the silence. "I guess I have to be a client of your firm to get a hug from my son?"

In response, Keith walked over and hugged her. It was a long and tight hug that was filled with the love that he remembered receiving as a child. It was such an emotional moment that he had to stop himself from shedding a tear. Keith and his mother hadn't always had the smoothest relationship, but there was no denying that he had missed her dearly.

"So, you gonna act like you got only one kid?" Maxine faked an attitude.

"Hush up, Maxine," Ma told her. She then looked and saw Tiny standing behind Maxine, trying to make herself invisible. "Max, what did I tell you about bringing your whores to my house?"

"I'm not a whore. I'm an escort," Tiny said proudly.

Ma pointed the bat at her like it was a sword. "Bitch, you'll be dead if you open that mouth one more time."

"Tiny, wait for me in the car. I'll be only a few minutes, and then we can get you to where you need to be," Maxine told her. Tiny rolled her eyes at Ma before sashaying back toward the Maybach. "Mama, why do you always have to be so rude to my girls?"

"Because I got no stomach for whores," Ma said flatly. "I wouldn't trust one around my man, and I damn sure wouldn't trust them in my house."

"But that doesn't stop you from taking your cut off my cathouses," Maxine shot back.

"Shit, it ain't but what you owe me. I raised, fed, and sheltered your ass for thirty years. The least you can do is give me a taste off the back end," Ma told her.

"I see ain't much changed over the years," Keith thought aloud.

"If it ain't broke, then don't fix it. Now c'mon in the house so we can get out of this heat." Ma turned and headed back inside.

The back door led Keith into the kitchen, where he was immediately sucked in by the smell of something tasty cooking. His mother had all four burners and the oven going. Keith's stomach rumbled. It had been a long time since he'd had a good home-cooked meal. Bernie could throw down well enough in the kitchen, but not on the level of his mother.

"Wow. It smells amazing in here!" Keith said.

"I ain't lost a step on these pots or behind the trigger." Ma gave him a wink. "Judging by how skinny you done got, it looks like you could use a good meal. What's the matter? That gal you been catting around with ain't feeding you?"

Keith couldn't hide his surprise. He had never really spoken to his mother about Bernie.

"Don't look so shocked. Just because you don't care too much for me don't mean I ain't been keeping tabs on you."

"Cut it out, Mama. You know it ain't like that," Keith told her.

"I only know what you show me, and that ain't a lot of love," Ma said seriously.

"Haven't you been getting the cards I send you every birthday and holiday?"

"Yeah, I've been getting the change you send me. It's greatly appreciated, but don't nothing compare to seeing the faces of your loved ones. Time isn't promised to any of us. Big Money being gone so soon is proof of that."

"Yeah, I can't believe he's gone." Keith paused for a moment. "You okay?" he asked. His mother had raised Big Money like one of her own sons, so even though she wasn't showing it, Keith knew she had to be taking it hard.

Ma shrugged. "The game gives, and the game takes. Big Money knew the stakes before he sat down at the table. Ain't much we can do about it at this point but make sure he's sent off properly and that those responsible for his death leave this world not long after."

"Mama, I don't think the whole eye-for-an-eye thing is the best way to go about handling this."

"That's because it wasn't your house his head was delivered to," Ma informed him.

Keith was speechless. When Asher had told him that Big Money had been killed, he'd left out the part about him having been decapitated. "I had no idea," Keith said softly.

"Cut that boy up like he wasn't even a person . . . like he was cattle," Ma said emotionally.

"Do the police have any leads?" Keith asked.

Ma laughed at the question. "What them pigs care when a black child is murdered in the streets? Nah, I doubt we'll be getting any help from them."

"I know some people with the NYPD. Maybe I can reach out and see if I can find anything out," Keith offered.

"What care the law got for the lawless? Savage blood has been spilled, and there must be a reckoning," Ma insisted.

"How? By shooting up a bunch of city blocks?" Keith asked sarcastically.

"Nope. Just the one them bitches who killed our family occupy," said Big John as he entered the kitchen. He was dressed in baggy shorts and Timberlands, and he had a duffel bag slung over his shoulder. "Good to see you, little brother." He hugged Keith.

"Good to see you too, John. I just wish it were under different circumstances."

"You know don't nothing get black folks together like funerals," Big John half joked.

"You get what I asked you for?" Ma asked her eldest child.

"Sure did." Big John laid the duffel bag on the table and unzipped it. Inside was a tommy gun. It was almost identical to the one Ma had used at the Fulton Fish Market robbery, but it had more bodies on it. The weapon had been in the Savage family since the twenties.

"About time I brought this old bitch out of retirement." Ma stroked the machine gun lovingly.

"And what do you plan to do with that, Mama?" Keith asked, though it was a question he already knew the answer to.

"Hopefully, some damage." She cackled.

"C'mon, Mama. At your age?"

"Keith is right," Big John agreed, much to everyone's surprise. "War is a young man's game. I done sent word out to our kin as far as Buras-Triumph, and they're all ready to join our cause."

"John, this isn't the Old West. You can't just roll into New York with an army and wage war on a drug crew," Keith pointed out.

"We don't need an army. Just a dozen or so men who don't mind dying," Big John declared.

"Amen to that!" Ma chimed in.

"This is nuts. Max, surely, you don't agree with what they're planning to do?" Keith turned to his sister. She looked hesitant.

"Max would never go against family. She's a Savage . . . a *true* Savage," Ma observed.

"And I'm not?" Keith challenged.

"That remains to be seen, but I gather we'll find out before all this is over," Ma told him.

"Mama, did you know there's birthday cake all over the side of the house?" Dickey Savage called as he barged into the kitchen. He sounded much like a child when he spoke. Dickey was a pump man with happy eyes and lips that looked like they were always ready to part into a smile. He wore a blue flannel shirt that was a size too small, jeans, and work boots, which had been lazily tied. Over his right eyebrow was a scar, marking the spot where a bullet and a piece of his skull had been removed.

"I know, baby. Your brother had a little accident with some of his fireworks," Ma told him.

Dickey was about to go into his speech about the dangers of setting off fireworks without taking the proper precautions when he spotted Keith. His eyes lit up like a kid's on Christmas before he lumbered across the room and grabbed his brother in a crushing bear hug. "Killer!" he squealed, spinning Keith around in his arms. "I missed you!"

"I missed you too, Dickey!" Keith said good-naturedly. Of all his siblings, his older brother Dickey was the one he was happiest to see.

Dickey was five years Keith's senior, but you wouldn't know it from the way he carried himself. He had the mental capacity of a twelve-year-old as a result of a vicious attack he'd been the victim of many years ago. It had been the same day their father was killed. Back then Dickey had been a notorious heist man. He had overheard his father planning to rob a jewelry store, and he'd wanted in. His father had initially refused, but Dickey had insisted, and Dickey Savage was a man who didn't lose arguments. On this job, Dickey drove the getaway car, while his father and two of his chums took down the jewelry store. They were on their way out of the store when the police appeared out of nowhere. Apparently, the person responsible for disarming the silent alarm had botched the job, and the robbers found themselves surrounded by cops. For reasons that to this day no one understood, instead of their father surrendering, he opened fire on the police. Their father and the other two burglars were gunned down, and Dickey took a stray bullet to the head. For his part in the crime, Dickey would spend the next six years in a prison mental ward, and when he was finally released, he was a shell of the man he had been.

"Did you bring me something from Atlanta?" Dickey asked excitedly.

"You know I did." Keith reached into the pocket of his suit jacket and produced a shiny key chain with a bedazzling peach hanging from one end of it.

"Wow. Thanks, Killer!" Dickey snatched the key chain and stared at it in amazement. It was little more than a trinket, but he cherished it as if it were found treasure.

"Glad to see my boys together again and bonding."
Ma beamed. "Now, if y'all will excuse me, I'm going
upstairs to catch a quick nap. I've been up since early this
morning, and I'm about pooped. Dickey, go out back and
tell Bug I said to help you bring your brother's bags in. I
got a room made up for him upstairs."

"Yes, Mama!" Dickey hurried off to do as he was told.

"I have a reservation at the Marriott," Keith said.

"Cancel it," Ma said. "Been years since I've had all my
children under the same roof. The next time it happens
will probably be for my funeral, so I want to enjoy this
time with y'all while I can." She was gone before he
could protest.

CHAPTER 14

When Keith stepped into the bedroom his mom had made up for him, he had to do a double take. It was a new house, but the bedroom was a replica of the one he had slept in all his life on Benton. All his trophies and awards were on display on the walls and shelves. His mother had even put a twin bed that looked like his old one in the room. Out of curiosity, Keith got on the floor and checked the legs of the bed. When he saw that one was missing, and the corner of the bed was propped up by textbooks, he realized that it didn't just *look* like his old bed. It *was* his old bed!

He continued wandering around the room, examining memorabilia from his childhood. He stopped at a framed picture resting on one of the shelves. It was a photograph of him and his high school baseball team, taken after they had won the championship. Keith couldn't pitch in the final game, because he had suffered a broken arm a few days before. Remembering the event that had caused the injury made Keith's blood boil as if it had just happened yesterday.

It had been the night of their junior prom. Keith and some of his gang had been hanging with their dates behind the school. They'd been smoking weed and sipping cheap whiskey from paper cups. Back then he'd been dating a girl named Darla, who lived next door. She came from a family that was almost as dysfunctional as his, which was probably why his mother liked Darla.

The kids had been so caught up in having fun that Darla stayed out past her curfew, which meant there would likely be trouble. Darla's dad, Charlie, was a piece of shit. He drank too much and worked too little. When he got drunk, he loved to take out his frustrations over his shortcomings on his family, especially Darla. It wasn't unusual to see Darla come to school with fresh bruises from fistfights she had gotten into with her dad. His excuse for hitting her was that she had a slick mouth, which she did, but it was really that Darla reminded him so much of her mother. She'd left her abusive husband and her kids when Darla was a freshman in high school.

Keith and Darla stole across the yard under the cover of darkness and headed around to the back of her house. The family tended to leave the back door open because Charlie was always getting drunk and losing his keys. Considering the neighborhood that they lived in, it probably wasn't the wisest thing to do, but it was better than having Charlie banging on the door and waking up Darla's younger siblings at all times of the night. Keith saw Darla to the back door, and they thought they were home free, until the kitchen light came on as they stepped inside. They found Charlie waiting for Darla.

"Oh . . . hey, Daddy," Darla greeted, trying to hide her nervousness.

"You know what time it is?" Charlie questioned. They could smell the vodka on him from across the room.

"I'm sorry. We were—"

"It was my fault," Keith said, cutting her off. "My brother was supposed to pick us up from the prom, but he never showed, so we had to take the bus," he lied.

"It figures," Charlie snorted. "Every time something bad happens in this city, one of you Savages is usually responsible." He shambled forward on shaky legs, glaring at Keith. "You think you slick, don't you?"

"Sir?" Keith didn't understand the question.

"I see the way you look at her . . . the way y'all are always whispering and giggling. She let you taste it yet?"

"Daddy!" Darla was embarrassed.

"Shut your mouth, tramp!" Charlie barked. "You just like ya mama, always gotta interject when men are talking. You're lucky I don't knock your damn teeth out for creeping in here at this hour." He faked like he was going to hit her and made Darla flinch. When she did, he smiled sinisterly.

Keith spoke up. "That's not necessary, Mr. Charlie."

"Fuck you say to me, li'l nigga?" Charlie growled, turning on Keith.

"Keith, just go home. I'll talk to you in school on Monday," Darla said as she ushered him toward the door.

"You sure you're good?" Keith hesitated.

"Listen to your little girlfriend and get your ass gone, before you get a taste of this grown man's business, boy!" Charlie snarled, threatening Keith.

Keith took a step toward the older man, but Darla blocked his path. "That'll only make this worse. Please, just go home and let me handle it."

Reluctantly, Keith let Darla push him out the back door. For a few moments, he stood in the yard, wondering if he had done the right thing. He had just convinced himself to leave when he heard shouting coming from the house, followed by the sound of glass breaking. Everything in Keith told him not to get involved, but he couldn't just walk away. He cared too much for Darla to leave her at the mercy of her drunken father. Against his better judgment, he went back inside the house. The kitchen was a mess. Broken dishes were scattered across the floor, and blood was splattered on the walls. Darla was curled up in a ball in a corner, while Charlie stood over her, punching her with his closed fist. There was no doubt in Keith's mind that if he didn't do something, Charlie would surely kill her.

Keith was good with his hands, but Charlie was older, more experienced, and outweighed him by about fifty pounds. When it was all said and done, both Keith and Darla ended up in the emergency room that night. Darla ended up with a black eye and a busted lip, but Keith caught the worst of it. Charlie had broken his arm in two places. When the doctors asked what had happened, the kids lied and said they had gotten jumped on the way home from the prom. Not long after they were released from the hospital, Charlie packed his family up and disappeared.

It was probably for the best. When Keith's brother Mad Dog found out the real story of what had happened, he was looking to kill Charlie. A few days after he graduated from high school, Keith received a congratulatory card from Darla in the mail, but he tossed it in the trash. Words on a card could do nothing for the hurt he was experiencing. He understood why Darla had to leave, but at the very least, she could've said goodbye to him. It was the first time Keith's heart had ever been broken, and it took him years to get over Darla.

"Damn! What you got in here? Bricks?" Fire Bug's voice startled Keith, yanking him from his thoughts. Fire Bug and Anthony were standing in the doorway with Keith's luggage.

"Thanks, boys. You can just drop them anywhere," Keith told them. The two teens dropped the bags and prepared to head back out, but Keith stopped them. "Bug, I need to holla at you for a second . . . alone." He looked at Anthony.

"I'll be outside. Bug, don't be too long. You know we got somewhere to be in a while," Anthony said, then gave Fire Bug a look before disappearing.

"So, what you think of your room? Mama did a good job making it look like your old one, huh?" Bug flopped on the bed.

"Yeah, I never realized how closely she paid attention," Keith said.

"Shit, you know that old bird don't miss nothing."

"So, what's going on with you lately?"

Bug shrugged. "Not too much. Out here hustling, like everybody else."

"How's school?"

"I wouldn't know. I ain't been there in two years." Fire Bug laughed. Keith didn't.

"Are you kidding me? You're only seventeen years old! Ma might be twisted in her ways, but she made sure all of us graduated. Why would she let you drop out?"

"Calm down, Killer. I didn't just drop out. I got my GED last year," Bug informed him.

"And what about college?"

"Nah. I've had my fill of school. I'm exploring other interests."

"You mean like getting tied up in the family business?" Keith gave him a knowing look. Bug's face said he was searching for a lie, but Keith saved him the trouble. "Maxine already told me."

"Damn! Max and her big-ass mouth!" Bug cursed.

"Bug, you're a smart kid with tons of potential. You can be anything you want in life. Why would you get caught up in this shit?"

"Same reason as you did back in the day!" Bug shot back.

No matter how much Keith wanted to, he couldn't argue with Bug's logic. Their parents had groomed them all to be criminals, and Keith hadn't been an exception. Granted, he'd eventually managed to break the hold his mother had on him, the same one she had on all her children, but there had been a time when he was every bit as Savage as the rest of his siblings. Back then, he'd been Killer Keith in name and deed, and some of the acts he committed as a teen had haunted him into adulthood. Keith had been a child who was exposed to too much, too soon; and apparently, his little brother was walking the same path.

"Maxine says that a job you and Big Money pulled may have been why he was killed." Keith paused for a moment. "Can you tell me what happened?" he asked.

"It was all fucked up," Bug sighed. "We were hired to whack this fuck nigga who was stepping on the toes of some important people, and it went to wrong. I laid a bomb for the target, and a kid got killed by mistake."

"Jesus, Bug!"

"It wasn't my fault. The kid got in the way of the target."

Keith remembered seeing a story on the news a while back about a car exploding in Harlem, killing a kid. It was a dark day in New York City. At the time the police had no solid leads, but they suspected it was a terrorist attack gone wrong. It had hurt Keith then to hear about the child's death, but it hit him like a physical blow now to find out that his little brother was behind it.

"How could you have been so careless?" Keith asked, his voice heavy with emotion.

"One thing I ain't is careless, Killer. I could set off a bomb in a room full of people, and the explosion would be so precise that it wouldn't touch anybody except my mark. That piece of work was for King James. It was just dumb luck that it was the kid who started the car instead of him," Bug insisted.

"So, you think it was this King James who killed Big Money?" Keith asked.

"If I had to guess, I'd say so. But it could've also been the cat who hired us, trying to clean up the mess," Bug suggested.

"Who hired y'all for the job?"

Bug was silent.

"Bug, I'm trying to stop a full-scale war from breaking out. Now ain't the time to go silent. Who dropped the bag on King James?" Keith said, pressing him.

"A guy named Shai Clark," Bug finally confessed.

This took Keith by surprise. He didn't know Shai personally, but his reputation preceded him. To the general public, he was a charismatic young businessman who ran a multimillion-dollar construction empire. There were rumors about him having deep ties to the underworld, but Keith had never put much stock in them. Shai was a man who had it all, legitimately, so his getting involved in street business didn't seem logical. Keith had first become aware of Shai Clark through his family's lawyer, Martin Scott, whom everyone called Scotty. Scotty had been a guest speaker at NYU when Keith was attending the university. Keith looked up to the man, because like him, Martin Scott had come from nothing and had become a prominent lawyer. In essence, Martin Scott had laid out the blueprint that Keith followed.

"How do you know Shai Clark?" Keith asked, not really understanding the connection between the millionaire and his family.

"I don't know him. Only met the man once, and that was when Mama brokered the job. A one-eyed priest put it together for us," Bug told him.

The one-eyed priest was someone Keith was familiar with. Priest was a reputed assassin who had a history with their family that dated back to before Keith was born. Priest and Keith's mother had a relationship that his father had never been comfortable with. It was as if they were spawn from the same pit in hell. Keith had met him a few times over the years, always when his father wasn't around, but he had never really cared for

the man. Something about the way Priest looked at Keith
had always given him the creeps. At least Keith now had
a starting point to try to unravel the mess his brother and
cousin had made.

"Any idea how I can get in contact with Priest?" Keith
asked Bug.

"Sure. Buy yourself a Ouija board. I hear he bought the
farm recently," Bug told him. "Now, are you finished giving me the third degree about all this? Me and Anthony
got a function to attend."

"Oh yeah? Where you boys off to?"

"Well, the family is going to do something for Big
Money after the second line tomorrow, but me and some
of the gang are gonna have our own thang tonight. Grab a
few bottles and burn some bud. Nothing too crazy," Bug
told him.

"Sounds like fun. Mind if I tag along?"

"Hell yeah, you can come. I'll get big-time props showing up with Killer Keith!" Bug said excitedly.

"How about we chill a little on the Killer and just go
with Keith?"

"Right, right . . . You wanna fly under the radar. That's
cool, but can I offer you some advice?"

"Sure."

"Dead the suit."

Keith looked down at the Armani number he was
wearing. "Boy, you're crazy! This is Armani."

"I dig it. That may work for them high-society parties
in Atlanta that you're used to, but the place where we're
going, the only people in suits are the Feds and the dead."

CHAPTER 15

After changing into jeans and a T-shirt, Keith jumped in Fire Bug's pickup truck and rode with the youths down to the Quarter. They parked in a lot off the main street and walked the rest of the way. As Keith passed through blocks that had once been so familiar to him, he couldn't help but feel like a fish out of water. It was so crowded with people crawling in and out of the bars along the strip that they had to walk sideways to avoid colliding with the drunks. Keith was used to the swarming crowds on Canal Street during Mardi Gras and the big gatherings during the Essence Festival, but this was a regular Friday night!

"Changed some since you were last here, huh?" Bug asked, picking up on his brother's discomfort.

"That's putting it mildly," Keith said, sidestepping a young woman who was puking at the curb.

"Got like this not too long after Katrina. When the money came in to rebuild the city, they dumped it into the tourist spots, instead of helping the folks who lost their homes," Bug explained.

"Turned it into a regular tourist trap, huh?" Keith observed.

"It's a trap, all right. When they get themselves good and wasted, it makes for easier pickings." Anthony gave a mischievous laugh.

"You a part of the family business too?" Keith asked.

"Have been since I was old enough to shoot a rifle," Anthony said proudly.

"And Asher is okay with that? He's always been a straight arrow," Keith told him.

"He don't like it, but ain't too much he can do about it. I'm a man, and men do what they gotta do to help their families. That's why you went off to become a lawyer, isn't it? To help the family?"

"In a sense, I guess."

The trio continued walking through the Quarter, with Keith looking around in amazement, like a tourist, as they went. He stopped when his eyes landed on a familiar location. It was a posh bar with windows that stretched from floor to ceiling, and it had an inviting neon sign that advertised its signature drink, which was the 190 Octane. The last time Keith had seen the place, it was a run-down saloon frequented by killers and thieves. The sign on the front now read B.B.'s, but Keith would recognize Black Magnolia's anywhere.

"Say, is that the Magnolia?" Keith asked as he stopped in front of the bar. The location brought back memories of when he was a wild youth, getting involved in things he shouldn't have.

"It used to be, but you see what they've turned it into now," Bug said in disgust.

"I haven't been inside this spot in years. I gotta go in and see if they still make the strongest One-Ninety in the Quarter." Keith started toward the door, but Bug stopped him.

"We'll pump you full of all the liquor you want when we get with the rest of the crew, but we ain't going in there. We ain't welcome," Bug informed him.

"Why not? This has been a Savage family hangout since before you were born."

"Things have changed since the last time you walked the Quarter, Killer. We stick with our own, and the muthafuckas in that spot ain't our own," Bug warned.

"That's bullshit, Bug. Whatever clan foolishness y'all have got going on has nothing to do with me, and I'm not gonna let it stop me from having a drink in a place that was once like my second home." Keith ignored Bug's warning and stepped inside.

B.B.'s was much nicer than Black Magnolia's had been. The old pillars had been knocked down, clearing space for a dance floor, and now there were two bars instead of one. Three large flat-screen televisions hung behind the bar, and all of them were tuned to the basketball game. Bug and Anthony hung by the door, screw facing everyone who wandered too close to them. Keith, on the other hand, made himself at home. He found an empty stool and ordered a 190 Octane from the attractive bartender. It was a cool spot, and Keith couldn't understand why Bug had been so adamant about not going inside. He would find out halfway through his drink.

"I've seen a lot of things in my young life, but until now I've never laid eyes on a ghost," a feminine voice called from behind him.

Keith turned on his stool, expecting to find some young chippie looking to try her hand with the new guy, so he was unprepared for the person he would lay eyes on. She was dark skinned, the color of natural chocolate. Booty shorts strained so much around her thick thighs that the seams threatened to burst. She now wore her hair in a short natural cut that suited her round face . . . a face that Keith had loved since he was a teenager and had never forgotten.

"Darla!" he gasped, not sure if his eyes were playing tricks on him or not.

Darla was across the room in two strides, and before Keith knew what was happening, she had leapt into his lap and wrapped her arms around his neck. "Please tell me this is real and you ain't a dream?"

"No, it's really me." Keith let her linger in his arms. He had forgotten how much he loved the touch of her. After an awkward few moments, she released her grip and climbed off his lap.

"When I heard tales that you were coming home to us, I thought it was a lie, but here you are, back where you belong!" Darla said, wiping tears of joy from the corners of her eyes.

"I ain't back, just passing through. Came to pay my respects to my cousin," Keith said coolly. He was thrilled to see Darla, but he hadn't forgotten her abrupt departure and how long it had taken him to pick up the pieces of his broken heart.

"I heard Big Money passed. Please give your family my condolences," Darla said sincerely.

"So, how long you been back?" Keith asked.

"A few years. After we had to leave New Orleans, we settled in Mississippi for a time. Things were okay until Daddy got fired from his job and we had to move again. We stayed in Texas until Daddy got himself killed," Darla replied, filling him in.

"Somebody finally put Charlie's old, mean ass in the ground, huh?" Keith hadn't meant to sound so cold. It was just the way it had come out.

"Got caught creeping with another man's wife. The guy shot him dead while he was still inside her," Darla revealed.

"Damn. That's cold. Sorry to hear it."

"It's okay. Not like we all didn't see it coming. My father wasn't a good man."

"Tell me about it." Keith flexed the arm that Charlie had broken all those years ago. "So did your brothers and sisters come back to New Orleans with you?"

"After Daddy got killed, we all kind of drifted apart. Marcus is down in Florida, and the twins are living up in

Boston. New Orleans held too many bad memories for us."

"So what made you come back?"

Darla shrugged. "I guess because it's the only place that ever felt like home. And it beat how I was living. I went through a few rough patches while trying to make it on my own. When things got really bad, I figured the best thing was for me and my son to come home."

"Your what?" Keith wasn't sure he'd heard her right.

"My son," she repeated. From the look on his face, she knew this had come as a surprise. "I assumed your sister, Maxine, had told you. She helped us out a lot when we first came back."

"No. She left that part out when she was bringing me up to speed. So, how old is he?"

"Five, going on fifty." She laughed. "I swear that boy has been here before. He's smart as a whip too."

"I'll bet his dad is proud," Keith said unenthusiastically.

"I wouldn't know. He cut out not long after he found out I was pregnant."

"Sorry to hear it."

"Don't be. We made that baby more out of lust than love. Besides Kyle, there is only one other man that will occupy a space in my heart." She made sure to look Keith in the eyes when she said it. "But enough about me. What's going on with you? I hear you're a hotshot lawyer in Atlanta now."

"I don't know if I'd call myself a hotshot, but I've got a pretty decent track record," Keith said modestly.

"I'm glad to hear it, but not surprised. One thing I always knew about you, Killer, is that you were going to make something of your life. You always had dreams bigger than New Orleans, and I'm glad you got to see them through. So how do you like living in Atlanta?"

"It's not New Orleans, but it's cool. It suits me."

"Bet you got at least half a dozen ladies trying to get your attention."

Keith smirked. "You know how that goes. Women outnumber men three to one in the A, but I only got eyes for one . . . Her name is Bernadette."

"Oh." The revelation stung Darla, as Keith had intended it to. "I hope she realizes how lucky she is to have you."

"She does," Keith said, reflecting on Bernie and how she had always been in his corner through thick and thin. It made him miss her even more.

There was an awkward silence between them.

"Keith, you know I never had a chance to explain to you what happened that night after junior prom."

"You don't owe me no explanations, Darla. Your dad made you guys move. Nothing you could have done to stop it."

"But there's more to it than that. I didn't want to leave. I swear to you, I didn't. Even when we got to Mississippi, I tried to call you, but my dad caught me and beat me damn near to death, then kept me locked in the basement until I healed. Took nearly two weeks. I had to sneak the card I sent you to the postman in order to get it out. That summer, when I was well enough, I ran off and came back to the only people who I knew would take me in and keep me safe. Your family."

"What?"

"I showed up on your doorstep with nothing but the clothes on my back and hope in my heart. I begged your mama to let me see you so I could explain what had happened, but she turned me away. She blamed me for the fight between you and Daddy. She called me a whore and told me that I was trying to ruin your future. She even pulled that old machine gun on me and told me that if I ever showed up on her property again, she would fill me with holes. Didn't she ever tell you?"

Keith was too stunned to answer. All these years he
had resented Darla for leaving him the way she had,
never knowing that she had tried to come back to him.
He wanted to call her a liar, but he knew that she wasn't,
because he knew his mother. No woman would ever
be good enough for her son. Just like that, all his old
resentments toward his mother forced their way to the
surface. "I'm so sorry," was all he could say.

"That ain't on you, Killer. Though the way she went
about it was fucked up, I know your mother was only
trying to protect you. You had a bright future, and me
and my bullshit had no place in your life. Had she let
me in, you probably wouldn't have gone on to accomplish
all that you have." She sobbed. This time the tears flowed
freely. "Look at me, going all to pieces like a silly schoolgirl."

"Don't cry, Darla. You know I hate it when you're
hurting." He wiped her tears away with his thumbs.

"Now, ain't this a touching sight." A masculine voice
was added to the conversation.

Keith looked up and saw another blast from the past
making his way toward them. He was a powerfully built
man with a shaved head and skin the color of night.
Tattoos covered his face, head, and arms. In his nose was
a gold hoop earring.

"Beau," Darla said nervously and moved away from
Keith.

"Don't break up your little reunion on my account."
Beau's hard eyes went from Darla to Keith. "The porters
told me they had taken the trash out, but apparently, they
missed some. How you be, Killer?"

"I'm good," Keith said in a clipped tone. He and Beau
had been rivals since they were kids. Beau's family, the
Toussaints, and the Savages had been at each other for
decades, though neither of them could tell you exactly

why. More often than not, Keith and Beau had found themselves on opposite sides in fistfights. The last Keith had heard, Beau Toussaint was locked up on a murder charge, but apparently, the rumor had been just that.

"Keith is back home for his cousin Big Money's funeral," Darla said nervously, trying to defuse the situation.

"Looks like he's come home for more than that." Beau pulled Darla roughly to him and cupped her ass. He was marking his territory. "You enjoying my hospitalities, Killer?"

"Not sure what you mean, Beau. I just popped in here for a drink," Keith replied.

"That's what I'm talking about. You know I own this joint now, right?"

"Nope, can't say that I did."

"I *persuaded* old man Johnson to sell it to me and remade the place in my image. Ain't it grand?" Beau boasted. Knowing him, that likely meant he had threatened or killed the man to take over his property.

"Yeah, it's pretty cool," Keith said, keeping his voice even. By then Bug and Anthony had spotted the confrontation and come over.

"Fuck you li'l niggas doing in my spot? Y'all know you're too young to drink. You trying to cost me my liquor license?" Beau glared at the two youngsters.

"Cousin Keith wanted to come in and get a drink. He doesn't understand how things are now," Anthony said sheepishly. He was clearly afraid of Beau, and with good reason.

"But the two of you do. Maybe you should've pulled his coat. We wouldn't want ole Killer to wander into the wrong spot and find himself in a bad way, would we?"

Fire Bug spoke up. "We're Savages, and we go where we please."

"Not in the Quarter, you don't," Beau said threateningly. Two members of his security team had appeared behind him. The situation was getting tense. "You should know the rules. Or maybe my boys need to explain them to you again?"

"Or I could get Mad Dog down here, and you could explain them to him," Fire Bug countered, bluffing. The sound of Mad Dog's name stole some of Beau's thunder. The last time Mad Dog had jumped on him, it had resulted in Beau needing almost thirty stitches in the back of his head.

"I came in here for a drink, not to have a pissing contest," Keith said. "Let me settle my tab, and we're gone." He reached into his pocket, but Beau stopped him.

"Savage money don't spend in B.B.'s. This drink is on the house," Beau said, but what he was really telling them was to leave before things got nasty.

"C'mon, Killer. It smells in this joint, anyhow," Fire Bug muttered.

Keith took another swig of his drink before slamming the glass on the bar, purposely splashing liquor on it. He gave Beau one last look before following Bug and Anthony to the door.

"See you again soon, Killer!" Beau shouted after him.

"Not if I see you first," Keith grumbled and then made his exit.

"What was that shit?" Keith asked Fire Bug once they were outside.

"I tried to tell you not to go in there," Bug replied. "Since Beau took over that joint, it's been a no-fly zone for anyone with the last name Savage."

"Fuck Beau. I'm talking about Darla. Did you know she would be there tonight?"

"Darla goes wherever her master does, like the good little bitch dog she is!" Bug spat.

"Watch your mouth," Keith warned him.

"Killer, I know you ain't still stunting that ho. She was dead to us the minute she started sleeping with the enemy. Forget about her. They'll be plenty of chicks when we link with my gang."

"I changed my mind. I'm gonna grab a cab and go back to the house." Keith stormed off.

"C'mon, Killer. Don't be like that!" Bug called after him, but Keith ignored him.

Keith was on fire. He had moved on with his life, and Darla had a right to do the same. But with Beau? She could've picked any number of men to be with, but the fact that she had chosen his childhood enemy was the ultimate betrayal in his mind. At that moment he could've walked back in the bar and killed Beau and Darla too. The demons buried in Keith's soul were chattering at a million miles per minute, demanding blood. If he didn't get out of the Quarter as quickly as possible, he would surely answer them.

CHAPTER 16

A loud boom outside his window jarred King James awake. Still half asleep and acting more on instinct than on conscious thought, King rolled from his bed and grabbed his gun from the nightstand drawer and crept to the window. When he looked out the window, he expected to see enemies closing in on him, but the streets were empty, save for a man dressed in an MTA uniform, who was making his way to work. He heard a boom again, and it drew his attention heavenward, where thick clouds blocked out the rising sun. It was thunder and not gunshots he'd heard. There was a storm coming.

King stood there for a minute, waiting for the adrenaline coursing through his body to dissipate. He wondered if he would ever get used to the quiet East Side neighborhood where he'd rented a tenth-floor apartment. King had gotten so used to living in the chaos of the prison system and the projects where he held sway that he was having trouble adjusting to the peace of his new neighborhood.

He'd leased the apartment a few months ago, after narrowly escaping a situation in the projects. When King came home from prison, he took up residence in the apartment he had once shared with his mother and his siblings. It was located in the center of his empire, and it allowed him to keep a close eye on his operation. When he began to grow in status and finances, the old man suggested that he move out of the hood, but King wasn't trying to hear it. The projects had been his home for as long as he had been alive. He felt safe there. This changed on a night when the madness he had created showed up on his doorstep.

This happened shortly after he had established the uneasy truce with the Clarks. The war was over, but the effects of it could still be felt. A cease-fire had been called, but bad blood still lingered between the two sides. King James was coming home in the wee hours of the morning, after hanging out at the strip club with Lakim, Dee, and some of the others. It was Dee's birthday, so bottles had been popped left and right. King James wasn't a big drinker, but in light of the special occasion, he'd allowed himself to indulge. That night was the drunkest King had been since coming home from prison.

When they hit the block, King parted ways with his crew, promising to link with them that afternoon. He was blitzed and needed to sleep it off. Before going upstairs to his apartment, King decided to hit the twenty-four-hour bodega and grab a sandwich. The bread would help soak up the alcohol he had consumed. While King was at the little window, placing his order, an addict approached him. He was dressed in tattered jeans, a dirty shirt, and sneakers with holes in them. The dude looked too young to be strung out, but King had been around long enough to know that addiction didn't practice age discrimination. He had seen both young and old hooked on the poison he sold.

"You holding, big bro?" the fiend said, walking up on King.

"Nigga, you're either new to the hood or stupid. You know I don't touch no drugs. Get the fuck away from me!" King snapped at him.

"My bad, big man . . . my bad," the addict stammered, then slunk away, giving King a dirty look. There was something familiar about him, which King wouldn't pick up on until after he replayed the night's events.

After getting his sandwich, King ambled across the street to his building. The streets were quiet, which was unusual. They sold crack twenty-four hours a day, so there was usually someone out looking to score from one of his workers, but on this night the streets were empty. He didn't even see the young worker named Jeff, who was supposed to be on the night shift. Knowing Jeff, he was probably tucked in one of the apartments with some young hood rat. When King caught up with Jeff, he was going to kick his ass for slacking on the job.

When King got inside the building, he hit the steps to walk up to his apartment, as was his routine. As he climbed the concrete stairs, an eerie feeling settled in his gut, but he ignored it. Had he not been so drunk, he probably would have paid it more mind. King's apartment door was right next to the stairwell, so he didn't have far to go when he stumbled onto his floor. As he was fumbling with his keys, the stairwell door on the opposite side of the floor opened. Instinctively, King went for the pistol tucked in the back of his pants. Out of the stairwell shambled the fiend who had approached him at the bodega.

"Sorry. Didn't mean to scare you," the addict said sheepishly.

"Fuck is you doing? Following me?" King snarled.

"Nah, man. I was just looking for somewhere to blast off." The addict held up his crack pipe for King to see. "Your boy downstairs hooked me up. And sorry about that business earlier. I didn't mean any disrespect."

"Whatever, man. Find somewhere else to smoke that shit." King dismissed him and turned his attention back to the lock on his apartment door. He had taken his eyes off the addict for only a second, but that was all the time the addict needed to make his play.

King James must've felt something was about to go down, because he managed to throw himself out of the way mere seconds before the addict tried to cut his throat. The addict swung the blade again, and in his drunken state, King instinctively raised his arm to block the blow. The knife bit deep into his arm, spraying blood onto his door and the wall behind him. The pain from the cut sobered him up. When the addict swung the blade again, King caught his arm in midair. Twisting with everything he had, he broke the man's arm at the elbow. The addict howled in pain and staggered backward. This gave King a chance to gather his wits. Seeing that the trap he was attempting to spring had failed, the addict tried to run, but there would be no escape from King James.

The addict bolted for the stairs. He managed to make it down half a flight before one of King's heavy boots struck him in the back and sent him flying the rest of the way down. The addict bounced off the concrete wall. Dazed and bleeding from the cut that had opened up on his forehead when he hit wall, he tried to run again, but King was on him. He delivered a powerful right cross to the addict's jaw, nearly breaking it. The addict tried to muster up the energy to fight, but there was little he could do to fend off the jackhammer-like punches King was raining down on him. The addict tried to wilt to the ground, but King would have none of that. He wrapped his massive hands around the addict's throat and lifted him off his feet. As King looked into the man's hate-filled eyes, he realized why he had looked so familiar. He had seen those eyes before.

"You?" King gasped.

The addict smiled, knowing that King had recognized him and now had an idea why he had come. "This is for Shorty!" the addict bellowed before producing a second knife from the pocket of his dirty jeans and ramming it into King's gut.

Pain shot through King's gut as the blade pierced the lining of his stomach. The strength faded from his arms, forcing him to release the addict. The addict poked King three more times as the big man dropped to his knees. He would've surely killed King James had one of the neighbors not come out to investigate the noise. The last thing King remembered seeing was the addict taking off down the stairs, and then everything went black.

The next morning King woke up in St. Luke's Hospital. Lakim was at his bedside. Dee and about half a dozen of the other young soldiers were in the waiting room, all screaming for blood. King told Lakim the story of how he had gotten caught slipping. When Lakim asked King if he knew his attacker, King lied and told him that he didn't. In truth, he had seen the addict before. His was one of the many angry faces in Shorty's mother's apartment the day King and his crew had gone to pay their respects after his murder. Shorty's family had blamed King for his death, and in a sense, they weren't wrong. Had it been anyone else, King would've unleashed his dogs without giving it a second thought, but for the addict, there would be no retribution. The addict had carved King up pretty bad, but at least King still had his life, which was more than could be said for Shorty. King chalked the stabbing up to a case of karma coming to pay him a visit.

"You okay?" Aisha's sleepy voice startled King, bringing him out of his reverie as he stood in the middle of the bedroom. She had been sleeping beside him but was now watching him nervously from the bed. Aisha was the girl King had been seeing off and on since he came home from prison.

"Didn't mean to wake you, Ma. I just had a bad dream," King lied.

"Do you usually try to shoot your nightmares?" She nodded at the gun in his hand.

PART III

Cross-Examination

CHAPTER 17

It was about 6:00 a.m. when Ma's full bladder stirred her from a peaceful sleep. She hadn't had an uninterrupted night's rest in over a decade. It seemed the older she got, the more the organ shrank. She lay there for a time, ignoring the sensation, until the mounting pressure forced her to her feet.

As she sat on the toilet in the bathroom adjoining her bedroom, Ma began to mentally tick off the things she needed to do that day, before the send-off. Ma had planned nearly a hundred home goings in her lifetime. None of them had been easy, but after so many, they had started to become routine. This one felt different, though. Not just because it was a family member. She had buried plenty of those. This was her sister's boy. The same sister she had given her word to on her deathbed.

Ma's sister, Paulette, had always been the black sheep of the family, and that was saying a lot, considering all the Savages were just naturally rotten in one way or another. Being the only two girls in a litter of ten, the sisters had always butted heads while they were growing up, and the rivalry had only intensified the older they got. Ma and Paulette had engaged in some epic battles over the years, with Paulette even shooting Ma in the legs during one of them. She had been a troubled girl with a weakness for hard drugs. Heroin, cocaine, crack, booze . . . If it could give her a buzz, Paulette was all in. She would sometimes disappear for weeks or months at a time, only to resurface with a hard-luck story to tell. Paulette reminded Ma of her son Mad Dog in that way. Trouble and hard times seemed to follow them wherever they went. Ma and Paulette couldn't stand each other, but they were still family and were bound by the Savage code to help out when a family member was in need.

So when Paulette showed up on Ma's doorstep, looking twenty years older than her actual age of thirty-five, with a young boy on her hip, Ma couldn't turn her away. It seemed that Paulette's way of life had finally caught up with her. Somewhere in her travels, she had contracted the HIV virus. Back then, not a lot was known about the disease, and most of the effective treatments that had been devised were reserved for those who could afford them. Paulette couldn't. It also didn't help that she was so heavily into her drug habit that by the time she started to realize she was sick, there wasn't much she could do about it, except get her affairs in order. By then Paulette had squandered everything she owned, and the only thing of some value that she had left was her son, Michael.

It was when Paulette realized that she had reached the end of the road that she showed up on Ma's doorstep with Michael. The moment Ma laid eyes on the boy, she knew that he was trouble. He had the same darkness about him that his mother had hauled around like luggage. Ma wasn't too keen on the idea of taking on her sister's boy, but he was family. As it turned out, Paulette passed shortly after dropping her son at her sister's place. They found her dead from an overdose in a crack house in Hollygrovee. Paulette had decided that if she was going to go out, it would be with a bang.

At first, Ma found having Paulette's son under her roof quite demanding. Dealing with the shenanigans of her own five children was already a large enough task. Adding a troubled child to the mix only made things harder. Paulette had subjected Michael to quite a bit of chaos at an early age, and as a result, he was constantly acting out. It seemed like every other week, Ma had to go up to the school to discuss something he had done, be it stealing or fighting with the other kids. It was like the boy couldn't keep his nose clean to save his life. He definitely had Savage blood in him. The boy was a natural criminal, and it was Ma who taught him how to apply his skills when she brought him into the family business. Michael wasn't a killer, like the rest of her boys, but everything else in the criminal spectrum he attacked with a zeal that made Ma proud. This was why she had given him the nickname Big Money. He was always after the next big score.

The fact that Big Money was no longer with them saddened Ma, but she couldn't say that she was surprised. Big Money was a Savage, but unlike the rest of her brood, he played the game with no honor. It didn't matter to him whom he crossed or stepped on in the pursuit of his next dollar. Ma had tried to warn him time and again about the way he moved, but her words had fallen on deaf ears. Now, as it was with his mother, Big Money's lifestyle had caught up with him.

By the time Ma had finished relieving herself, she was wide awake. There was no way she would be able to go back to sleep, so she figured she may as well get her day started. She pulled on her bathrobe and shuffled down the stairs, headed for the kitchen. As she neared it, she noticed a familiar smell. It was weed. She had warned Bug and Anthony about getting high in her house. She grabbed her baseball bat from the hall closet, prepared to hand out some Savage-style discipline. She entered the kitchen and switched on the light, expecting to find one of the teenagers. She was surprised to see Keith.

"Killer?"

Keith looked up at his mother with red-rimmed eyes and flashed what she assumed was a smile. "Morning, Mama." Her straight-as-an-arrow son was sitting at the counter, toking on a joint and sipping Jack Daniel's straight from the bottle. Keith hardly drank, and she couldn't recall ever seeing him smoke weed, so she knew something was wrong.

"What you doing sitting down here in the dark all by yourself?" she asked.

"Drinking and thinking." He hoisted the bottle and took another swig.

"And stinking up the place." She fanned at the smoke.

"Found this stashed in Bug's room. Pretty good shit." Keith offered her the joint.

Ma took the joint from her son and hit it twice before handing it back. "You know I've got a strict no smoking rule in my house."

"Savages don't live by anyone's rules," Keith replied, repeating what his mother had always told them when they were growing up.

"Thought you were a Davis," she said sarcastically, taking the stool across from him.

"For years the Hulk masqueraded as Bruce Banner. Keith Davis is the mask my monster hides behind." Keith paused for a moment. "Would you like to meet my monster, Mama?" he asked sinisterly.

There was something Ma saw in Keith's eyes at that moment that made her nervous. "What's wrong with you, boy? You drunk?"

"Drunk as a fiddler's bitch." He laughed. "Can I ask you something, Mama?"

"Sure."

"How come you never treated me like the others?"

"What you mean? I love all of you the same," Ma insisted.

"That's not what I asked you. When we were growing up, you let Big John, Mad Dog, and Dickey literally get away with murder, but you were on my ass for everything I did. Whether it was my grades in school or how I performed during jobs, I always gave my best effort, but it never measured up for you. What was the matter? Wasn't I Savage enough for your standards?"

Ma thought about the questions before answering. "It was actually the opposite. Of all my children, you were the most like a Savage."

"I don't understand."

"Big John was cunning, Dickey was as fearless as they came, and Mad Dog had a mean streak a mile long. They all had one trait or another of the Savage men who came before them, but it was you who embodied them all. You were the one most fit to lead this family into the next generation, which is why it hurt me so bad when you abandoned us."

"I didn't abandon you, Mama. I went to college."

"And you never came back. Killer, I never had a problem with you going off and getting your feet wet in the world. Anyone with eyes knew you had dreams that were bigger than the Lower Ninth Ward, and I guess I'd always hoped that this family would fit somewhere in those dreams. You were my knight in shining armor, but you traded your legacy in for a suit."

"A legacy of blood and destruction," Keith snorted. "Thanks, but I'll pass."

"Spoken just like your daddy. He never had the heart for this life, either."

"Don't talk about him like that," Keith warned.

"What? I'm just speaking the truth," Ma said. "Your father was an amazing lover, but he was a half-assed criminal. He didn't have the heart or the stomach for our type of life, so I guess it's no wonder he killed himself."

"What the hell are you talking about? The police killed Daddy," Keith told her.

"Yes, your father died by those cops' bullets, but his death was his own design," Ma told him. "Tell me something. In all the years Dickey was right in the head, did you ever know him to miss even the smallest detail when it came to a job?"

"No," Keith said honestly.

"So, has it never struck you as odd that your father fucked up on one that was supposed to be so simple?" Ma asked.

Keith shook his head. "That wasn't Daddy's fault. The man handling the cutting off of the alarm system—"

"Was your dad," she said, cutting him off. "He was an electrician, remember? Your dad could hack through just about any kind of alarm system without even having to try. That alarm didn't go off by accident. It was by design."

"What are you trying to say?" Keith asked. He didn't like where the conversation was going.

Ma sighed. "I'm going to share something with you that I've never shared with another living soul except Mad Dog. Your father was a broken man. I don't know if it was the pressure of this life or whatever personal demons he was battling, but they had worn your father down. I knew something was going on inside him, but I figured it would pass. I never realized how bad he was hurting until I got the word that the police had killed him. Your daddy was tired, baby. So tired that he couldn't go on anymore. So he ended it."

"Suicide by cop." Keith put his head in his hands. His brain was reeling. His father being killed by the police was part of the reason Keith had decided to become a defense attorney, instead of sitting on the opposite side of the bench. His dad had been his motivation to wage war against police corruption. He would make them all pay for what they had done to his father, and now he was finding out it had all been a lie. "Why didn't you tell me before?"

"And tarnish the image of the man you thought was a god? I couldn't do that to you. I know you think I'm a sour old bitch, but you have to believe me when I say that everything I've ever done in life was to protect you," Ma said sincerely.

"Is that why you never told me about Darla coming to look for me?" Keith asked. He could see in her eyes that the question had caught her by surprise. "You don't have to lie about it. I saw her tonight at B.B.'s, and she told me everything."

"It was for your own good, Killer. That girl and her whole family were bayou trash. Had I let her get her claws in you, then you may not have been able to run off and become a fancy lawyer. Hell, I'd think you'd be grateful."

"Grateful for robbing me of my freedom to choose?" Keith snapped.

"Free will to choose what? To run off with Darla to whatever imaginary bullshit the two of you used to dream up while you were fucking like rabbits under my roof? Before long, you'd have fucked around, got that girl pregnant, and ended up working some shit job in the city, instead of chasing your dreams. News flash for you, Killer. Ain't no happy endings in the ghetto. Ain't that the reason you ran off?"

"I ran off because I didn't want to end up either a sociopath, like Mad Dog or, worse, like Dickey!" Keith shouted.

"My sons may not be model citizens, but at least they're men. When this family needed them, they stood tall and handled what needed to be done. They did not run off and hide like some pussies!" Ma fired back.

Before Keith even realized what he was doing, he was on his feet. He slid one of the knives from the rack near the sink and took a step forward. The deadly look Ma gave him stopped Keith in his tracks. It was then that Keith realized his mother had been goading him all along. And just like when he was a youth, his mother knew better than anyone else how to bring out the worst in him.

"There he is." Ma smiled wide, exposing the gold tooth in her mouth. "I knew my Killer was still hiding in there somewhere."

"I'm not your anything." Keith tossed the knife on the counter.

"You trying to convince me or yourself? Some nerve on your part, coming in here, trying to judge us for how we survive, when your fingernails are just as dirty as those of the rest of us, if not more. You think I don't know what you left buried on Conti Street?"

The accusation slapped Keith sober. He searched his mother's eyes for signs that she might be tricking him into confirming whatever she suspected, but her stare was unwavering. Ma Savage wasn't the type of woman to ask questions she didn't already know the answers to. As he stood there under his mother's gaze, Keith suddenly felt stripped as bare as the day he was born.

"Ain't nothing my boys can hide from me, including what's in their hearts." Ma picked up the bottle of Jack Daniel's and took a healthy gulp. "You might be using your daddy's name, but it's Savage blood your heart pumps."

"You're a twisted and evil old woman!" Keith spat.

"Maybe so, but at least I know what I am. Can you say the same?"

Keith had had enough. "I had a feeling you were gonna pull something like this, which is why I'm glad I didn't cancel my hotel reservation. I'll be back for Big Money's home going, and then I'm on the next thing smoking back to Atlanta." He stormed toward the door. Before he left, his mother had some parting words for him.

"That's right. Do what you do best and cut out when the shit gets too thick for you. But I'll tell you this, Killer Keith. You can run from here to the ends of the earth, but you'll never be able to escape from yourself."

CHAPTER 18

King hated early mornings. When he was in prison, he was always up at the crack of dawn either so he could get started on work assignments or so he wouldn't miss chow. He had promised himself that when he was free, he would see what it felt like to sleep in for a change. And it felt great. The only thing that irritated him more than getting up early in the morning was being summoned. But when the summons came from Shai Clark, you didn't gripe. You just showed up.

"Why the fuck this nigga always wanna meet in West Bubblefuck?" Lakim said from his position behind the wheel of the SUV.

"Queens ain't that far," King told him. They were in Astoria, which was a short hop across the East River, but to cats like Lakim, who never left the hood, they might as well be on Mars.

"Still don't see why he couldn't have met us in Harlem," Lakim replied, continuing to gripe.

"Yo, chill, God. I'm not really with that Angry Smurf shit this morning," King said harshly.

"What's good with you, King? You been in a foul mood since I picked you up this morning." Lakim knew King well enough to be able to tell when something was troubling him.

King looked at his friend, wondering how much he should reveal about the source of his worries. "I guess I just haven't been sleeping much lately, and it's starting to make me cranky."

"I get like that, too, especially if I've been hanging with Dee for a few days. The past couple of days, we been at this spot called Hades. Word to mine, that shit is super live!" Lakim revealed.

"Word? What is it? A strip joint?"

"Nah, B. This shit is on a totally different level than a strip club. Anything goes on at Hades. I don't care if you like coke, dope, pussy, or asshole . . . they got it all at Hades."

"How the hell did you discover someplace like that?"

"Dee put me onto it," Lakim told him. "It's a members' only spot. Son was on the waiting list for, like, three months before they let him smell the rooms past the bar. They said the dude that owns it is that Tinkerbell nigga Christian from up on the Hill. You remember, the guy that used to run with Ghost and them."

King knew Christian Knight by name, but he didn't know him personally. He was said to be a pimp and a pill pusher mainly, but he was also a person who could make just about anything happen for the right price. Though King had never met Christian, he was familiar with a guy who ran with his crew, a man by the name of Frankenstein. He bore a resemblance to the fictional monster in terms of both his looks and his build, right down to the lightning bolt–shaped scar across his forehead. Frankenstein had passed through Attica during King's stay. The man was a real head case, and the guards had handled him with the delicacy shown a serial killer. At that time Frankenstein had been up for a murder, but two years into his bid, he had had his conviction overturned. If Christian had muscle like that rolling with him, it was no wonder people thought twice about crossing him.

"I don't know," Lakim continued. "I was thinking if everything goes right between you and ya man in there, we could do something like that with your spot. We'd make a killing just off the strength of the bitches we could recruit to work there."

"Ain't gonna happen," King said flatly. "I told y'all that this spot is going to be clean. I don't want none of this dirt we stirring up on the streets touching it."

"I hear you, man, but I still can't figure out why you'd be interested in opening a legit business all of a sudden, if it ain't to run money through. For all that, you could just keep selling crack, and in half the time, you'd make three times what it'll make."

"Yeah, and end up dead or in prison," King noted.

"Man, you bugging."

"I'm not bugging. I'm paying attention." King looked at the construction site they were parked in front of. Planted in the dirt was a sign that read AFFORDABLE HOUSING COMING SOON. Beneath it was the unmistakable logo of Clark, Lansky & Co. "Gotta start somewhere," he mumbled.

"What was that, God?"

"Nothing," King lied. "Yo, when is the last time you spoke to that broad Pam?"

Lakim thought about it. "I dunno. Probably not since I paid her the bread for that info." Pam was the girl who had told King James that Big Money was behind the car bombing.

"She still hang around the neighborhood?"

"I see her from time to time, but not like that. Why the sudden interest in Pam? You thinking about trying to hit that again?"

"Nah. Just wondering, I guess. You know she's probably the only person who can tie us to what happened to Big Money."

"You thinking maybe it's time for her to go?" Lakim asked, hoping that he wasn't. Pam was a cool chick that both he and King had known for a number of years. That was a call he wouldn't look forward to making.

King thought about it for a long moment. "I don't know, man. I'm just thinking out loud. Let me run up in here and take care of this business." He slid from the vehicle.

King picked his way carefully across the overturned ground and gravel, making his way to the back of the structure that was being built. Workmen milled about, tending to their assigned tasks. None of them even spared King a second look. Their employer always paid his employees a little extra to take no notice of the comings and goings of strangers on their job sites.

A few yards away stood three men. They were huddled around a table sitting on a dirt mound, going over what King assumed had to be blueprints. One of them was the foreman. He was wearing a white hard hat and khakis. He seemed to be leading the conversation. The second man was older, with silver hair. A salmon-colored suit hung over his thin frame. Every so often he would nod at whatever the foreman was saying. This was Sol Lansky. He was an old-world gangster, with a reputation that stretched back to the sixties. These days he was a semiretired businessman whom people paid handsomely for his counsel. The third man wore no suit. He was dressed in jeans, a white polo shirt, and white sneakers. Though he didn't look it, he was the most important man in the city, and the only person who could put out a summons that King would answer.

Shai must've felt King standing there, because he suddenly looked in his direction. Then Shai whispered something to the foreman, who walked off. Sol, however, remained. If the old man was sitting in, then, King reasoned, it was going to be an important conversation.

"Good morning, gentlemen," King greeted as he approached the two men.

"Always a good morning when there's money being made." Shai smiled broadly and shook his hand. From the way he had received King, you'd never know that only a few months ago, they had been going out of their way to kill each other. "You eat breakfast yet? We got some bagels and shit inside."

"With all due respect, Shai, I'd rather just get to the business of why you called me out here, so I can get back to the hood," King told him.

"A fish out of water," Shai remarked. "Anyhow, let me start by saying that I appreciate the job you've been doing with making sure your guys are all playing by the rules. A wise man once told me that partnerships are more profitable than wars."

"Sounds like some real-life game," King replied, wishing Shai would get on with it. They weren't currently feuding, but there would always be a part of him that longed to kill Shai Clark.

"This same wise man once told me that when someone does you a kindness, you should return it." Shai motioned to Sol. The old man reached inside the pocket of his suit jacket and produced an envelope, which he handed to King James.

"What's this?" King looked at the envelope suspiciously.

"A while back, you came to me and asked if I would use some of my connections to grant you a building permit. Sadly, I wasn't able to get them to agree. Some of my associates aren't as forgiving as I am," Shai said.

"So what is this? An 'I'm sorry' note?" King asked sarcastically. He opened the envelope, pulled out a document, and scanned it. It was the deed to a property in Harlem, and the property was registered under the name King Enterprises. "What is this?"

"A friend of mine who owns a restaurant uptown incurred a debt that he couldn't pay. He's still in the red with the bank for a few payments, and there will probably be fines that need to be taken care of, but that will all fall on the new owner, who is you," Shai explained.

King was stunned.

"Just because my partners wouldn't finance your dream doesn't mean you shouldn't have it," Shai commented.

"Why are you giving me a restaurant?" King still couldn't believe it.

"I think the correct response should be thank you, kid," Sol interjected.

"I'm sorry. I don't mean to sound ungrateful . . . truly, but why? With all the history between us, why pay me such a kindness?"

"I want you to know how serious I am about putting this thing between us to bed and getting back to this money. I may not like your ghetto ass, but I can't deny the fact that you project niggas know how to flip a bird. The working relationship between us has been profitable, and I'd like to ensure we keep it going, and that means showing you how to separate yourself from the trash. The fact that you came to me to make it happen in the first place shows me that you're serious about it. You just needed a little direction. Now it's up to you to see it through."

"I will."

"But it does come with a few conditions." Shai smirked. "I get five points per month off everything you make in the first three years."

King should've known anything Shai gave him wouldn't come without a catch. "Anything else?"

"Yes, there is. I don't want any of the shit in your backyard spilling over into mine. Do you understand?"

"Shai, you do what you do, and I do what I do. Outside of my people buying drugs from yours, our paths shouldn't need to cross like that."

"I don't think you fully understand what's happening here. I'm extending an olive branch. By me doing this for you, it creates a link between us. What you do from here on out will send a vibration up the chain. I don't want to feel your problems, so make sure your backyard is clear of anything that could make me regret our arrangement. Leave no stone unturned in making sure."

"You got it. Now, if there's nothing else, I gotta skate," King said.

"Before you go, I got a question for you, kid," Sol interjected. "Of all the businesses you could've considered getting into, why a restaurant?"

"For my mom," King answered sincerely. "Back in the days, she used to cook and sell plates to the people in the neighborhood. I always told her that when I got my weight up, I was going to buy her a restaurant."

"God bless your heart, kid. I know she's gonna be proud when you tell her." Sol gave him an approving nod.

"My mother passed a few years ago," King replied, darkening the mood.

Sol nodded. "I'm sorry."

"Thanks. I'll catch you on Monday, Shai," King said before he walked off.

"What do you make of that one, Sol?" Shai asked once King had gone.

"Had you asked me a few months ago, I'd have told you that he was a rabid dog that needed to be put down. Now . . ." Sol shrugged. "I'm not so sure. What I do know is that I'm glad the two of you have stopped trying to kill each other. Putting a leash on him was smart. Just don't ever make the mistake of letting him off the chain again."

"I won't, Sol . . . Trust me, I won't."

***

By the time King left Sol and Shai, he was in a far better mood than he had been in when he showed up. He had never imagined that the person who would help him realize his dream would turn out to be the one who had inspired it in the first place.

During the time King had been feuding with Shai, he had also been studying him. He knew Shai's story backward and forward, from how his family had started out to the real story of how Shai had inherited his father's throne. He didn't like Shai as a person, but he had a great deal of respect for how he moved. Not only did Shai have money on the streets, but he was also doing very well for himself through the businesses he owned. He had found a way to reap the benefits that came from being in the streets while insulating himself from the bullshit. That was the model King needed to adopt. King had no illusions about the crack game lasting forever, and he knew that when and if the walls to his kingdom fell, he had to have a plan B. The restaurant was to be the foundation of the world he was going to build for his child.

Thinking of his unborn child made him recall Shai's warning about making sure his backyard was clean. To his knowledge, there was nothing going on that could hurt his relationship with Shai. Then he remembered Big Money. King had always suspected that it was Shai who was behind hiring the Savages to hit him. If Lakim was right and his family decided to make a stink, King had to make sure there was no way they could connect Big Money's death to him.

"How'd it go?" Lakim asked once King was back in the ride.

"Everything went smooth. I got my spot," King told him.

"Say word? Shai came through on the building permits?" Lakim asked excitedly. He knew how bad King wanted this to happen.

"He did me one better, but I'll explain later. Do you remember that thing we were talking about earlier? The thing with the girl?"

"Yeah. What about it?"

"Make it happen."

"Okay," Lakim reluctantly agreed. He liked Pam, but King was his brother. "You got anybody in mind for this?"

King thought about it for a minute. "Put Dee on it. As a matter of fact, not Dee. Put the little Philly nigga on it. He should be about ready to cut his teeth. Besides, if something goes wrong and we gotta get rid of him too, it won't hurt as much as losing one of our own."

"Damn! You on some real Hitler shit, trying to kill the whole world at one time," Lakim half joked.

"Leave no stone unturned."

CHAPTER 19

By the time Keith checked into his room at the JW Marriott on Canal, he was out on his feet. It had been a long night and, thanks to his mother, an even longer morning. All he wanted to do was crash.

He stripped off his clothes and jumped into the shower. He pressed his head against the tiles and let the hot water wash over him. It felt good, loosening his tense muscles and clearing up some of the Jack Daniel's–induced fog in his brain. Drinking all that whiskey had been a bad idea, especially on an empty stomach, but he had desperately needed something to take the edge off.

After showering, Keith came out of the bathroom, intent on putting on fresh clothes before lying down. It was then that he remembered that in his rush to get out of the house, he had forgotten to collect his luggage. It was still too early for the clothing stores on the strip to be open, so until they were, there wasn't much he could do about it except wait. Once again, in his attempt to spite his mother, he had ended up with the short end of the stick.

Keith slipped into one of the hotel's complimentary bathrobes and flung himself across the bed. On the nightstand, he noticed the notification light blinking on his phone. He retrieved his message and was surprised to see he'd missed a call from Bernie. She hadn't bothered to leave a voicemail. He pondered calling her back, but what would he say? Keith's head was so screwed up that he didn't even know where to begin in repairing his broken relationship. He blamed his mother for that. He had almost believed the old woman's "making amends" routine, until she showed her true colors. He had been a fool to believe that a leopard could change his spots, but what did that say about him? Was she right? Was he trying only to run from who he really was? Those were Keith's last thoughts before drifting off to sleep.

As he slept, Keith was haunted by a terrible nightmare . . . a memory, really. He was a young man again back in New Orleans, and it was shortly after Mrs. Winston's funeral. The police were still doing a half-assed job of solving her murder. But thanks to an anonymous tip, they had managed to capture one of the boys who was responsible for her death. The other one was still on the loose. Though the boy the police had caught refused to rat on his accomplice, the whole hood knew who else had been involved in the crime. It was a boy named Tate Jones. While Mrs. Winston was rotting in the ground, Tate Jones was still breathing God's good air, and it frustrated Keith to no end. Something had to be done, and if the police wouldn't handle it, he would.

He spent the next week or so looking for Tate. He had gone into hiding, but boys like Tate never strayed too far from what was familiar to them. Keith got a tip from a crackhead that Tate had been hiding out in a dope house over on North Villere in the Seventh Ward. Keith spent the next few days sitting across the street in a car he'd stolen for his task, watching the house and waiting. Tate never seemed to leave the house, and for a while, Keith thought he was going to have to go inside Rambo-style and drag him out. Then an idea hit him. He found a pay phone a few blocks away, placed a call, and then went back to the house to wait for the inevitable.

"Five-oh!" Keith heard one of the lookouts shout just before the wagon screeched to a stop in front of the house. Both addicts and dealers scattered like roaches, trying to avoid capture.

When Keith saw Tate slip out the back door and hop the fence into the next yard, Keith took off after him in his car. He followed him for several blocks before pulling alongside him.

"Yo, is that Tate?" he called out the window.

Tate came to a stop. "Who that?" he asked nervously, prepared to take off running again.

"It's me, Killer, from school," Keith said in his best gullible teen voice. This seemed to put Tate at ease.

"What's your square ass doing round here?" Tate ambled up to the car.

"Trying to score," Keith lied.

"I thought you was on some athlete shit and didn't get high?" Tate asked suspiciously.

"It ain't for me. I got girls waiting for me who are looking to party, and the Ninth is bone dry."

"How much you need?" Tate asked. Most of his stash had gotten caught up in the raid, but he had a few loose bags of coke in his pocket that he could sell to Keith. That should hold him over until he could figure something else out.

"I'm not real sure. I've never done this before." Keith went into his pocket and produced several crisp hundred-dollar bills. The bills were counterfeit, but they looked real enough to stoke Tate's greed. "How much will this get me?"

"Enough to make sure you and your bitches have the time of your lives." Tate hopped into the passenger side of the car without waiting for an invite. "I can get you what you need, but you'll have to run me across town, to my stash spot, to get it." He knew just the spot to lure Keith to so he could relieve him of his bankroll.

Tate and Keith rode a few miles east, through the Seventh Ward and out past Willie Mae's Scotch House. The whole ride, Tate was running his mouth about how he had become the man on the streets since dropping out of high school. Keith smirked and acted like he was interested, but all the while he kept seeing Mrs. Winston's smiling face. Being that close to her killer made Keith so mad that he had to grip the steering wheel with both hands to keep them from trembling.

Tate directed him to a large house on Conti Street. The place was dark and was falling in on itself. It obviously hadn't been occupied in quite some time. Keith pulled the car around to the back of the house, which was overgrown with thick weeds, and killed the engine.

"You sure this is the place?" Keith asked, giving the house a queer look.

"What? You spooked or something?" Tate teased him. "I like to keep a low profile. Can't have everybody in my business, feel me?"

"Yeah, I feel you," Keith said, playing along.

"Give me the money, and I'll run inside to get the stuff. Shouldn't be more than five minutes," Tate promised. He wanted that money so bad, his palms were sweating. He planned to get in the wind as soon as it was in his hand.

"Here ya go," Keith said and produced a gun instead of the money.

"What the fuck?" Tate was shocked. There was no way that Keith could've known that he was planning on ripping him off.

"Sorry to spoil your plans, but I've got plans of my own," Keith said coolly. "Out of the car."

"You're making a mistake," Tate warned.

"Nigga, I said get out!" Keith clubbed him on the side of the head with the butt of the gun. Tate stumbled out of the car and spilled on all fours into the weeds.

"If it's money you want, you're shit out of luck," Tate told him.

"This ain't got nothing to do with money. This is the devil collecting what's due to him," Keith said in a low tone. "March," he ordered.

He kept the gun pointed at Tate as he marched him through the yard and into the house. The whole place stank of mold, like most of the houses in the neighborhood. A lot of them still suffered from heavy water damage as a result of the last big flood. He understood why Tate had picked this as the spot to spring his trap. It was so isolated that you could literally get away with murder. He forced Tate into the kitchen. It was as good a place to die as any.

"If you'd just tell me what this is about, maybe we could work out some sort of deal. At least give a nigga a chance," Tate pleaded.

"Did you give Mrs. Winston a chance before you and your punk-ass homeboy killed her?" Keith spat.

"Is that what this is about? The teacher?" A light of recognition went off in Tate's eyes. "Look, man, I was there, but I didn't kill her. That was all Steve! He's the one who should be standing here, not me!"

"I can't get my hands on Steve, so I guess you'll have to do."

Keith chambered a round into the gun. Keith paused, finger hovering over the trigger. He had replayed what the moment would be like at least a dozen times in his head, but now that it was at hand, he was unsure. He wanted Tate dead, but he didn't know if he had the heart to follow through. Keith had shot at people before, but this was an execution. Keith's moment of hesitation was all Tate needed. He lunged at Keith and slapped the gun away. It discharged when it hit the floor. Keith tried to go for it, but Tate was on him.

"Ole pussy-ass nigga!" Tate yelled as he punched Keith in the face. "You drawn your gun on me like you built like that!" He hit him again.

Tate hurled punches and curses at Keith, while Keith tried as best he could to protect himself. He had to admit that for a skinny dude, Tate hit hard as hell. Keith managed to land a blow on Tate's chin, but the punch was thrown awkwardly and didn't do much to help him. The next thing he knew, Tate had him bent over backward on the counter and was choking the life out of him. Keith's hand slid across the counter, looking for something . . . anything that would get the man off him. His fingers ran across something cold. It was a broken plate. Keith grabbed it and swung as hard as he could. He had meant only to get Tate off him, but the edge of the dish opened up a nasty gash in the soft flesh of the man's throat. Tate dropped to his knees, fingers clutching futilely at the wound, which was spraying blood all over the kitchen floor. With a death rattle, Tate fell over, dead, and it was done.

It took Keith a minute to catch his breath. Cautiously, he used his foot to turn Tate's body over. A gaping wound stretched across his throat, exposing white flesh and tendons. The sight of it was so grotesque that it made Keith retch. He barely made it to the kitchen sink before the chicken sandwich he'd eaten earlier that day spilled out in a river of bile. He wanted Tate to suffer for what he had done to Mrs. Winston, but until then he hadn't been sure how far he was willing to go with dishing out the punishment. He paced back and forth like a caged animal. He hadn't planned on killing Tate, only giving him a good beating or maybe crippling him, but things had gone too far, and the man had forced his hand. Now he was faced with a problem that he had no idea how to handle: what to do with Tate's body. If he left him there for the police to find, he might wind up going to jail. The thought of spending the rest of his life behind bars scared Keith more than when Tate was choking him. He needed to do something, but he wasn't sure what, so he called someone who would know.

The minutes seemed to tick by like hours as Keith waited. He jumped when he heard the sound of footfalls coming from near the back door. He scrambled for the gun Tate had knocked away, and hid himself in the shadows of the kitchen, holding his breath.

Mad Dog appeared in the doorway. He was dressed in dark coveralls and work boots and was wearing latex gloves. In one hand he carried a bucket, and in the other, a curved saw. Keith recognized it as one of the tools his father had kept in the shed behind their house. They would use it to trim the branches of the sycamore tree in their backyard when it started growing out of control.

"You in here, Killer?" Mad Dog called in his deep voice.

Keith appeared from his hiding spot, both shaken and relieved.

Mad Dog's eyes went from Tate's body to his little brother. "What the fuck happened?"

Keith gave Mad Dog the short version of the story. "I didn't plan on killing him. I . . . I only wanted to rough him up . . . maybe scare him a bit."

"Looks like you did more than that. How many times I tell you about trying to play grown folks' games? Give me that fucking pistol." He snatched the gun from Keith's hand and tossed it into the bucket.

"It was a mistake. I'm sorry," Keith said, on the verge of tears.

"Snatching a life is the one mistake ain't no apologies for," Mad Dog shot back. Seeing how rattled his brother was, Mad Dog softened his tone. "Look, I'm gonna need you to pull yourself together so you can help me clean this mess up." He knelt beside the upper half of Tate's body, ignoring the blood soaking into the knees of his coveralls. Keith went to Tate's feet and grabbed him by the ankles. "Boy, what the hell are you doing?"

"Helping you move him," Keith said.

Mad Dog laughed. "Man, you must be out of your mind if you think I'm gonna risk walking around, carrying a damn body, even in this shitty neighborhood. Where he fell is where he'll rest." He handed Keith the curved saw.

"What am I supposed to do with this?" Keith asked, unsure if he was ready for the answer.

"We'll need to chop his hands off and knock out his teeth. This way, even if someone discovers the body, they'll have a hard time identifying him," Mad Dog explained.

"I can't." Keith tried to hand the saw back to his brother.

"You can, and you will." Mad Dog refused the saw. "I warned you, but you wanted to play in the big leagues, so here we are. This is your mess to clean up, not mine. Get to cutting, or I'm gone, and you can deal with the consequences on your own."

Reluctantly, Keith did as he was told. First, he knocked out Tate's teeth with the handle of the saw. Then he closed his eyes and tried to imagine he was back home in the kitchen, cutting up raw chicken for his mother, but sawing through a human bone was much harder than cutting through a chicken's. By the time Keith had finished sawing off Tate's hands, he was tired, sweaty, and disgusted. It would be a long time before he was able to eat meat again, if ever. Mad Dog wrapped the hands in plastic and tossed them and the teeth into the bucket.

"What about the rest of him?" Keith asked.

Mad Dog ignored Keith and began rummaging in the bucket until his hand came up holding a jar of peanut butter, which he began smearing all over Tate's body.

When Keith saw the first of the rats creep out and begin sniffing at Tate's body, he understood what Mad Dog was planning for Tate's remains. The thought of the rodents devouring Tate made Keith so sick that he threw up in the sink again.

The ride back to the house was spent in silence. Keith was happy that his brother had come to his aid in his time of need, but he was also very disturbed. He had always known that Mad Dog was no saint, but back at that dilapidated house on Conti Street, he had seen a side of his older brother that until then he had only heard whispers of on the streets. Back at that house, face-to-face with that dead body, Keith had expected Mad Dog to give him a lecture or maybe even slap him around, but he hadn't done either. In forcing Keith to dismember the body, Mad Dog had taught him a lesson.

All his life Keith had looked up to his brothers. They were both feared and respected on the streets, but until that night he had never fully understood at what price those things came. His brothers were not only Savages in name but also in their actions. It was that night that the first seeds of doubt were sown in Keith. No matter how much he wanted to live up to the family's expectations of him, helping Mad Dog dismember Tate's body had made him realize that he couldn't. If that was what it took to be a Savage, Keith wanted no parts of it.

CHAPTER 20

The sound of someone banging on his hotel-room door drew Keith out of his slumber. He looked over at the alarm clock on the nightstand. It read 1:00 p.m. He had been asleep for almost six hours, but it felt like moments. He dragged himself out of bed and shuffled over to the door. When he opened it, he was surprised to find Ulysses standing on the other side.

"What the fuck?" Keith cursed.

"Good morning to you too." Ulysses invited himself into the room. Slung over his shoulder was Keith's garment bag, which contained two of his suits.

"What are you doing here?" Keith asked in an irritated tone.

"Making sure you don't show up at the funeral naked." Ulysses tossed the garment bag on the bed. "Get yourself together. Your sister is going to kill me if we show up at Big Money's home going late."

"And where is my dear sister at the moment?" Keith asked. He couldn't wait to see her to ask why she hadn't told him about Darla.

"She had some business to take care of this morning and will be meeting us at the house."

"What is she doing? Recruiting another whore for her stable?" Keith asked sarcastically.

"Less questions and more dressing, please," Ulysses urged. "I'll be downstairs waiting."

Ten minutes later Keith was dressed and walking out the hotel lobby. He drew quite a few stares in his tailored black suit jacket, over a black shirt and a black tie. The outfit was perfect, save for the white tube socks barely visible at the cuffs of his pants. Ulysses had brought Keith his suit but had neglected to grab the bag containing his undergarments, so he had to make the best out of what he had to work with.

He scanned the cars out front, in search of Maxine's Maybach, but saw no signs of it. He was about to go back inside the hotel to see if maybe he had missed Ulysses in the lobby when he heard a car horn beep twice. It was then that Keith noticed him. Ulysses was behind the wheel of a box-shaped red Chevy Caprice sitting on twenty-three-inch rims. The bass from Lil Wayne's "Fireman" rattled the windows of the car, drawing unfriendly stares from hotel guests and staff alike.

"Damn. How many cars does my sister own?" Keith asked when he slipped into the cream- colored leather passenger seat.

"Three, but this isn't one of hers. It's mine," Ulysses said proudly.

"Funny, you don't strike me as somebody who would ride in something like this."

"Why? Because I'm white?" Ulysses laughed. "Hang around me long enough, and you'll find that I'm full of surprises," he stated and peeled off into traffic.

As Keith rode in the car, he listened to Ulysses's colorful playlist. He bumped a variety of music, from artists as current as Migos and as classic as the Manhattans. None of the music playing in that car was anything Keith figured a man like Ulysses would be listening to. He was a strange nut indeed.

As he drove, Ulysses reached between the driver's seat and the center console and produced a silver flask.

Keeping one hand on the wheel, he unscrewed the top of the flask with his teeth and took a deep swig. He noticed Keith watching him from the passenger seat. "Care for a taste?"

"You think it's wise to be drinking while driving?"

"Dealing with your family, a stiff drink from time to time is how I make it through my days." Ulysses sighed. "Go on and take a swig. I ain't got cooties," he teased.

"Fuck it," Keith said, taking the flask. There was no way he could show up at the house totally sober, given what he was about to deal with. He took a drink and damn near choked. He wasn't sure what was in the bottle, but it was nothing they sold in local liquor stores. "What the hell is that? Gasoline?" He handed the flask back.

"Close. It's my own special vintage. I brew it in a still in the woods behind my house," Ulysses told him. He hit the flask one more time before putting it back in its hiding place.

"Can I ask you something?"

"What's up, Killer?"

"Keith," he said, correcting him. "What's your story?"

"How do you mean?"

"I mean, what is someone like you doing mixed up with my family? Is it a 'rebelling against Mommy and Daddy' thing by hanging out with gangsters?" Keith meant it as a joke, but Ulysses's reply was serious.

"If you must know, my mama died when I was a kid, and my daddy is spending the rest of his natural life in prison. As far as hanging out with gangsters, I grew up in Fifth Ward, Houston, not counting the time I spent busting heads for a guy named Hog in Dallas. I been the cream in the coffee all my life. It was actually a black woman who pulled me out of the cold and raised me to a man."

"I didn't mean any disrespect," Keith said, clarifying matters.

"I don't get offended easily. You think you're the only person who wonders how my white ass ended up on retainer to a female pimp with the last name Savage. It's actually a funny story, if you know it."

"I'd say we got at least thirty minutes before we reach the house. I'm all ears."

The story of how Ulysses had come into Maxine Savage's employ was something that Keith would have to fact-check later, because it sounded like a work of fiction. She had been playing in a high-stakes poker game down in the Quarter. Her stiffest competition was a gangster from out of Texas who was known as Hog. Hog was well known in the underworld circles throughout the South and fancied himself criminal royalty. He loved cocaine, money, and fast women. Except for the cocaine, Maxine fit the bill.

The whole time they were playing cards, Maxine had one eye on the pot of cash and the other on the handsome white boy who had come to the game with Hog. He never strayed too far from the hustler, and his cold blue eyes watched everything and everyone who came within spitting distance of Hog. A time or two, Maxine caught Ulysses checking her out in her too-tight dress, but he never let his eyes linger for too long.

Though Ulysses hadn't remembered at the time, the card game wasn't his first brush with Maxine Savage. About a year or so before, she had been in Texas on business. She had been looking to diversify her portfolio and had decided to dabble in moving cocaine. The coke in New Orleans was lacking, to say the least, so she followed a lead she had gotten from a friend, and that lead brought her to an associate of Hog's. Maxine was a good pimp, but a poor drug dealer, and she ended up getting burned on the deal. With Hog's reputation on the line, he dispatched his pet guard dog to make it right. Maxine was not only refunded her money and given a fresh package, but she was also gifted with the index finger of the man who had tried to dupe her. The way she heard it, the finger had been Ulysses's idea. When asked his reasoning for dismembering the man, he simply said, "It was a matter of honor." Maxine admired the man's methods, and she had been keeping tabs on him from a distance ever since.

Hog was a skilled poker player, and he had been getting the better of everyone in that poker game, including Maxine, for most of the night. This had built his confidence, and he decided to raise the stakes. There was one hundred thousand in the pot. It was too rich for the blood of most of the other players, so they folded their hands, but not Maxine. She saw his hundred thousand and raised him an extra fifty grand. Hog's hand was strong, and he reasoned there was little to no chance of losing against the girl, but that was because he didn't know Maxine. When the final cards were laid down, Hog found himself in debt to Maxine for nearly a quarter of a million dollars.

As it turned out, Hog was more flash than cash. Paying Maxine everything he owed that night would've hurt him financially, but not paying her would've hurt him physically. Everyone in that room knew that Maxine Savage wasn't someone you wanted to cross. After some bartering, Maxine came up with a solution that would both allow Hog to save face and ensure that the debt was paid. She would take his bodyguard on retainer until they were square. Hog got up from the table and left New Orleans, feeling like he had fleeced Maxine, but little did he know that his money was never what had motivated her to place herself across the poker table from him that night.

"It wouldn't be until years later that I would find out it was never Hog's money Maxine was after in the first place. She'd come for me. I had been exclusively on retainer for Hog for over a year by that point. Maxine knew there was no way he was going to let me go, so she played on his sense of greed to trick the contract away from him," Ulysses explained.

"Leave it to my sister to figure out how to win a *man* in a poker game." Keith laughed. "So, I'm guessing Hog never had a chance to come back for you?"

"Hog skipped out, owing Maxine Savage a quarter million. What do you think happened to him?"

"Knowing Max, I'm sure she didn't let him die easy." Keith shook his head.

"No, I actually made sure he died quick and clean."

"Wait, so you're telling me you took out your former boss?" Keith looked at Ulysses in a whole new light.

"Hog was never my boss. He was a client, until he wasn't."

"And what is my sister to you? Just another client?"

"Max will never be *just a client* to me," Ulysses said and turned his attention back to the road, letting Keith know he no longer cared to talk about it.

Ulysses was an interesting character, that was for certain. From the moment Keith met him, he knew he was no regular street dude. He could read it in the way Ulysses carried himself, always on guard, always respectful, and never saying more than what was necessary. If Keith had to guess, he'd say the man was ex-military or possibly law enforcement. A dangerous man, indeed, but no more dangerous than at least a dozen others who were loyal to the Savage clan. What made this outsider so special, to the point where Max would put such trust in someone who wasn't family? Keith wondered. Something about the man didn't sit right with Keith, and he planned to keep a close eye on him for the remainder of his trip. If Ulysses proved to be anything more than he let on, Big Money's killers wouldn't be the only men hunted by Savages.

CHAPTER 21

Genesis found that he had trouble sleeping that night. Tomorrow was to be the first day of his new life, and he was both excited and nervous. Since moving from North Philly to the family's new home in the General Grant housing project in New York City, he had been admiring King James and his crew from a distance. The first time he saw King, Lakim, and Dee posted up in the courtyard, there was no question as to who the controlling factor in the neighborhood was. Everyone, from the soldiers to the residents, treated King James's inner circle as if they were royalty. Genesis would watch dudes younger than him drive nice cars and creep in and out with women who were way out of their leagues. All because they were with the winning team.

Sometimes Genesis would fantasize about being a part of King James's crew, being doted on with free pussy and favor. He had been a nobody all his life, and he saw getting in with King James's crew as an opportunity to change that. To get next to King James, Genesis would first have to find a way to put himself on his radar. He started subtly, making sure he was around whenever the crew was on the block. Often King or one of the others would need someone to go to the store or run some other errand, and Genesis was always the first to volunteer. The day Lakim first approached Genesis and asked if he was interested in making a few dollars was the day that Genesis had been waiting for and scheming about for a while.

Genesis leaped at Lakim's offer and got right to work. He hated the shitty job of watching the exits, but he knew that it would be a means to an end. If he stayed down and showed he was loyal, bigger opportunities would come, and they did, sooner than later. When he was offered the promotion, he jumped on it. Though King was not clear about what his new responsibilities would entail, it didn't matter to Genesis. He was ten toes down. The bump in pay would help, but more importantly, King James had finally taken notice of him. He was finally on his way to becoming somebody.

Genesis climbed out of bed before sunrise, ready for whatever awaited him. He had just finished dressing for the day when his prepaid cell phone vibrated on his nightstand. He didn't recognize the number but answered anyhow.

"Be downstairs in five minutes," said the voice on the other end. It was showtime.

When he came out of his bedroom, he found his mother and his little sister on the couch. His sister was watching television, while his mother had nodded off. She was still wearing her MTA uniform. She had worked a double shift the day before and appeared to have passed out before she could change her clothes. He was glad she was asleep. It meant she wouldn't have a chance to press him about where he was going. Genesis crept to the front door, careful not to wake his mother, but his sister had other plans.

"Hi, Genesis!" his sister greeted, loud enough to disturb his mother. When she stirred, his sister gave him a mischievous smirk before turning her attention back to the television.

"You going somewhere?" his mother asked him sleepily.

"Oh . . . I was just gonna run to the store right quick," Genesis lied.

"Funny, you always seem to be going to the store, but you ain't never got no money," his mother said in a suspicious tone. "Did you ever fill out that job application I brought home for you?"

"I haven't gotten around to it yet."

"Then when do you plan on it? You can't expect to go through life living off the mercies of others."

"I ain't living on nobody's mercies. I'm a man!" he declared.

"Men go out and work. They do not keep late hours with hoodlums."

"C'mon, Ma. Why you sweating me?" Genesis sighed.

"Because that's what parents do. They sweat their children to try to keep them out of trouble," she shot back.

"I'm not in any trouble."

"Not yet, but you're likely to find some with that crowd you've taken to running with. Those boys ain't nothing but gangsters."

"You think everybody who lives in the hood is a gangster," Genesis retorted. He laughed it off.

"Not everybody, just the ones who make their living by breaking the law."

"You tripping, Ma. I ain't into none of that."

"Not yet, but you don't think I see the path you're walking down? Genesis, I know you may think that because I'm old, I don't know what I'm talking about, but it's the fact that I've lived to be this old that makes me an authority on this. I used to be out there in them streets too, thinking I had it all figured out, until reality hit and the streets took everyone that I loved, including your father."

"I ain't my father," Genesis spat.

"That's obvious to a duck. Your father knew how to play them streets, and still, he got himself killed. So imagine what could happen to someone like you," she said.

"You trying to say I don't know how to handle myself?" he asked defensively.

"No, baby. I'm sure you'd stand tall if your back was against the wall, but why even bring it to that? The streets are merciless and will eat you alive if you get in over your head, which is what you're doing by throwing your lot in with those neighborhood boys."

"You're right. I'm not." "I'm better," was what he wanted to tell her, but he kept it to himself. "I gotta dip." He headed for the door.

"You do what you feel you have to do, son. Just remember that trouble is easy to get into and hard to get out of."

Genesis was in a sour mood when he came out of the building. He was sick of his mother being on his back, like he was some punk kid and not a man of eighteen. Ever since he had opted not to go to college, his mother had been on his back about looking for a job. He had been filling out applications and dropping off résumés, but other than being offered low-paying gigs for short hours, he hadn't gotten many hits back. They could keep their shitty jobs, because Genesis had bigger plans. It hurt him that his mother didn't have confidence in him to do what needed to be done to provide for their family, and this had only motivated him to hit the ground running on the streets. Once he started making real money with King James, he would show his mother and everyone else who had doubted him.

Once he was outside his building, Genesis started looking for Dee, as he was the one he was supposed to meet this morning, so he was surprised when he found Lakim waiting for him. He was posted up on the avenue, leaning against an idling Ford Explorer. Genesis headed over.

"Peace, God." Lakim gave him dap.

"Sup?" Genesis replied. "Where's Dee? I thought I was supposed to be meeting him so he could show me what I'm supposed to be doing on the block."

"Been a change in plans. You ain't hitting the block today," Lakim told him before jumping behind the wheel. Genesis climbed in on the passenger side, not sure what to make of this.

Lakim pushed through traffic and jumped on the northbound lane of the Henry Hudson Parkway. They were headed to the Bronx. To Genesis's knowledge, King didn't have any territory in the Bronx, so he wondered why they were going there. Then an idea hit him. Maybe King was looking to expand, and Genesis's new responsibilities would include looking over their new territory. This filled Genesis with a sense of excitement. He had already started planning in his head how he would run their new turf when Lakim broke the silence.

"Yo, I wanna tell you that the hard work and dedication you've shown to this crew hasn't gone unnoticed. Both me and King are proud of you, son," Lakim told him.

"Thanks, La. It's like I told you when you recruited me, I won't let you down."

"And so far you haven't. I know shit can't be easy for you, watching your mom struggle with working all types of hours. What she make an hour? Eleven . . . maybe twelve dollars an hour? That's hardly enough to take care of y'all."

"I know, and that's why I've been busting my ass day and night, trying to get this money up. I want to help my mom out," Genesis said.

"And I respect that. It was the same way for me. I got tired of watching my mother struggle, so I had to go out and do what I had to do. I felt like less of a man when I was watching my old earth break her back for peanuts. Feel me?"

Indeed, Genesis did feel him. It made him feel like shit, having to watch his mother work such long hours. Sometimes when she got in from work, she was so tired that she didn't even have the strength to feed them. Those were the nights either Genesis or his sister had to cook dinner.

"Yeah, it's been rough, but I ain't complaining. I'm just happy y'all put me in a position to put a few dollars in my pocket," Genesis said.

"So long as you keep doing the right thing, you're going see more than a few dollars. I can see you with your very own seat at the table," Lakim told him.

"Really?" Genesis asked excitedly.

"True indeed. I was just telling King how much you reminded me of myself when I was your age. I was down to do whatever, wherever, when it came to my team eating."

"And I feel the same way," Genesis said.

"I believe you, but unfortunately, I'm not the one who needs convincing. You got people who been down with us longer than you who ain't happy about you being promoted so quickly. They feel like maybe you haven't done enough to deserve a seat at the table. Their gripes have made it back to King James's ears, and I'm thinking he might be second-guessing your promotion." Lakim cut him a look to make sure he wasn't pouring it on too thick.

Genesis was suddenly filled with dread. His promotion was to be his opportunity to show his mother and everyone else that they had been wrong about him, and now some haters were threatening to snatch it away. "Lakim, just tell me what I gotta do, man. I'm with you. I promise."

"Those are strong words, but this crew is based on actions." Lakim paused. "How far are you willing to go to prove yourself?" he asked, already knowing how Genesis would answer.

"All the way," Genesis said with conviction.

The trap had been baited, and the mouse had gone for the cheese, just as King James said he would.

Pam was feeling restless, which was nothing new. For the past few weeks, she had been holed up at her sister's house. Her sister lived in a one-story house on Allerton Avenue in the Bronx. It was a nice neighborhood, and it was quiet there, but Pam missed her beloved Harlem and longed for the day she could go back.

The exile on Allerton Avenue was a self-imposed one. A while back she and her friend Tiffany had been on a double date with these two country dudes that hadn't gone so well. Pam and her guy, Big Money, had gotten along fine, but Tiffany and Fire Bug, Big Money's cousin, had gotten into an exchange of words over his sexual performance . . . or lack thereof. Things had got heated, and more words had been exchanged, which resulted in the two guys throwing Pam and Tiffany out. Pam had been embarrassed and hurt. Not because she had gotten thrown out, but because it had happened in front of Tiffany. Tiffany was like a little sister, and she looked up to Pam. She took everything the older girl said as gospel, so it had made Pam look bad when she got handled that way by the bumpkins. She had to get them back, but how?

It was then that she remembered a conversation Tiffany and Fire Bug had had while pillow talking. Tiffany had told her all about it. In a moment of foolishness, Fire Bug had boasted to Tiffany about a hit he and Big Money were a part of in Harlem. The hit was supposed to be on a dude Pam used to sleep with named King James, but it went wrong, and a kid was killed as a result. King James had offered cash to anyone with information about who was behind the hit, and that was where Pam saw her opening. To get back at Big Money, she dropped a dime to King James about Big Money's involvement in the hit. She did it more to be petty than to get the reward. It wasn't until after she heard that Big Money had been killed that she realized the seriousness of what she had done. That was when she decided that it might be best for her to get low until things blew over.

Tiffany had teased her about hiding out at her sister's house. King James's right-hand man Lakim had assured them that they had nothing to fear, but Pam didn't trust this. Tiffany was young and didn't know any better, but Pam understood men like King James and how they operated. Even if Lakim had been being truthful, she didn't see any need to tempt fate.

Outside of Tiffany, the only other person who even had an idea where she was staying was her weed man. Pam refused to smoke anything other than Purple Haze, and there was none in her sister's neighborhood. Though it may not have been the wisest move, she had hit her weed man up the night before and had had him make a delivery. It was only once, and Pam had met him five blocks from her sister's house, so even if someone did press him about her whereabouts, all he would be able to say for sure was that she was somewhere in the Bronx. Still, she'd had an uneasy feeling in her gut ever since meeting up with him.

She had learned a long time ago to follow her instincts, so with this in mind, she packed a few things in her bag and left her sister's house. She headed to the train station, where she was going to catch the number two train to the Port Authority. Once there, she would board a bus that would take her to Connecticut. A dude she had been seeing had an apartment in Bridgeport, and he wouldn't mind her crashing there so long as he could get his dick sucked whenever he liked.

She was heading up the street toward the train station when her phone rang. It was her girl, Tiffany. "What's up, bitch?"

"Ain't nothing. About to head to the laundry." She paused. "Your ass still hiding in the Bronx?" Tiffany asked.

"I ain't hiding. I'm just staying out of the way," Pam said, correcting her. "If you were smart, you'd do the same."

"I been at my cousin's house on Dyckman, but I been through the hood a few times, and everything is quiet. I even seen Dee the other night, and he acted like nothing was wrong. You're worried over nothing."

"Whatever you say, Tiff," Pam replied, brushing her off. She was still walking and talking when she noticed a green Ford Explorer coasting alongside her. She flipped her hair and threw on her sunglasses. The last thing she had time for was entertaining some thirsty Bronx nigga who was trying to get her number.

"Yo, Pam, what's good?" a familiar voice called from the SUV. She almost shit her pants when she saw Lakim behind the wheel.

Pam contemplated running, but she was in the middle of a long block. Lakim would surely be on her before she made it to either end. Choking down her heart, which was trying to escape her chest, Pam smiled and played it cool. "Hey, La! What you doing way up here?" She dropped her phone into her bag but kept Tiffany on the line. She wasn't sure what to expect.

"I'm coming from picking up some work, but I could ask you the same. Ain't seen you on the block in a minute." Lakim eyed her.

"Oh . . . I got this new job, and it doesn't allow me much time to hang out. I'm actually on my way to work now," Pam lied.

"Get in. I'll give you a ride," Lakim offered.

"No thanks. I work all the way in White Plains. I don't wanna put you out of your way." Pam attempted to cross the street, but Lakim cut her off with the SUV.

"Nonsense. Get in, and I'll at least give you a ride to the train station." It was more of a command than an offer.

Seeing that she had little choice, Pam climbed in the Explorer. It wasn't until they had pulled out into traffic that she noticed Lakim wasn't alone. There was a young dude in the backseat who had a familiar face, but Pam didn't know his name. She had seen him on the block only a time or two.

"Hey," she said, trying to break the ice, but the young man didn't respond. Something wasn't right. She only hoped Tiffany hadn't hung up.

"So, besides working, what you been up to?" Lakim asked.

"Nothing much. Just trying to stay out of the way," Pam told him, trying to keep her voice steady. She then noticed that they had blown past the train station. "Hey, you missed my stop!"

"I know, and I'll spin you back. I got something I need to holla at you about real quick," Lakim told her. He continued driving until they found an isolated block, where he pulled over and killed the engine. "I know by now you heard what happened to your boy, Big Money."

"I told you, I've been working. I haven't had a lot of time to see what's going on in the hood," Pam lied.

Lakim gave her a look. "C'mon, Pam. You and I both know you keep your ear to the ground no matter where you rest your head. Don't insult my intelligence."

"Listen, La, I ain't trying to get no deeper into this shit than I already am. I don't know nothing and don't wanna know nothing, so if you're worried about me opening my mouth—"

"Is that what you think this is about?" Lakim said, cutting her off. "C'mon, Pam. How long have we known each other? Of all the bitches in the hood, I know you're solid. You running your mouth is the last thing I'm worried about. It's your girl Tiffany that I'm worried about."

"Tiffany ain't gonna say shit, either. She's solid, La," Pam insisted.

"Just the same, I'd like to hear it out of her mouth."

"If you want, I can give you her phone number," Pam offered.

"I was thinking we could have a face-to-face conversation. You don't have to come with me to her house or anything. Just tell me where she stays," Lakim said.

"La, please. Don't make me do this," Pam pleaded. Pam knew that because of her friendship with Lakim, she at least had a chance to talk her way out of this, but Tiffany would have no such luck.

Lakim turned to her. "Maybe I'm not making myself clear. Now, you can either give me your homegirl's address or—"

Bang!

There was a deafening roar in the car. Lakim's eyes winked closed only seconds before Pam's brains and hair splattered on him and the dashboard. He turned around in wide-eyed shock to see Genesis holding a smoking gun.

"What the fuck? I wasn't done questioning her!" He wiped blood from his eyes with the back of his shirtsleeve.

"Like you said, the bitch is solid. Wasn't no way she was going to give her friend up," Genesis said.

"I guess we'll never know now, huh? Stupid . . . just fucking stupid." Lakim shook his head. "You're gonna clean this fucking car and dump it too."

"I told you, whatever this crew needs, I'm all in."

CHAPTER 22

By the time Keith and Ulysses arrived back at the house, Keith was good and buzzed. There were dozens of people gathered at the Savage house. Cars filled the driveway and spilled over onto the road leading to the house. Keith was quietly impressed by the turnout for Big Money's funeral, as he knew the man had never been very well liked. He wondered how many had come to pay their respects and how many were there just to join the war party Big John was trying to form.

Keith walked into the house to find it crawling with people. A few of his wayward family members greeted him warmly, while others just stared, as if he had shown up to borrow money. He hadn't seen some of these people in years, if ever, so he couldn't imagine what he could have done to them. Keith ignored the mixed signals and continued his search for Maxine. He couldn't let go of what Darla had told him, and wanted to have a word with his sister.

In the thick of the gathering, he found his little brother, Bug. Bug had combed his hair for once and was dressed in a fire engine–red suit. It was hardly appropriate for a funeral, but at least he had tried. As the boy got closer, Keith noticed a bruise under his eye.

"What happened to you? Did that sucker Beau do that to you after I left the Quarter?" Keith asked angrily. That would've been all the excuse he needed to go back down there and stomp his rival.

"I didn't get this from Beau. Me and Anthony got into it today."

"Y'all were as thick as thieves last night. What changed in the past couple of hours?" Keith wanted to know.

"Just some bullshit. No big deal," Bug said, but his tone let Keith know that he was lying.

"C'mon. Spill it." Keith nudged him.

"We got into a fight over you."

"Me? What do I have to do with you two fighting?"

"Well, people have been talking lately," Bug began in a heavy tone. "They're saying that you ain't planning to ride with us on Big Money's killers . . . that you ain't a Savage no more. I told them that's bullshit and there's no way Killer would turn tail on a fight, but they kept talking shit . . . calling you soft. When Anthony joined in with the bullshit, I hit him, and that's how we started fighting."

"Bug, people are always gonna talk. Fuck them and their opinions. What's important about a man is his character, not people's opinions of him, feel me?"

"I feel you, Killer. I told them they were wrong about you, but maybe they'll respect it more coming from you." He gave a sigh. "Tell them muthafuckas you down to ride, same as always," Bug urged him.

"It isn't that simple, Bug. I agree that the men who were involved in Big Money's death need to feel some justice, but not in the way Big John is planning. If they ride off into New York like a bunch of cowboys, the end result will be us burying more Savages in the family plot. We need to—"

"It's true, ain't it?" Bug said, cutting him off. "I heard Mama talking shit about you having changed, but I always thought it was Mama just being bitter. You've really turned your back on us."

"Bug, let me explain." Keith reached for his brother's arm, but Fire Bug jerked away.

"You ain't gotta explain nothing to me, *Keith*. I see we ain't on the same side of the line no more," Bug spat before walking out the front door.

Keith started to go after Bug but decided against it. Bug had a hot temper, and pressing the issue at that point would probably make it worse. He would wait until he cooled off, and then he would talk to him again. The idea of Bug being in the streets and following in his family's footsteps troubled Keith more than anything else that was going on. In a sense, he felt like he had failed his little brother. Had he bothered to come back home sooner and to offer his brother some sort of guidance, then maybe Fire Bug wouldn't have turned out the way he did. Keith accepted that and would do what he could to fix it. He just hoped there would be time for him to get through to Fire Bug before he ended up like so many of the Savage men—dead or in prison.

Across the room, Keith spotted his mother. She was sitting in a chair, while his brother Dickey kneeled in front of her while she struggled to fix his bow tie. Wearing a black dress and a shawl, her silver hair done up in big curls, she looked more the kindly old grandmother she should be than the snake that she was. He didn't feel good about the way things had ended between them that morning. He might not have liked what she had to say, but she was still his mother, and he had been very harsh with her. He was standing there, contemplating whether to say something to her or avoid her until after the funeral, when Dickey robbed him of the choice.

"Over here, Killer!" Dickey shouted across the room, waving his thick arms in the air to make sure Keith saw him.

Keith crossed the room and hugged his older brother warmly. This time Dickey didn't snatch him off his feet. The brothers broke their embrace. Then Keith's eyes went to his mother, whom he had felt watching him the whole time. "Mama," he greeted her.

"Killer," she responded dryly.

"Can you help me with this, Killer?" Dickey waggled the two loose ends of the bow tie, which neither he nor his mother could seem to figure out.

"I told you to wear a regular tie or a clip-on, but your ass wanna dress up like a butler," Ma commented.

"Clip-ons are for babies, and bow ties are for gentlemen. I'm a gentleman," Dickey said proudly. "Say, Killer, you know who else wears bow ties?"

"Who?" Keith asked, as if he didn't already know what his brother was going to say.

"Sammy Davis Jr. He's my favorite actor, ya know?"

"I know." Keith smiled.

Years ago, their mother had taken Dickey to see Sammy Davis Jr. perform. This was not long before the legendary entertainer passed away. Dickey had found himself smitten with the charismatic icon's style. Ever since then he had always tried to imitate Sammy Davis Jr., opting to wear bow ties whenever the opportunity to dress up presented itself. His fascination with Sammy Davis Jr. was one of the things Dickey's brain had seemed to retain after the shooting. Keith tied Dickey's bow tie for him, then smoothed it over with his fingers.

Keith studied his work. "There you go."

"Thanks, Killer." Dickey looked at the tie proudly.

"Dickey, why don't you go and fetch ya mama a drink? I'm feeling a bit parched," Ma said.

"Sure thing, Mama." Dickey skipped off across the living room.

"Looking at that poor fool, you'd never know he was the mastermind of over a dozen bank robberies." Ma shook her head sadly, remembering the man her son once was.

"And God knows how many check-cashing spots," Keith added. "Do you remember the time Dickey wanted to rob that mail-carrier plane for those postal money orders?"

"Shit, yeah, I remember. My Dickey has come up with some crazy ideas over the years, but that one took the cake," Ma replied.

"It actually wasn't a bad plan. Stash himself on the plane, rip them off while they were in the air, and then fly off like a superhero." Keith made a swooshing motion with his hand. "Only thing that stopped him was the fact that nobody in the hood knew how to get hold of a parachute." He chuckled. "Do you think he'd have really gone through with it?"

"Knowing Dickey . . . absolutely. He was fearless, same as all my boys. One thing none of my children lack is heart," Ma said proudly.

Keith took a seat in the chair next to his mother. "Mama, about last night. I owe you an apology."

"For speaking your mind? No you don't. I'd rather you have gotten it off your chest than hold it in and let it fester. I think we both needed to get some things off our chests, and I'm glad we did."

"Still, I was a little harsh in my delivery, and I'm sorry. I never meant to disrespect you," Keith said.

"Thank you for that, Killer . . . I mean Keith."

For a long while, the mother and son sat in silence. They watched the various branches of their family tree move about the house. They all wore different faces and had different personalities, but they were bound by one common thread. They were Savages. Keith had once been so proud of that name, but what it now represented to him filled his heart with dread.

"Looks like Big John has got his army," Keith observed, finally breaking their silence.

"Seems so," she agreed.

"Can you imagine how powerful we could be if we banded together for good things like we do when it's time to put in work?" Keith reflected.

"We?" Ma gave him a look. "I thought you wasn't a Savage anymore?"

"I guess I can't escape from myself," Keith replied, alluding to her warning from that morning. Though Keith hated to admit it, his mother was right. He may not be able to run from his family legacy, but he shouldn't have to. He was the son of a Savage, but he was still his own man.

"So all of a sudden you're down for the family cause again?" Ma asked suspiciously. She fished her pack of cigarettes from her bra and tapped one out.

Keith shrugged. "I don't know about the cause, but I'm always gonna be down for my family. This is why I need you to stop this before we lose anyone else."

"You know I can't let the men who killed Big Money just walk away." She lit the cigarette.

"I know you can't, Mama. I'm just thinking maybe we can find another way to handle this. A way that doesn't cost us any more Savage blood. Today we're burying Big Money. Tomorrow maybe it'll be John or, God forbid, even Fire Bug, because if this goes down, you know he isn't going to ride the bench. Your baby boy is gonna be right in the thick of this shit. Is that something you can live with?"

Ma didn't answer immediately. She sat there smoking her cigarette and looking over the sea of Savage faces. There was truth to what Keith had said. Big John's assault on New York was sure to be a bloody one, and there would be no shortage of casualties. However, if the family didn't react in true Savage fashion, they would be looked at as soft, and that wasn't something that appealed to Ma.

But the thought of more of her boys dying on the front line was less appealing. "You think you know a better way to deal with this?"

"Honestly, no. But I'm willing to try to figure one out."

"I'll speak to Big John."

"Thank you, Mama."

"Don't thank me just yet. Big John ain't gonna like the idea of not going to war, and I can't guarantee that he'll call it off. All I can do is promise you that I'll do what I can to avoid him riding into New York with an army of Savages." She got up and walked away.

Keith rose from his chair and continued his search for his sister, Maxine. He finally spotted her moving toward the kitchen. He intercepted her just as she was about to go through the swinging door. "I need to talk to you."

"Okay, but it can wait for a minute. I've got something for you that I hope will pick your sour-ass spirits up." Maxine smiled.

"Why didn't you tell me?" Keith asked, totally ignoring what she had just said.

"I kind of wanted to keep it a surprise. I came by this morning but—"

"A surprise that Darla was in town?"

"Darla? What the hell are you talking about?" Maxine was confused.

"I saw her in the Quarter last night, and she told me everything. Told me how you knew she was back in town and how you even were helping her out. What? Darla sells pussy for you too now?"

Maxine looked at Keith as if he had taken leave of his senses. "Killer, I don't know if you're high, drunk, or both, but you need to take a minute and listen to what I'm trying to tell you."

"That's the problem with the women in this family. You do too much talking and not enough listening!" Keith stormed. "You kicked all that shit about the importance of family, and how we should stick by each other, and I find out you've been conspiring with the girl who broke my heart into a thousand pieces!"

"Killer, right now you acting like a little bitch. If you got a problem with me, we can damn sure talk about it, but now ain't the time or place. You need to tone that shit down," Maxine said, trying to quiet him down. People were beginning to look.

"Don't try to quiet me like I'm one of your whores!"

"You better watch it. You dancing a very fine line right now," Maxine warned him.

Big John came over, intent on finding out why his brother and sister were showing their asses in front of all these people. "What the hell is wrong with the two of you?"

"I'm airing out a grievance, big bro. Mama always said that when two Savages have an issue, they should bring it to the table, so that's what I'm doing. Or is that rule good only for Savages who are still actively robbing, killing, or selling pussy for a living?" The minute Keith said it, he knew he had gone too far, but it was too late. Maxine slapped him so hard that his ears rang. They now had a full audience.

"How dare you disrespect me like that!" she barked. "I don't know who we picked up at the airport, but it surely ain't Killer Keith. No way the little boy whose ass I wiped and secrets I kept would be standing here talking to me like that."

"Max, I didn't mean it like—"

"Did I say I was done?" she snapped, cutting him off. "My entire life has been spent looking after your ungrateful ass, tending your wounds, helping you with your homework, and even lying for you when I had to. And you got the nerve to be stunting me because I helped a friend of the family who had fallen on hard times? What you and Darla had was done with over ten years ago. She's moved on, but apparently, you haven't."

"Who's Darla?" a soft voice asked from behind Keith. When he turned and saw Bernie standing behind him, he could've fainted. He wasn't sure how long she had been standing there, but the look on her face said long enough.

"Surprise, asshole!" Maxine shoved past Keith on her way into the kitchen.

CHAPTER 23

Keith sat on the edge of his three-legged bed, watching Bernie, who sat on a metal folding chair across the room. An awkward silence hung between them.

"So, when did you get here?" Keith asked, breaking the silence.

"A few hours ago. Maxine picked me up from the airport this morning," she replied.

"I'm happy you decided to come, but I must admit I am surprised to see you."

"Probably just as surprised as I am that I actually came. I wasn't sure I'd go through with it until the plane was actually taking off," Bernie admitted.

"I know it took a lot for you to make the trip. Thank you for being here for me, Bernie," Keith said sincerely.

"Who says I came for you?"

"I'm sorry. I'd assumed you came to give me moral support."

"Like you assumed that I wouldn't accept you if I knew the truth about your past?" she retorted.

"Bernie, I told you that it's complicated. My story isn't a pretty one," Keith said.

"I know. While I was waiting for you to show up, your mom and me finally got a chance to talk."

"What did you guys talk about?" Keith asked, hoping his mother hadn't offended her.

"A little bit of everything. Mrs. Savage is a very interesting woman, to say the least."

"You don't know the half," Keith said sarcastically.

"After talking to your mother, I think I understand you a little better, but there's still so much that I'm unsure about," Bernie admitted.

"I'll tell you anything you want to know. All you have to do is ask."

"I want to know who you are." Bernie got up from the chair and crossed the room. Keith thought that she was coming to join him on the bed, but she walked right past him. He watched her as she walked around the replica of his old bedroom, familiarizing herself with his past history. She looked over the posters on the walls, his sports trophies. She gently plucked up the picture from the night of junior prom and stared at it for a time. "Is this her? Darla?"

"Yes."

"She's pretty." Bernie placed the picture back down. "I can see why you fell for her."

"Darla is old news."

"That's not what it sounded like downstairs."

"Bernie, it's—"

"If you say *it's complicated* again, I'm probably going to punch you," Bernie warned. "Do you still have feelings for her?"

A lie sprang to Keith's lips, but he decided not to tell it. "Yes."

Bernie laughed to cover the sting of his admission. "At least you are honest about that."

"Bernie, I care about Darla, but not in the way you're thinking. We've just got some unresolved history."

"Seems like you've got a lot of unresolved issues these days."

"You could say that, but there's only one issue I'm concerned about right now, and that's finding out where we stand." Keith got up and moved closer to her.

"We *stand* in your bedroom." She took a step back.

"Quit playing."

"I assure you that I'm quite serious, Keith. Don't think that just because I showed up in New Orleans for the funeral, things are okay between us."

"I thought you came down here so we could work things out?"

"I came because it was the right thing to do. I knew you having to face whatever demons chased you out of New Orleans in the first place wasn't going to be easy, and I wanted to be there for you. That's what a good woman is supposed to do. Hold her man down in times of need," Bernie told him.

"So, you still love me?" Keith was hopeful.

"Of course I do, Keith. I can't just turn that part of my heart on and off. But that doesn't change the fact that you're a lying piece of shit, and I don't know if I'll ever be able to trust you again."

"Ouch." Keith rubbed his chest, as if her words had struck him physically. His attention was drawn away from her when he noticed Ulysses standing in the doorway of his bedroom.

"It's time," Ulysses announced.

The sun had been shining the entire day, but as soon as Big Money's service was about to get under way, thick storm clouds materialized, making it look like early evening instead of the middle of the afternoon. Thunder crashed in the distance, warning of an impending storm.

Keith escorted Bernie out into the backyard, where Big Money's home-going service was to be held. The moment the two of them appeared in the doorway, they could feel the stares and hear the whispers. Keith ignored them and walked Bernie down the aisle formed by all

the chairs that had been set up, to the front row, where
the immediate family was seated. Big John gave them an
approving nod, and even Bug offered a smile of greeting
to Bernie, but Maxine didn't even look their way. She
was still angry, and she had every right to be. It was yet
another relationship Keith would have to repair before it
was all said and done.

Keith was about to take the seat next to his mother, but
she motioned to him that Bernie should sit there. When
Bernie was seated, Keith was surprised to see his mother
close her hand over that of his fiancée, as if giving and
receiving comfort. As he took the seat on the other side
of Bernie, he wondered what had passed between them
before he showed up at the house.

Ma Savage had spared no expense in laying Big Money
out. His casket was a shiny green custom box, stamped
with dollar sign emblems. Inside it he rested on hundreds
of dollars in shredded bills. Stuffed in his crossed hands
were wads of cash. He had finally gotten his big score.

The preacher gave a good sermon, though he had to
yell at certain points to be heard over the roar of thunder.
He went on and on about how good a man Michael
Savage was, and he even gave a spiel about him being
a pillar of the family and the community. That went to
show how little he knew about the deceased. The high
point of the funeral was when two women, both claiming
to be Big Money's baby mama, met for the first time.
The women's children were about the same age. They
nearly got into a fistfight, and as they circled each other,
they nearly knocking the casket over. It took Ulysses, Big
John, and Fire Bug collectively to separate the women.

While this was happening, Keith turned to Bernie
and found her stifling a laugh. It was the first time he
had seen her smile since they were reunited. Once the
women were separated, and everyone sat back down,

the pastor continued. Ten minutes later, just as the pastor was winding down, the storm made good on its threat. But the drizzle that fell was not what captured everyone's attention.

Everyone was drawn to a commotion that had broken out near the house. They watched as the two gun-wielding men who were guarding the property attempted to block a homeless man from crashing the ceremony. He was dressed in frayed jeans that looked like they had never been washed and a dirty green parka, one much too heavy for the New Orleans heat. His hair was wild and matted and matched his thick, dust-filled beard. He appeared to become violent with the guards, and this was when Big John stepped in. He said something to the armed men, and the homeless person was allowed to enter the property.

Bernie watched with a look somewhere between disgust and pity as the homeless man shambled down the aisle. All eyes seemed to be on him. When he passed the seats in which she and Keith were sitting, she could smell the heavy stink of must and cheap booze. The homeless man reached the casket and stared at Big Money's corpse for a long while. A lone tear ran down his dirty cheek. Once he had paid his respects, he turned his attention to the family. His eyes scanned each one of their faces, as if he was trying to remember them. They lingered on Keith slightly longer than on anyone else. The homeless man stepped away from the casket and stopped in front of Ma. To Bernie's surprise, he fell to his knees, dropped his head in the older woman's lap, and begun to weep uncontrollably. Ma somehow squeezed out of her seat, then excused herself and got Big John and Maxine to usher the homeless man into the house.

Bernie turned to Keith, who wore a worried expression. "Who was that?"

"My brother . . . Mad Dog."

CHAPTER 24

The drizzle had stopped by the time Big Money was put in the ground. Everyone went back into the house for the repast. There was plenty of food and liquor, all of which the guest helped themselves to. Before long the living room, den, and even the front yard and the backyard were full of people carrying on. There was no shortage of stories being swapped among members of the Savage clan, but the story most were interested in hearing was being told in the kitchen.

After showering and changing into some fresh clothes—jeans, boots, and a sweatshirt—Mad Dog Savage looked more like himself. He still sported the shaggy beard, but at least he had allowed Maxine to comb it. Mad Dog had always been a handsome man, with rich brown skin, a nice build, and perfect teeth. Girls loved him even more than Keith when they were growing up. He wasn't quite the pussy hound that his younger brother was in those days, though. He had a steady girl that he had been seeing since middle school, and he only had eyes for her until the day she was taken from him.

Keith watched from the doorway of the kitchen as Savages young and old vied for the attention of his mother's favorite son. Mad Dog showing up at the funeral had ended up overshadowing Big Money's passing. It had been nearly a year since anyone in New Orleans had laid eyes on him, longer still since he and Keith had spoken. Ma had made Mad Dog a healthy plate of chicken, greens,

potato salad, and jambalaya. The way he was devouring
the food at the kitchen table, seemingly not bothering
to swallow, said that it had been some time since his
last meal. From what Keith gathered, he had been living
on the streets for a while. Mad Dog had always been
somewhat of a nomad, but it wasn't like him to neglect
his personal hygiene in such a way. Keith couldn't help
but wonder how his brother had fallen into such a state.

Bernie walked up beside him. "You okay?"

"Yeah, I'm cool," he lied.

"So, where you been, Mad Dog?" Dickey asked. He
had been sticking to his brother like a shadow since he
showed up.

"Here and there," Mad Dog replied in between bites of
food. "After that business with the Feds, I figured it was
best I get ghost for a while. Spent some time hustling
with some jokers I know out in Baton Rouge. When
the spot out there got busted, I made my way north.
Found some work at the shipping yard when I was in
Shreveport, and finally, I ended up in Dallas. Purely by
chance, I happened to run across cousin Oliver when he
was passing through Dallas on his way to New Orleans.
He was the one who told me about Big Money and made
sure I got here in time for the funeral."

"We tried to contact you, but nobody seemed to know
where you were. We were afraid that something had
happened to you," Maxine told him.

"World can't do nothing to me that ain't already been
done," Mad Dog stated, then finished off his plate and
motioned for someone to fill it up again. His mother
placed a fresh plate in front of him, and he dug in. "So,
you just gonna stand there gawking, or are you gonna say
what's on your heart?" he asked Keith without looking up
from his plate.

"Just glad to see you home, Mad Dog," Keith said,
somehow unable to think of anything else.

"Likewise." Mad Dog licked the gravy from his fingers. "I'd heard you were lost to us."

"Not lost. Just finding my way," Keith said.

"That yo' lady?" Mad Dog looked at Bernie.

Bernie stepped forward and took the initiative. "I'm Bernadette." She extended her hand. Mad Dog looked at her hand for a minute, and she wasn't sure if he was going to bite it or shake it.

Quite unexpectedly, Mad Dog stood up from the table and hugged her. "Family don't shake hands. We hug. And you kin now, ya hear?"

"Thank you." Bernie blushed.

"Glad to see your taste in women has improved since the last girl you brought home to meet Mama, Killer," Mad Dog said. Keith knew it was a shot at Darla.

"Bernie is going to make a fine wife," Ma said sincerely, which surprised Keith. She had never paid a compliment about any woman he had dated. Whatever she and Bernie had talked about before he got there must have left quite an impression.

"I don't suppose we should expect an invitation to the wedding. Keith ain't too big on family, but I'm assuming you know this by now," Mad Dog said to Bernie.

"I'd be lying if I said Keith exactly glows when the topic of family comes up, but what family doesn't have its issues? I've got relatives that I don't necessarily like, but I love them because they're family. When Keith and I are married, you guys will become my family too, good, bad, or indifferent," Bernie told Mad Dog.

Mad Dog cracked a sly smile. "You are a wise and kind woman, Ms. Bernadette. Far too good for the likes of a Savage."

"Your brother seems to feel the same way," Bernie half joked. "Well, I know you guys have a lot to catch up on. I just wanted to make sure I introduced myself properly. It was nice meeting you, Mad Dog."

"Likewise, Ms. Bernadette." Mad Dog gave her a parting hug before Bernie left the kitchen. "That's quite a woman you got there, Killer." He sat back down at the table.

"I tell myself the same thing every day," Keith said.

"To be young and in love. Must be nice, huh?" Mad Dog said.

"It has its moments," Keith replied.

"Hold on to that one, Killer. Protect her and keep her close. The thing about love is, it's such a rare thing that there are those out there who will try to snatch it from you if you take your eyes off the prize. Losing a loved one is a pain that can be dulled, but it'll never go away. You'll walk around with that hole in your heart for all your days. It never heals. Only stops spreading. You follow where I'm going?" Mad Dog gave Keith a serious look.

"Indeed, I do." Keith nodded. Mad Dog, in his way, was addressing the elephant in the room. It was the reason why two brothers that had once been so close hadn't spoken in years.

"No need digging up old bones," Ma said, cutting in. "We're just glad you're back home with your family, son."

"And speaking of family, Savage blood has been spilled. I'm sure I don't need to tell anyone in this room what that means." Mad Dog looked over the faces of those who had gathered around.

"It means Fire Bug make the trap go boom!" Fire Bug sang.

"That you will, little brother . . . That you will." Mad Dog cosigned. "So, anybody know where I can get a line on these walking dead men?"

"Hold on, Mad Dog. We still don't have all the facts. We've already decided that it's a bad idea to run off half-cocked," Keith told him.

"We ain't decided shit, since I wasn't here for whatever conversation y'all done had. And the only facts we need to know are that somebody touched Big Money and that they gotta die. No more to be said."

"Amen to that shit!" Fire Bug added.

"Watch your mouth in front of Mama," Big John said, checking him.

"Why does everyone in this family think the only way to solve a problem is to kill it?" Keith was frustrated.

"Because it's our way . . . the Savage way," Mad Dog said, as if the answer should've been obvious. "Guess you'd know that if you hadn't turned your back on this family."

"I didn't turn my back on anyone. I went off into the world to try to better myself. I'm not apologizing for wanting more out of life than this shit!" Keith snapped.

"So, that's what we are to you now? Shit?" Mad Dog questioned.

"That's not what I meant, and you know it, Mad Dog."

"Hard to tell with you sometimes, Killer. What you say don't always match up with what you do," Mad Dog said.

"And what's that supposed to mean?" Keith asked defensively.

"Do I really need to say it?" Mad Dog got up from the table and stood in front of Keith.

"Boys, please!" Ma exclaimed, trying to defuse the situation.

"No, Mama. If your precious favorite son has a problem with me, then let him get it off his chest." Keith was tired of Mad Dog's shit and was ready to lay it all on the table.

"That's fine," Mad Dog said. "See, the rest of the family dances around your uppity-ass feelings, but I ain't afraid to call a spade a spade. You might share our blood, but you ain't no Savage, Killer. Ain't been since you put the life of another muthafucka over that of your brother."

The gauntlet had been thrown.

"You still on this shit, Mad Dog? Look, I'm sorry about what happened to her. You have every right to be mad at me for getting in the way of what you were planning, but as God is my witness, I did it only because I was trying to save you." Keith was emotional.

"And instead, you broke me!" Mad Dog slammed his fist against the table so hard that it tipped and dishes spilled onto the floor. When he next spoke, his voice was thick with hurt. "Do you know what it was like for me, knowing that someone I loved had been murdered and there was nothing I could do to make it right? Of course you don't, because when them boys killed your precious teacher, you settled that debt. Even had me help you clean it up."

"What the hell is he talking about?" Maxine asked. What had happened to Tate was a secret that no one in the family knew except Mad Dog and Ma.

"I'm talking about misplaced loyalties," Mad Dog spat.

"There's a difference between being disloyal and being compassionate," Keith fired back. "What kind of man would I be if I had stood by and let you kill an innocent family over a death you caused?"

"Watch it, Killer," Mad Dog snarled.

"What? The truth hurts? We were all fucked up when we found out Michelle was killed, but let's be honest about this. Those bullets were meant for you, not her. If you wanna place blame somewhere, why don't you start by looking in the mirror!"

Before anyone even realized that he had moved, Mad Dog was on Keith. He socked his little brother in the jaw so hard that Keith flew across the room and crashed into the china cabinet. When he closed in, Keith countered with a combination to Mad Dog's chin. The two of them barreled around the kitchen, breaking dishes and knocking over silverware, beating each other like two strangers in the street.

Bernie came back into the kitchen to investigate the noise and found Keith and Mad Dog in a tangle on the kitchen floor, with Keith on top. In his hand he held a butcher knife, which he pressed to Mad Dog's throat.

"Keith!" Bernie screamed.

Bernie's voice brought Keith back from wherever his mind was visiting. He looked down at the knife in his hand, as if he was seeing it for the first time. Mad Dog looked up from beneath him, bloodied and smiling triumphantly.

"Go on. Finish the job," Mad Dog taunted him. "Show that nice girlfriend of yours the true face of the man she's fixing to marry!"

"I . . . I . . . ." Keith couldn't even compose his thoughts. The walls of the kitchen felt like they were closing in on him, and he found it hard to breathe. Keith rose from the floor, stood on shaky legs, and backed toward the door.

"Keith." Bernie reached for his arm to steady him.

"Don't," he said as he snatched his arm away. "I'm sorry . . . Look, I just need some air."

"I'll come with you," Bernie offered.

"I'm fine, Bernie. Really, just give me a few minutes to get my head together," he told her and then walked out the back door.

Keith stumbled down the driveway in a blind rage. Rain was falling now, and the drops mixed with his tears and stained his cheeks. He couldn't believe that he had almost killed his own brother. What the hell had he been thinking? But that was the point. He hadn't been thinking, only reacting. Keith knew better than to think he could take Mad Dog in a fight. His brother had baited him, and Keith had fallen for it, hook, line, and sinker.

At the foot of the driveway, Keith was blinded by the lights of the Camaro that had just pulled up. He shielded his eyes and made out a figure getting out on the passenger side. When the headlights went off, he was able to make out Darla. She had been noticeably absent from the funeral.

"Killer, that you?" Darla called out.

"What are you doing here?" Keith asked rudely.

"I came to pay my respects to Big Money."

"The funeral ended hours ago."

"I know . . . I just figured that maybe I wasn't too welcome and I should keep my distance. Darla noticed the tears on his cheeks. "Are you okay?"

"I'm fine," he lied.

"Killer, if you need to talk—"

"Darla, if you came to pay your respects to Big Money, then I suggest you go inside and handle your business. I'm good," Keith said, dismissing her.

Darla opened her mouth to say something but decided against it. She recognized the darkness in Keith's voice and knew him well enough to leave him alone when he got like that. She shook her head sadly and walked up the rest of the driveway to the house.

Keith felt bad about the way he had spoken to Darla. She had only been trying to make sure that he was okay, and he had acted like an ass. It was all spillover from the fight with Mad Dog. The longer he stayed in New Orleans, the more of himself he lost. He would be happy to be on a plane back to Atlanta tomorrow. He sat on the hood of the Camaro and rested there, collecting his thoughts. The car's horn suddenly blared, startling him to his feet. He turned around and saw Beau's smug face behind the wheel.

"Wouldn't want you to fuck up my new paint job," Beau said from inside the car.

"Sorry," Keith mumbled.

"Indeed you are, but I ain't one to judge," Beau taunted and got out of the car. He looked at Keith, in his disheveled state, and whistled. "Man, looks like the day ain't been kind to you. Funerals are always hard, especially when you're burying family. The once mighty Savage clan seems to be getting smaller by the day. Soon won't be none of y'all left."

"Beau, I suggest you leave me the fuck alone. If you're waiting for your bitch, you might want to do it from inside the car," Keith warned. He was in no mood for Beau's shit.

"Oh, now she's a bitch? Wasn't too long ago that she was the love of your life. I know you ain't one of them ole bitter exes," Beau taunted him. Keith ignored him. "Yeah, Darla had it bad for you. Probably still does. You know, for the first few months I was trying to get at her, she wouldn't let me hit it. I guess she was saving herself for you, hoping her childhood crush would swoop in and rescue her from all this poverty. We see how that played out, didn't we?"

"Last warning, Beau."

"I'm only messing with you, Killer." Beau flashed a crocodile grin. "Darla is actually a good little bitch. She ain't too smart, but she got a shot of pussy that keeps me coming back. That girl stays as wet as the Mississippi. Yeah, she's got some pussy, but her favorite hole is her mouth. We got this little game we play, where she lets me blow my load on her—" That was as far as Beau got before Keith snuffed him in the face.

Hitting Beau made Keith feel good. So good, in fact, that he hit him again and again and again. Beau found himself the recipient of all Keith's pent-up anger. All his pain, his dashed hopes, his shortcomings . . . Keith rained them all down on Beau's face. Beau tried to defend himself, but he was no match for Keith's rage. He wasn't sure how long he had been pounding on Beau before Ulysses came out and dragged Keith off him. Beau was unconscious, and his face had swelled to the size of a basketball.

"Two fights in one night? You're worse than me during Mardi Gras." Ulysses pulled Keith farther away from Beau. "What's going on with you, Killer?"

"I need to get out of here. Can you drop me and Bernadette back off at my hotel?" Keith asked.

"No problem, kid. I'll go in the house and get her for you. Stay put, and for the love of Christ, please don't hit that boy anymore. That chicken is already done," Ulysses said before heading back to the house to fetch Bernie and Keith's bags.

A few minutes later Bernie and Keith were in Ulysses's Chevy, getting ready to go back to the hotel. Bernie questioned Keith about the unconscious man in the driveway, but Keith didn't answer. All he wanted to do was get away from his family. As they were pulling out of the driveway, Keith spared a glance back at the house. He saw Mad Dog standing at the top of the driveway with a beer in his hand. It was dark, so Keith's couldn't be sure, but he could've sworn his brother was smiling at him. Ma Savage wasn't the only one who knew how to bring out the worst in him.

CHAPTER 25

As soon as they got back to Keith's hotel, he took a long, hot shower. It felt like every bone in his body was aching, and the knuckles on his right hand were badly swollen. He hoped that he hadn't broken the hand. One thing he had to admit, though, was that letting out some of that anger had felt good.

When he came out, he found Bernie sitting on the bed. She had slipped into one of the hotel's complimentary bathrobes. Near the door, there was a room-service cart. She had also taken the liberty of fixing them two drinks from the minibar. One thing he loved about Bernie was that she always seemed to know what he wanted without him having to ask.

"Thanks, babe." Keith took one of the drinks.

"I wasn't sure if you had a chance to eat back at the house, so I ordered you some room service. All they had at this hour were sandwiches, but I guess it beats going to bed hungry," she told him, trying to lighten the mood.

"I'm not real hungry. I just want to get some sleep and get ready for that flight." Keith threw himself across the bed.

"What was that business about back at the house?" Bernie asked. She had never known Keith to be a fighter, yet all he had seemed to be doing since she got to New Orleans was fight.

"With who? Beau? He's just some shit-talking nigga who has never liked me since we were kids," Keith told her.

"I'm not talking about Darla's boyfriend," Bernie said, letting him know that she was more informed than he gave her credit for. "I'm talking about you getting into it with Mad Dog."

"Just some old shit he can't seem to let go of," Keith said, downplaying it.

"Are we doing this again?"

"Doing what?" Keith pretended not to know what she was talking about.

"Omitting the truth. I haven't totally forgiven you yet, but the fact that I flew down here says I'm open to the idea. If we've got any shot at a future, I'm going to need you to start being honest with me. Is this about Michelle?"

Keith looked surprised when Bernie mentioned that name.

"I heard you yell her name when you and Mad Dog were arguing," Bernie explained. "Does she have something to do with all this?"

"She has everything to do with it."

A little-known fact about the Savage children was that they were all well educated. Ma had made sure that they all spent just as much time studying the books as they did learning how to rob banks. She hadn't given two shits about what they did in the street, but school was something she had never allowed them to slack off on.

All the Savage children, with the exception of Fire Bug, had graduated from college. Keith had spent time at Texas A&M before graduating from NYU and then getting his law degree, Big John had gone to Louisiana Tech, and Maxine had received her undergraduate degree from Northwestern. All three of them had college degrees, and it was no different with Mad Dog. He had surpassed them all not only by being accepted to Tulane University but also by graduating at the top of his class. Despite his reputation as a vicious killer, Mad Dog was also a borderline genius. He even graduated high school a year early. When he got his degree from Tulane, Mad Dog Savage had been poised to go on and do some amazing things with his life until the night that changed everything.

Mad Dog and Michelle had dated off and on since middle school and had gotten serious in high school. Next to Ma, she was his biggest supporter. Michelle knew who Mad Dog was and the things he did. Though she didn't approve of his lifestyle, she stuck around because she believed that he had the ability to change. And for a while, it looked like he would.

On the day of his Tulane graduation, the family threw Mad Dog a big party at the house. At some point, that night Mad Dog and Michelle slipped away from the party and went off to have a private celebration. That was the night Mad Dog was prepared to propose to Michelle. He planned to marry her and whisk her away from New Orleans, so they could start a new life, one that didn't involve him being an enforcer for the family. Much like Keith, Mad Dog knew the only way to truly put the Savage name behind him was to leave New Orleans, but unlike Keith, he would never have the chance.

Mad Dog took Michelle to one of her favorite places, a restaurant called August. He had never really cared for the food, but Michelle loved it, so he endured. They had a quiet dinner and shared a bottle of expensive red wine. Mad Dog picked the right moment and got on one knee and asked for Michelle's hand. Of course, she accepted. It was one of the happiest days in both their lives, but their moment of joy was short lived.

On the streets of New Orleans, Mad Dog had no shortage of enemies. He had killed many men in the name of his family, and it was only a matter of time before his karma came back to haunt him. Apparently, one of his enemies had spotted Mad Dog and Michelle in the restaurant and had lain in wait for them. When Michelle and Mad Dog came out of August, the two men exchanged words right in front of the restaurant. Michelle pleaded with Mad Dog the whole time to leave it alone. She was making progress until the man Mad Dog had been arguing with called Michelle a bitch. Without even thinking about it, Mad Dog gunned the man down. It was when he and Michelle were making their escape that things went sour. An armed security guard who worked at the bank next door to the restaurant had seen what happened. Michelle and Mad Dog managed to reach the car and get in, but as Mad Dog was pulling away from the scene, the guard fired two shots, one of which hit Michelle in the back of the head. She died instantly.

Mad Dog was inconsolable. Michelle's death broke him in mind and spirit. Day and night he could think of nothing but revenge against the man who had murdered his lover. It didn't take long for the Savage family to find out everything they needed to know about the man. He was a working-class citizen who had taken the job at the bank as a second source of income to feed his wife and six kids. That didn't matter to Mad Dog. He wanted the man to suffer as he was suffering. And instead of killing him, Mad Dog planned to kill his family.

Keith was the only one Mad Dog shared his plan with. Keith tried to talk Mad Dog out of it. He was fine with Mad Dog killing the security guard, but the family should be off-limits. They were innocent, but Mad Dog would hear none of it. The sentence had been passed, and the executioner planned to carry it out. Keith knew that if Mad Dog got caught, he would surely get the death penalty. There was no way he could stop his brother by force, so Keith came up with another solution.

When Mad Dog left the house on the day he planned to carry out the execution of the family, Keith called the police and reported his brother's car stolen. After the police stopped Mad Dog, they arrested him for possession of a firearm and a stolen car. It took a while for the police to sort out that Mad Dog had a gun permit and that the car was his own, and the few days they held him was enough time for Keith to go to the man and explain to him in no uncertain terms what would happen to him if he and his family remained in New Orleans. By the time Mad Dog was released from the city lockup, the man and his family had vanished.

Keith told Bernie all of this.

"I denied Mad Dog his revenge, and he's never been able to forgive me for it," he said with a heavy heart.

"Keith, you saved the lives of an entire family. You should be proud," Bernie replied, trying to ease his pain.

"Yes, but it came at the cost of my brother. Mad Dog was angry, and rightfully so, but I know my brother. Even if he'd gotten away with it, he never would have been able to live with the stain of what he'd done on his soul."

"If you had it to do over again, would you still warn the man?" Bernie asked.

"Yes," Keith said honestly.

"Then you did the right thing. You guys haven't seen each other in a while, so the wound may still be fresh, but you're brothers and you can get through this."

"How?" Keith asked.

"Go to him and explain it to him like you've explained it to me."

"You don't think I have? I tried to tell him when it first happened. I ain't gonna keep kissing his ass."

"Time has a way of healing certain wounds. Be the bigger person. Go to your brother, bare your soul, and beg for his forgiveness," Bernie urged.

"And if he isn't willing to forgive me?"

"Then at least you tried."

Keith and Mad Dog had been on the outs for far too long. Keith loved his brother, and though Mad Dog didn't always show it, Keith knew Mad Dog loved him too. Bernie was right. It was time to fix things.

"I'm going to start making amends for the things I've done. To my family . . . to you."

"Keith, this isn't about me," Bernie told him.

"Yes it is. I was wrong for lying to you, Bernie. No matter how I thought you would react, I should have told you the truth. I'm sorry for that."

"I know you are, Keith, but it's going to take a bit more than words to make this right. I need to know that you can be honest with me, like I am with you. What do we have if not trust?"

"You're right, Bernie, and moving forward, I'm going to do everything I can to show you that it wasn't a mistake for you to give your heart to me. That's if you're still willing to have me."

"Keith Savage," she said, calling him by his real name for the first time, "I can't imagine a life without you, jacked-up family and all."

"Thank you for understanding . . . and forgiving." He hugged her.

"I understand, but forgiveness is going to require you putting in some major work."

"I'd do anything for you, Bernie. Just tell me where to start," Keith told her.

She opened her robe, revealing her nakedness beneath it. "I've been in New Orleans for a whole day, and you've yet to give me a proper welcome. How about you start there?"

CHAPTER 26

Keith and Bernie were up bright and early the next morning. He'd changed his flight so that he and Bernie could fly out together later in the day. The plane wasn't scheduled to leave until 5:00 p.m., so he had more than enough time to go by the house and make peace with his family.

When they got downstairs, Ulysses was waiting for them. He was driving the Maybach again. He helped them load their bags into the trunk and then opened the back door for them. Keith was surprised when they got inside the car and found Max waiting.

"Hey," Keith greeted.

Maxine didn't respond. She was still mad at him. She looked at Bernie. "So, how was your time in New Orleans?" she asked Bernie.

"It was eventful, I'll say that," Bernie joked.

"Well, hopefully, it won't take somebody dying to get you down here again. You've got an open invitation. With or without my brother, you are always welcome here."

"Thanks. I'll be sure to take you up on that invitation, Maxine."

"Maxine is for my employees. You are family, so call me Max." She patted Bernie's knee.

The rest of the ride was spent with the girls talking among themselves. Keith tried to engage his sister several more times, but she continued to ignore him. He may as well have been invisible. When they got to the house, the girls walked ahead, but Ulysses motioned for

Keith to hang back. He had something he needed to say to him that wasn't for everyone's ears.

"You know you hurt her, right?" Ulysses told him.

"Yeah, I know," Keith said shamefully.

"Do you *really*? In all the years I've been working with Max, I've never seen that woman cry until after you embarrassed her at the house. That was some real foul shit you said."

"I know. I guess I was just in my feelings," Keith admitted.

"I guess you think you're the only one who has them, huh? You know, when you first showed up in town, I wasn't sure how I felt about you. Everyone has been telling me these stories about the notorious Killer Keith, but you haven't really lived up to my expectations."

"Sorry to have disappointed you," Keith said sarcastically.

"My opinion ain't worth too much shit. It's Max who you should be sorry for disappointing. The whole while you've been in Atlanta, I've watched Max defend you to everyone else who seems to have written you off. Can't say nothing bad about Killer Keith without Max jumping in your shit. I thought you would be a stand-up dude, but you're nothing but the spoiled brat with Mommy issues that everyone has made you out to be."

"You don't know me well enough to judge me."

"I don't know you, but I know your type. You run around like it's your family that's all fucked up, but there's going to come a time when you have to take responsibility for the part you've played in all this. I'd suggest you start with making things right with Max."

"Why does hired muscle care so much about what goes on between me and my sister?" Keith asked.

"Because the hired muscle is also her husband." Ulysses walked away, leaving Keith standing there with a stunned expression on his face.

***

Things were quieter in the house that morning. Most of the relatives that had descended on the Savage house either had gone or were in the process of leaving. He searched the house for Fire Bug and found him in his bedroom. He was sitting at his worktable, scooping what looked like gunpowder into empty ink-pen cases.

"What you doing?" Keith asked as he entered the room.

"Working on a new project," Fire Bug said without bothering to turn around.

"Can we talk for a second?"

"Talk. I'm listening." Fire Bug continued his work.

"I'm sorry," Keith began. "Not sorry for failing to live up to the great expectations placed on me by this family, but for failing you. Regardless of what my personal feelings toward Mama are, I should have been there for you."

"It's all good, Killer. I had Big John and Mad Dog to raise me up while you were off living the high life." Bug snorted.

"And that's exactly what I mean. Kids grow up to mimic what they see. If all you had around you were people doing wrong, then how could you possibly know any better?"

"So, you saying there's something wrong with my brothers teaching me how to survive out there in the world?" Bug asked defensively, stopping what he was doing.

"I'm not saying that at all, Bug. A man needs to know how to survive in the world, but he should also have an idea of just how big the world is. There is so much more to life than just the trap."

"What if that's all I know?" Bug asked seriously.

"Then it's up to me to teach you," Keith replied. "Bug, I know I missed out on a lot in your life, but if you're open to it, I'd like to change that. After we get past all this, I'd like you to come spend some time with me in Atlanta.

Maybe you can even hang around my office a few days and watch your brother work."

"I don't need your pity, Killer."

"It's not pity, Bug. It's love," Keith said sincerely. "Just think about it, man. When you decide you're ready, I'll fly you up."

"Sure," Bug said unenthusiastically.

Keith hung his head and headed out of the room. He knew repairing his relationship with his brother would take time. But he was willing to put in the work.

"Killer," Bug called after him. "I'm glad you're back, even if you are a square now." He smiled and went back to his work.

Keith went into the kitchen, where he found his mother and Big John sitting at the table, drinking coffee.

"Morning," Keith greeted them.

"Morning, Killer," Ma replied. "Are you and Bernie hungry? I could whip you up something if you like."

"No. We're good. And we can always get something at the airport later."

"Well, it's been good having you home, and I hope it doesn't take another dead body to get you to come back," Ma joked.

"No, I'll be back again soon. I miss being around you guys, and I promise not to stay away so long the next time," Keith said. "And about the way I've been acting . . . I owe all of you an apology."

"You don't owe us any apologies, Killer," Ma told him.

"No, I think I do. I've been acting like a real brat." He thought back to his conversation with Ulysses. "We haven't always gotten along, but we're still blood. That should trump any petty differences that we've had over the years. Being here again made me realize how import-ant family is."

"Sounds like you're finally starting to grow up." Big John slapped him on the ass playfully.

"Better late than never." Keith smiled. He looked over at the broken china cabinet, and memories of the night before came flooding back. "Say, is Mad Dog around? I'd really like to talk to him before we leave."

"Mad Dog is long gone. He left sometime in the wee hours," Ma informed him.

"Really? He only just came back. I thought he'd have stuck around for a while this time. Where did he go?"

"To New York City. Got some family business that needs handling." Big John flashed a sinister grin.

Keith was shocked. "Ma, you gave me your word that you would talk to Big John about not sending an army into New York."

"And I kept my word. We ain't sent no army. Just Mad Dog," Ma said, clarifying matters.

Keith felt dizzy. Sending Mad Dog to New York was like taking the leash off a rabid pit bull in the middle of Times Square on New Year's Eve. An army of Savages going to New York would've been bad, but Mad Dog's wrath would be one thousand times worse.

"Ma, you've got to stop him!" Keith told her.

"How? Mad Dog ain't exactly the cell phone–carrying type. Besides, even if I could reach him, you know once Mad Dog has been loosed ain't no calling him off."

"We've got to do something." Keith began pacing nervously.

"Ain't much we can do at this point but stay out of Mad Dog's way," Big John joked, as if it was all a game.

"I'm not just gonna sit by and watch while my brother gets himself killed or thrown in prison," Keith vowed.

"Tell you what. Since you're in the business of saving lives instead of taking them these days, I'll give you a sporting chance." Ma looked at the clock on the wall. "Depending on how big of a head start he's got on you, I'd say you've got about forty-eight hours to find Big Money's killers before Mad Dog does."

EPILOGUE

New York City . . .

New York had been hit with thunderstorms for the past couple of days, but now the sun was finally starting to shine again. The minute the sun reappeared, the business of selling drugs was back in full swing. It was Genesis's first day holding down the block.

When King James had mentioned giving him a promotion, Genesis had figured it would entail selling drugs directly or bagging up drugs in one of the stash houses. Unbeknownst to him, King had had something more sinister in mind. Genesis had agreed to complete the mission, but he hadn't been sure he'd be able to go through with it when the time came. Surprising himself and Lakim both, he had completed the task. He had taken a life.

Genesis had thought initially that he would be haunted by what he had done, but he wasn't. Lakim hadn't been too thrilled at the prospect of taking Pam out, but it hadn't mattered to Genesis. To him, she was a nameless face . . . a stepping-stone to where he needed to be. He didn't feel much different after killing Pam, except for experiencing a feeling of liberation. Holding power over life and death made him feel like a god, and there was a part of him that couldn't wait to experience it again.

Dee walked up on him. He had a new position as shift manager, so he was the kid whom Genesis answered to. "How we looking?"

"Five packs gone and five to go. We're gonna need another re-up before the night shift comes on."

"Damn! You're a hustling little muthafucka," Dee said proudly. "At the rate you're going, you'll be in off the block in no time."

Their conversation was broken up when an addict approached. He was a bearded man wearing a baseball cap, tattered jeans, and an overcoat that had holes in it. Genesis had never seen the man before, but he knew he had to be a drug user because of the unmistakable crazed look in his eyes. They were the eyes of a man jonesing for a fix. "Say, man, y'all up?" he asked in a voice that carried a hint of an accent.

"Yeah. What you need?" Genesis asked in a tough tone, trying to impress Dee.

"I got about fifty to spend, but it's gotta be good. The last time I copped from one of you boys, the work was weak."

"Fuck is you talking about? King James don't sell no bullshit," Genesis declared.

"Oh, so you hustle for King?" the addict asked.

"Everybody in this neighborhood hustles for King James. Where the fuck are you from? Mars?" Genesis teased.

"No. New Orleans, actually." The addict's coat flew open, and he produced a sawed-off shotgun.

"Oh, shit!" was all Genesis was able to blurt out before Mad Dog Savage painted the side of the building with his brains. Just like that, his run in the game was ended.

Dee moved to run, but Mad Dog turned the shotgun in his direction, and Dee froze him in his tracks. Mad Dog walked up on the boy and pressed the hot barrel of the shotgun to his chin. "I'm gonna ask you a question. Answer true and you live. Lie to me and . . ." He glanced over at Genesis's corpse. "Where can I find King James?"

"I don't know, man. Nobody has seen him in a few days," Dee told the gunman.

Mad Dog searched Dee's eyes for signs that he was lying. The boy seemed to be telling the truth. It confirmed the information he had gathered. King James had gone underground. "Listen, tell your boss that all your operations are shut down until he comes out of hiding and dances with me. Every corner, every trap house . . . I'm on your ass for all this shit. You understand?"

"Yeah, man," Dee said nervously.

"Oh, and one more thing. Tell King James that Big Money Savage sends his regards from hell," he told Dee before knocking out his front teeth with the butt of the shotgun.